GALERIE

OTHER BOOKS BY
STEVEN GREENBERG

Enfold Me
Galerie

www.stevengreenberg.info

STEVEN GREENBERG

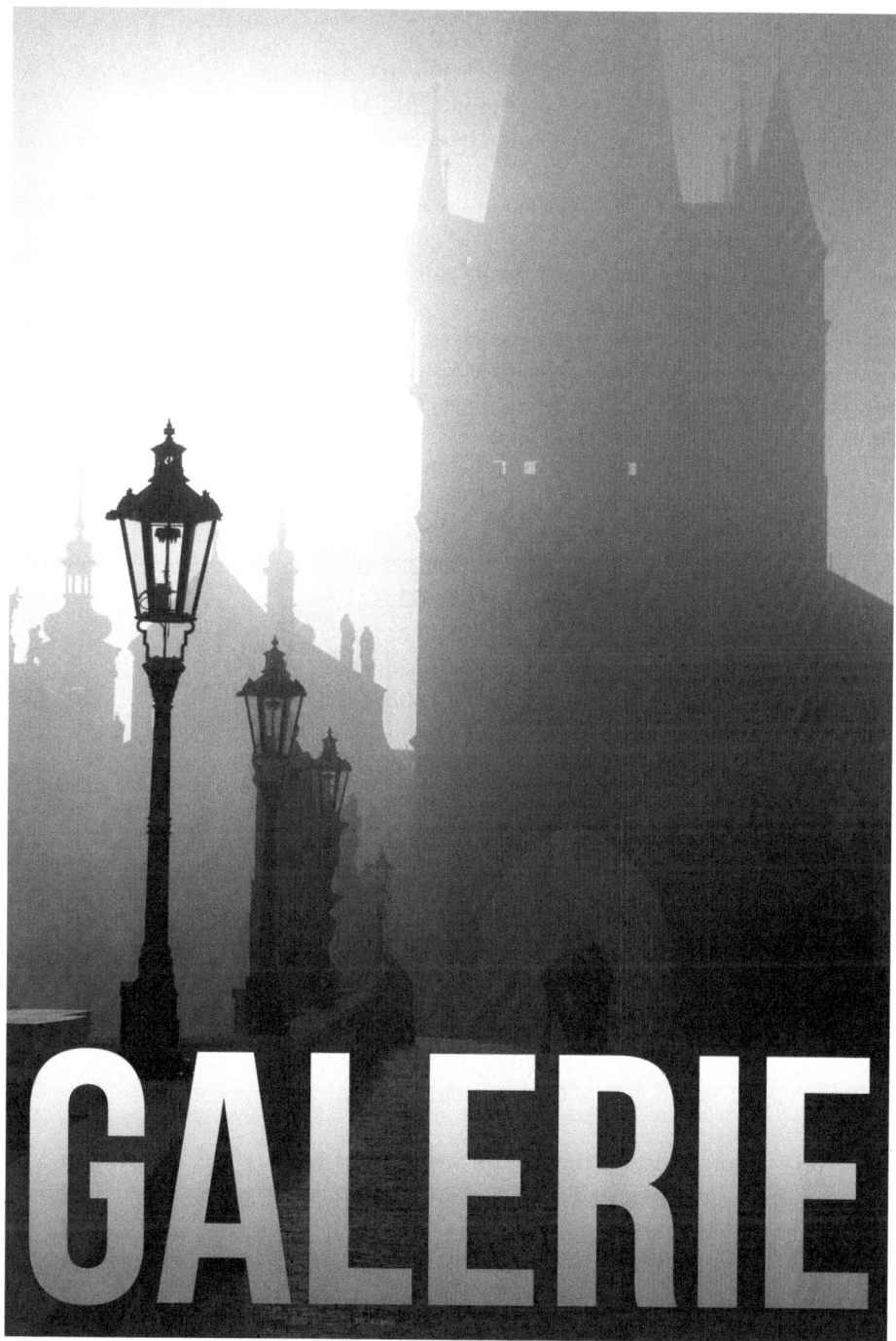

GALERIE

GALERIE
Copyright © 2015 Steven Greenberg
Cover Art Copyright © 2015 Mallory Rock
Interior Design by D. Robert Pease

FIRST EDITION PAPERBACK
ISBN: 1622532216
ISBN-13: 9781622532216

Editor: Michelle Barry
Senior Editor: Lane Diamond

Printed in the U.S.A.

www.EvolvedPub.com
Evolved Publishing LLC
Cartersville, Georgia

This is a work of fiction. Names, characters, places and incidents are products of the author's imagination, or the author has used them fictitiously

Printed in Book Antiqua font.

For Segev — the best travel companion, researcher, editor, plot consultant, and son that any man could hope to have.

PROLOGUE

Prague, 1943

Despite the basement room's damp November cold, the boy dripped with sweat. His breath fogged out in gasps as he rocked, face huddled between spindly knees that peeked out through his threadbare trousers like two dim streetlamps in an otherwise dark alley. He'd drawn himself into a ball, hugging his legs so tightly with his stick-like arms that the tips of his dirty fingers had gone white.

He'd already seen more than a twelve-year-old should have to witness, let alone process.

He grasped the individual details of the scene, many of which were by themselves familiar: the table, the flickering bare bulb dangling from the ceiling as if on an umbilical cord, his father's sharp and varied tools.

They'd been familiar sights, but when his father had moved aside, no longer obscuring the boy's field of view—that was when the whole had become incomprehensibly greater than the sum of its parts. That was when his heart leapt out of his skinny chest, commanding the scuffed leather-clad feet to run, run, RUN!

And he had run. Back to the empty basement storeroom, with stone walls that sweated in the summer and radiated cold in the winter. He'd spent more time down here in the basement, as the weather had grown colder, rainier, and more dismal. Since it was no longer possible to play outside in the building's small, dingy courtyard, he'd turned the mostly

1

empty building into a personal playground. From nooks like his current subterranean roost, up to the attic rooms whose small dormer windows, reached eagerly *en point*, provided a glimpse of occasional passersby on the narrow cobblestone street below — the boy knew the limestone-faced building inside-out.

Now, he drew closer to the building's main sewage pipe, which provided faint warmth that always comforted, as long as he didn't dwell on its origin. He shouldn't have been anywhere near his father's workshop in the sub-basement, the equivalent of several floors below his current refuge. "Never pass this door, do you understand? Promise me." His father had made him promise, out loud.

And he never did pass the heavy metal door with the symbol engraved on it, which led to the brightly lit staircase curving so steeply down. But at twelve years old, with no people around, he was lonely and bored, not to mention relentlessly curious. It hadn't taken him long to find the wide ventilation ducts that let him move surreptitiously throughout the building, down to the basement where he now hid, and even to the massive sub-basement. Today, the workshop door had been left open — irresistibly so — just wide enough for a small eye to peer through the crack....

His breathing slowed and he raised his brown-curled head tentatively, opening first one eye, then the other, checking the safety of his surroundings. The small stone storage room sat empty, and he was alone. For now.

He'd been alone the first months, too. Father had not had any time for him, between long hours in his workshop and seemingly constant dealings with the man who came several times a day, regal and straight-backed in his black woolen overcoat, fedora, leather gloves, and silver lapel pin that bore the same strange symbol as the door. Father always showed the man respect and gratitude, and made the boy do the same, because if they were polite and worked hard, the man would bring Mother. She'd been left behind in Terezin, but remained warm and secure.

The beginnings of a smile budded on the boy's chapped lips. Soon, at least, he wouldn't be alone. More people would come. They always did. He liked meeting them, these new people. They were kind, and hopeful, and they told stories with funny accents, which he sometimes couldn't understand, and had strange clothes and smells. He rose to his full height, brushed the dust from the seat of his trousers, and started toward the door.

As he left the room, he turned and looked back, the light of child-like curiosity just beginning to eclipse his dark visage. He imagined the room full again with voices, smells, and hopes. *Yes*, he thought, now smiling fully, *new people would make it so much better*.

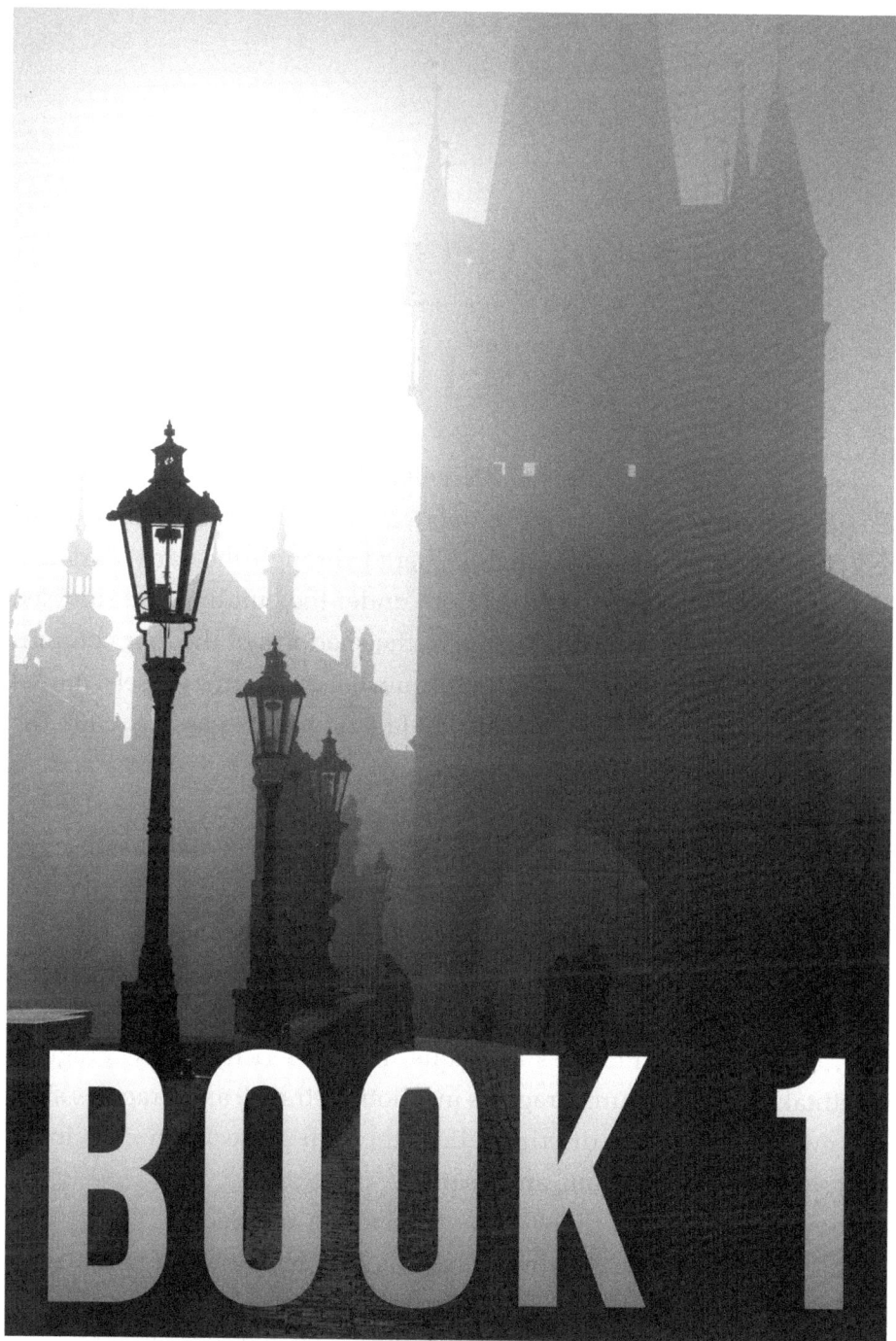
BOOK 1

CHAPTER 1

SWEETNESS

Prague, December 1991

A rickety tram wiggled by, its unpainted metal roof mismatched to its red paneled sides. Dual headlights peered through the early darkness like serpentine eyes as it emerged from under the building and rumbled by Vanesa Neuman. From her perch in the shadows of the four columns of the Church of the Holy Savior, the squeal of the tram's wheels, muted by a crunchy dusting of snow, quickly faded with its passing. Only the sharp smell of electricity from the tangle of overhead wires remained, as if to preserve its memory.

For Prague in 1991 was a like a memory, she told me before she even left Tel Aviv—and not a good memory. She'd never been to the city, and had never intended to come. She'd heard all she needed to hear over the years from her father. She knew what she needed to know, and had never once felt a need to learn more about the city. All her life, she'd heard of Prague's beauty, Prague's mystique, Prague's rich history, Prague's breathtaking architecture, Prague's insidious betrayal, and Prague's slow downward spiral from discrimination, through persecution, into inhuman realms of misery, pain, and death.

No thank you, she'd thought. No need to see *this* place.

Yet here she was, and damn it, he was late. She must be in the right place, for there was only one Church of the Holy Savior in Prague, on Krizovnicka Street, across from the iconic Charles Bridge. He was supposed to meet her right here, in the shelter of the church's massive columns, at five o'clock. The impassive eyes of the six marble statues above Vanesa, white-cloaked in fresh snow, gazed disdainfully down at her. It was already five-thirty, and almost fully dark. Still she, and the statues, waited.

Huddled deep into dark coats and scarves, pedestrians flowed by. Streetlights flickered on, as did the gay Christmas decorations strung between the lampposts, throwing shadows dangerously into the paths of oncoming Skodas.

Vanesa pressed deeper underneath the meager shelter that the columns afforded. They loomed over her, heavy, their menace unabated by the veneer of holiday cheer that draped the city. She pulled her long wool coat tighter around her petite frame, and tugged the hat further down over her ears, making her dark curls stand out at crazy angles. Still she shivered, stamping her booted feet halfheartedly in a futile attempt to warm them.

She'd never really known *actual* cold. In a lifetime of nearly year-round Tel Aviv sunshine, cold—at least *biting* cold, like Prague's December air—was an unknown commodity. Tel Aviv cold nipped lightly at you. The Golan Heights cold, which she'd encountered in her army service, snapped at your chin, numbed your earlobes and toes. The damp Jerusalem cold could actually get into your bones. Prague cold, however, clamped right down and *gnawed* on you, like a Piranha going after aquarium-dipped fingertips.

She hadn't wanted to come, she told me, to this land where her parents' family had lived for over 500 years, to this land from which some 85% of Jews were eradicated at places she'd read about, or heard mentioned in hushed Czech whispers when her father spoke to friends or customers at the shop.

"Of course I remember Luba!" either he or the friend would gush, confronted with a just-discovered mutual acquaintance. This elation inevitably preceded an understanding blink, a subtle nod in her direction, and a lowering of eyes, as either one or the other knowingly whispered the words—usually "Auschwitz," but sometimes "Maly Trostenets," "Sobibor," "Izbice," or simply "the transports."

She'd come to Prague not out of want, but out of *need*—a need that led her to wait on this frozen street corner to meet a man she only knew through Uncle Tomas, and who's gravelly, authoritative voice she'd only heard briefly over a scratchy international telephone line. She needed to make sense of her father's dying gift, to fill in the vast empty space that was his life during the war. She needed to put some sort of face on this man who had raised her after her mother died—a face not lit by gaudy Tel Aviv sunshine, but rather by the same fading, winter-gray Bohemian light that currently lit her own face.

She sighed. Her primary contact in Prague was a no-show, leaving her the lone actor in a slowly-fading street scene.

A tram lumbers by, she narrated to herself, attempting to alleviate her boredom and forget the cold. *A faulty streetlight flickers. Tourists straggle off the Charles Bridge, closely followed by artists lugging wares in cleverly-designed carts. Another tram, this one with a squeaky wheel. Cue more cars. Cue pedestrians. Enter boy on a bike, slipping in the patchy snow: Fewer and fewer pedestrians now. Finally, following an agonizingly slow fade, the spots darken, the street grows silent. The curtain falls.*

At six-fifteen, she gave up and turned to walk the half kilometer back to her hotel next to Old Town Square. Halfway down Platnerska Street, she could already see the mismatched twin spires of the St. Nicholas Cathedral peeking from above the buildings and leafless trees. Her footsteps, squeaking occasionally on the patches of foot-packed snow, had begun to echo on the deserted street.

Unlike in the movies, she told me later, she'd never even heard another set of footsteps. She'd never spotted a shadowy figure trailing her, had never seen a suspicious car with a figure in a dark hat glancing furtively in her direction as it glided by. She was simply walking one second, and being pulled into the alley the next second.

Two men, both bald, both in high, black, military-style boots, grabbed her. One stank of garlic; the other reeked of alcohol, likely vodka. Once off the street, Garlic grabbed her from behind, pinning her arms behind her back, his rank breath on her neck. Vodka clamped a cold hand over her mouth. They ignored her admirable yet futile attempts at resistance, pulling her deeper into the alley and through a low doorway into what had to be a garbage room, based on the ripe stench. A metal-grated door clanged shut, abruptly cutting off any remnants of city sounds audible over Vanesa's silent struggling.

>——⫻

When her father told her that her mother had died, alone at night in the off-green sterility of Tel Aviv's Sourasky Medical Center, Vanesa had not cried. Neither had she cried at the funeral, nor during the *shiva* — the traditional seven-day period of mourning. She'd never been an "emotional girl," she told me, because she'd always known — and frequently been reminded — that whatever her current tribulations, they paled in comparison with her parents' experiences. What right had she, a girl who'd always had clothes to wear and food on her plate, to complain to two Holocaust survivors... about *anything*? Who was she to mourn a lost toy, a stubbed toe, an insult, even a single death, when her childhood memories were as populated by the ghosts of her parents' past as by living souls?

"So, from a young age, I fought epic battles with tears," she said. She'd won, but it had been a Pyrrhic victory. The tears, once defeated, were disinclined to return, even when needed.

Only Uncle Tomas had managed to elicit a dribble of tears from the dry well of twelve-year-old Vanesa. Uncle Tomas, with his wool coat that had in those years always smelled vaguely of carrion, and the fading blue-black number on his forearm that she'd long ago committed to memory — A-25379. His stiff Germanic manner was, she believed, only a frozen exoskeleton that the Mediterranean sun had not yet thawed. Her father seemed to alternately despise and grudgingly admire Uncle Tomas, always keeping him at arm's length, but never farther. Despite his family status as closest living relative, Uncle Tomas wasn't really even a relative, but rather her grandfather's business partner, co-owner of the cramped shop on Nahalat Binyamin Street in south Tel Aviv's working-class Florentine neighborhood.

Nor had the tears returned of their own volition when her grandfather Jakub died four years later. They'd found him slumped over his work-bench in the dingy back room of the shop, a single bare bulb reflected in the stainless steel scraping tool he still clutched in one hand, his forehead resting lightly on his other hand.

Again, only in the comfort of Uncle Tomas' stiff embrace could she mourn, as if he held some secret key to the floodgates of her grief. Thankfully, he had always been beneficent in his duties as gatekeeper.

If her parents were closed books, her grandfather had been to Vanesa a locked library, a restricted section cordoned off with gaily painted steel mesh that was superficially decorative but ultimately foreboding. Vanesa had never met a more silent person, yet he always smiled sweetly when she waltzed into the shop after school on her way home, the family apartment being just one floor above. He would look up from whatever he was scraping, stretching, or trimming, with a distracted smile, as if he'd forgotten something and her arrival had pleasantly jogged his memory — a vague "aha!" moment. Then he would lower his head, wordlessly turning back to his work, leaving her to poke around the shop until she found the piece of hard candy he placed in a different hiding place each day.

"It was like I learned, both in the shop and in my life, to look past the silence and find the sweetness," she told me.

But no sweetness could be found in what Vodka and Garlic did to Vanesa in that dark Prague garbage room, just as there had been no sweetness whatsoever in the untimely death of her father at age 60, just six months previously.

No sweetness, and still no tears.

CHAPTER 2

WELCOME TO PRAGUE

Prague, December 1991

They flung Vanesa to a cold concrete floor. She slid backwards over the frozen film of garbage juice until the back of her head connected with a filthy brick wall, the unhealthy *thunk* making her teeth rattle.

Her head cleared slowly, and an ominous silence followed. Her eyes adjusted to the semi-darkness, picking up wisps of light floating in through the rusty mesh metal door.

The two hulking silhouettes loomed above her, sufficiently backlit that she could see the swastika tattooed on one's neck when he turned. Neither made any effort to hide his face. They stared at her, as if impressed with their accomplishment thus far but unsure how to proceed. Garlic finally took the lead, speaking in unaccented Czech.

"So, bitch, Miss...." He looked at the palm of his hand, as if reading what was written there but then deciding not to vocalize it. He looked sideways at Vodka for encouragement, turned back to Vanesa, smiled — showing a number of sickly black teeth — and adopted a quasi-formal, oratorical tone. "Uh... welcome to Prague, the jewel of Bohemia. As part of our city's welcoming package to intrusive cunts like yourself, we'd like to enlighten you as to certain local rules and customs. The very first rule is that too much curiosity can piss people off." He spat in her direction, again turning to Vodka for reassurance.

11

Vodka nodded sagely, wringing his hands in undisguised anticipation.

Vanesa pressed herself tighter against the damp coldness of the brick wall, which provided faint reassurance, simply owing to the fact that it was *not* tall, muscular, swastika-tattooed and looming.

Garlic began to unbuckle his belt, looking back at Vodka with leering satisfaction. With her defiance now supplanted by visible fear, he was pleased with himself, and continued. "...and pissing people off in Prague has historically held somewhat unpleasant consequences, as you may know."

"*Prosim,*" she stuttered in Czech. "Please...."

As the two men closed in on Vanesa, the remaining inky light left the fetid room like a final solemn breath.

>—/

Wisconsin, 1981

When I first met Vanesa Neuman, she had more questions than answers, and a clear willingness to ask them. I once joked that her truly insatiable curiosity made her a sort of bottomless intellectual sinkhole, swallowing anything thrown into her. She lived her interrogatory life in a kind of stream-of-consciousness, one question inevitably leading to another. A discussion about peeling paint could easily unravel into the Allegory of the Shadows, meander back to the inner life of mosquitoes, flit to the merits of that evening's dining hall fare, and roost thereafter on the branch of Mongolian falconry.

As the years passed, Vanesa's question-to-answer ratio slowly tipped. In the way of zealots, technocrats, taxi drivers, and the clinically insane, she gained too many answers. They pushed her questions aside, as if her intellectual storeroom had finite volume. And she grew further and further away from me.

Nonetheless, the touch of some people who intersect your life never completely fades. In the summer of 1981, more than a decade before I'd even heard the word "Galerie," Vanesa became one such person.

I was an oh-so-serious nineteen-year-old college student, working as a counselor for high school-aged kids, in a sleepover camp tucked back in the woods two hours north of Chicago. The camp's ample grounds snuggled at the edge of a still wooded but increasingly urbane subdivision that had sprung up uninvited on one side. On its other side ran a copse of dense forest whose depths even the most adventurous camper dared not plumb. To the east, the property hugged a mud-bottomed lake with a trucked-in sand beach, which boasted a speedboat and small catamaran, not to mention a number of canoes and paddle boats renowned for providing only the illusion of movement.

Donna, the waterfront director, lorded over the lake. Her word, inevitably reinforced by an eardrum-piercing whistle, was absolute — as absolute, it was irreverently rumored, as her prodigious posterior, which was said to have once crushed an errant kitten that made the regrettable life choice of napping on the lifeguard chair.

Vanesa was a quintessential sixteen-year-old, a camper in the oldest group in which I was a co-counselor for a boys cabin. She stood 162 centimeters in her All-Stars, shorter and slightly chubby compared to the Madonna wannabes in her cabin. But you could feel the fire in her at a glance — in the way her eyes met yours without a shred of hesitation, without an inkling of self-consciousness, probing you like a district attorney and then delivering judgment like a Wild West hanging judge. She had a way of tossing her dark, shoulder-length curls when she argued, of leaning her small-chested figure in to engage you when she spoke — as if not just her mind, but her whole body tried to prove her point.

I was instantly smitten, and remain so today — less with what she's become than with what she still is to me, which is, of course, sixteen years old.

My pimple-faced, hyper-hormonal yet laudably under-experienced campers — this was the 1980s, after all — lived for the duration of each month-long camp session in a rickety wooden cabin, together with my co-counselor and myself. The cabin — the camp brochure called it "rustic" — boasted screen-only windows quite effective at keeping the mosquitoes in the cabin, gaps in the floorboards wide enough to accommodate the entrance of almost any spider or vermin, and a screen door whose industrial-strength spring slammed it closed with a bang loud enough to grace the finale of the 1812 Overture.

Teenage boys being teenage boys, my campers lacked interest in much beyond sports and girls. So I was drawn to chatting with the girl campers during my free time. They were strictly off-limits romantically, and I maintained the propriety of the camp rules, but what nineteen-year-old straight male would not enjoy the fawning admiration, chaste though it may be, of a gaggle of boy-struck teenage girls?

Vanesa did not penetrate the inner circle of the girls' cabin intrigue. Neither did she linger on the fringes. Instead, she struck me as standing some three meters above. She sat apart reading, writing in a journal she kept in a simple spiral notebook—not a pretentiously locked and frilly girl-diary—or just gazing at the sky, with a gently curving nose flaring out to meet cheeks that retained just the right accent of baby fat. Sixteen, perfect, and untouchable—I was staff, after all—and she was a visiting Israeli camper.

We had no hope romantically. Or so I thought that summer.

Vanesa was born in Israel, a true *sabra*, which made her all the more beguiling to a young American Jew like me. Her father, Michael Neuman, was a Czech immigrant to Israel, which explained her impressive command of not only Hebrew and English but also Czech, which she spoke at home. It also explained her real name, Limor, which she used only in Israel—or so she told me at the time. Vanesa was actually her mother's name. She said she'd adopted it because "it's easier on your American ears and tongues."

Later, I learned the real reason, but she has always remained Vanesa to me.

>—⸦

Prague, December 1991

With his belt opened and his fly now unzipped, Garlic continued. "In accordance with rule number one—which, you'll recall, is that in Prague, pissing people off has consequences—we have a message for you. An important message," he continued. He nodded to Vodka, who followed Garlic's lead and unbuckled his own belt. "You see, in Prague, if you piss off the wrong people, you can end up in a whole world of mess." He chuckled and nodded in Vodka's direction. "And not just any mess, but, in fact, a whole world of piss."

At this, both men, having unzipped and taken themselves in hand, began urinating on Vanesa. Steam rose from the horse-like streams as they sprayed her and laughed.

She cowered silently, scooting away from them, squeezing into the corner of the room, trying to shelter her face and head from the relentless, sickly-warm torrent. It was no use. Her face, hair and torso were soaked in a matter of seconds. An incongruous passing thought of how much these two must have had to drink before meeting her flashed through her brain, defying both the gravity of the situation and her gagging disgust.

When the drenching waned and stopped, she raised her dripping head to look defiantly at her attackers, wiping the liquid from her eyes with the back of one garbage-congealed hand. As she did so, Vodka hocked and spat directly onto her forehead. The viscous liquid ran down over her eyebrows and dripped onto both cheeks.

Now it was Vodka's turn to speak. He leaned in and raised a hand as if to backhand her, and she shrank from him. "Bitch! Go home. If you don't, there will be worse for you next time." Satisfied, he re-zipped his trousers and joined Garlic at the mesh metal door.

They chuckled and exited the garbage room, leaving Vanesa's sodden, steaming, gasping figure on the floor in the corner.

CHAPTER 3

A KLADNO SCHOOLGIRL

Kladno, 1941

My Vanesa's mother—I took to calling her Vanesa Sr. when we spoke of her, which was infrequently—was born Vanesa Rokeach in 1930 in Kladno, a medium-sized industrial and mining town north of Prague. Both sides of her family had lived for more than four generations in Kladno. Her father's surname still reflected the fact that, some one hundred years prior to her birth, her great-grandfather had been a noted apothecary, serving both Jews and Gentiles, despite being officially limited to doing business in the Jewish section of the town. Like thousands of Jewish communities across Europe, Bohemia's Jews—the Kladno Jews among them—had for centuries been regarded with suspicion and dislike, at best. Tolerated for their commercial usefulness, they were treated with varying degrees of severity and persecution, depending on the whim of the current ruler and fickle public sentiment.

Vanesa Sr., dark-haired with warm eyes that carried the precursor of the fire that blazed in my Vanesa's eyes, was the daughter of a seamstress and a machinist. Her father's profession was unusual for a Czech Jew, but less so in Kladno, the center of Bohemia's industrial heartland—a heartland later coveted by the German war machine for its iron and steel works. Vanesa Sr. left Kladno once, when she was twelve, and never returned. Kladno was, to the day of her death, the very embodiment of betrayal—much as Prague became for her future husband, Michael, my

16

Vanesa's father. Every memory that Vanesa Sr. related to her daughter, every happy moment, every personal childhood triumph, every family achievement, was tainted, inevitably qualified with "...but that was, of course, before *they*...."

The "they" Vanesa Sr. referenced constantly was amorphous and nameless, but terrified my Vanesa as a child. Were "they" also the menace who had attacked Israel on Yom Kippur of 1973, when my Vanesa was just eight—old enough to still remember both the scary sirens and the sweets the kind man next door had shared with her during their hours in the neighborhood bomb shelter? Were "they" the menace against whom Vanesa Sr. double-locked the doors of the small Tel Aviv flat, refusing to leave the apartment unless absolutely necessary so "they" wouldn't come and take, burn, destroy, or worse? Certainly, "they" were the menace against whom my Vanesa contrived her bedroom's childhood guardian force, comprised of conscripted teddy bears and warrior dolls armed with popsicle-stick swords. "They" had made Vanesa Sr.'s childhood itself seem like poison to her daughter, something to be put away on the back of a high shelf, toxic to the touch.

Vanesa Sr.'s memory, like wood smoke in a winter forest, floated wispy yet pungent in my Vanesa's mind. My Vanesa carried mental snapshots of her mother that sparkled, soundbites that crackled, and grainy videos that wept. Mostly wept. For my Vanesa's overwhelming memory of her mother was of crying, tears in endless permutations of liquid grief. In the open, and more often behind closed doors, she'd let flow tears of frustration, tears of longing, tears of remembrance, tears of remorse, and later, tears of fear. At the end, as Vanesa Sr.'s body shut down, the tears had dried up, and her deathbed weeping had been dry, inconsolable and empty.

Vanesa Sr. was nine years old when she stood on Kleinerova Street on a rainy March day in 1939, looking up wide-eyed, huddled between her parents' overlapping umbrellas. Her brother's chubby hand, clutched tightly in her own, was so clammy that she had to keep releasing it to dry her own hand on her skirt. Vanesa Sr. watched her parents, far more interested in their stony faces than in the seemingly endless line of grey tanks and troop transports rolling into Kladno, shaking the ground, clouding the air with diesel fumes. She did look up, however, as several cars and troop transports stopped first—as they would later do in Prague—at the looming limestone façade of local Czechoslovak Central Bank, where they made a one-sided, cripplingly large transaction.

In Prague, the German *Reichsbank* special commissioner accompanying the invading forces "persuaded" the directors of the Central Bank there, at gunpoint, to transfer some twenty-three tons of gold to *Reichsbank* accounts. In Kladno, the withdrawal was smaller, but monstrous nonetheless.

"We often forget," my Vanesa told me one evening in her best university-lecturer voice, "the strictly economic considerations of the Nazi invasion of Czechoslovakia, and indeed of all Europe. In today's popular consciousness, the Nazi period doesn't carry the stain of pillage. Of terror, certainly. Of genocide. Of betrayals and petty reprisals. But the fact was that Germany stole billions of dollars from the countries they invaded—just plain stole, like sticking up a convenience store, but on a national scale."

Vanesa Sr. understood that the Nazis' coming was a bad thing. She recalled her father's fury the previous year when he read of Chamberlain's cowardly Munich Agreement, in which Czechoslovakia's most loyal allies sacrificed her on the altar of Nazi appeasement. She understood and feared the armed troops, with their large black guns, fierce helmets, long coats, and uncaring eyes. What she never understood, even after numerous and patient parental explanations, was the nature and purpose of that second Nazi army, armed to the teeth with boxes and boxes of pens, papers, forms, and regulations. Vanesa Sr. could understand guns, but over the next ten months, every time she waited in an endless line with her mother or father for some bespectacled clerk to examine, sign, stamp, or reject in angry guttural German yet another piece of paper, she wondered how it was that this strange army's power to change her life was so vastly superior to the first's.

This army of bureaucrats had changed her very identity. Whereas before she'd just been Vanesa Rokeach, a Kladno schoolgirl who'd never lit a Sabbath candle in her life and never seen the inside of a synagogue; now their papers and their forms had transformed her.

She was no longer a nine-year-old girl that liked lollipops, loved to play *Pesek*, and tried to avoid brushing her hair before bed.

Now, she had become this "*Jude*" word. It was written on the yellow star that her mother had sewn to her coat with such tight, small stitches. At first, she didn't really understand what this word *was*, but she quickly learned what *it meant*. It meant she couldn't go to her school anymore, that she couldn't play in the park with the high slide, and that there was no meat for dinner. It meant Father stayed home more frequently, unshaven and often cross.

Soon it would come to mean much, much more.

In 1941, the Central Office for Jewish Emigration, under the personal supervision of the notorious Adolf Eichmann, changed gears. The office and its bureaucratic procedures had been created, first in Vienna and later in Prague, to "assist" Jewish families in leaving the Reich. This was allowed following payment of all relevant levies and taxes — generally amounting to well over 80% of a given family's net worth. Now, the office focused primarily on systematically relocating the Jews of the Protectorate of Bohemia and Moravia into a 150-year-old, sparsely-populated but sprawling garrison town named after the mother of Austrian emperor Joseph II, Maria Theresa. The Jews of Kladno, Vanesa Sr. and her family among them, would be some of first offered "relocation" to this new Jewish *Reichsaltersheim*, paradise ghetto, in Terezin — better known today by its German name, Theresienstadt.

>—/

Prague, December 1991

Tears or no tears, horrific yet mute wartime experiences notwithstanding, my Vanesa knew that her mother's strident European sensibilities would have been gravely offended at her current state — hair matted, coat smeared with garbage floor grime, reeking of urine. She almost laughed at the thought, but the laugh came out as a muffled sob, which she choked back with no small effort as she passed a couple walking arm in arm in the arctic Prague dusk. This was decidedly not how she had expected this evening to turn out.

She had expected to find answers. Like a porter carrying a load up endless flights of steep stairs, she had fervently hoped to finally set down the list of questions she'd been accruing since childhood. It was a list that had ballooned since her father's death a month previously, since she'd inherited the shop, since she'd received the diary.

She walked on with increasing urgency, occasionally breaking into a stumbling, shivering trot. She tripped on the stairs of her nondescript hotel, looking up as she caught her balance at the façade whose architectural glory was intact yet well concealed under decades of Soviet-era grime, as was much of the city. Prague's most notable color in 1991 was grey. The bright colors of centuries past had faded with the neglect of collective ownership and the exhaust from two-cycle engines in East German *Trabants*, the cars with the quasi-cardboard body that had descended on Czechoslovakia in recent years.

It brought to mind the story about Everybody, Somebody, Anybody and Nobody: there was an important job to be done, and Everybody and Anybody were asked to pitch in. However, since Everybody was sure that Somebody would do it, in the end Nobody did. Until the Velvet Revolution of 1989, only two years previously, Nobody had done much in the way of preserving Prague's architectural heritage because, after all, it was Everybody's responsibility.

The night clerk barely acknowledged her as she brushed through the lobby. Far worse than the corruption, oppression and poverty the Soviets had brought with them from the East was the uniquely Russian ability to utterly ignore anyone they didn't feel like seeing.

Vanesa recalled her foray to the Information desk of the *Intourist* section of the Prague airport after she landed at 3 a.m. *Intourist* had been the Soviet agency responsible for handling incoming tourism to the empire. Among the agency's goals had been to minimize exposure of Soviet citizens to decadent Western influences. This had been accomplished in Prague, as in many other Soviet airports, by completely segregating Westerners. In Prague, they used a separate wing of the airport. In less central Soviet-era airports, they literally herded foreigners into corrals populated by rough wooden benches and surrounded by three-meter high corrugated metal walls, often erected right in the middle of a busy terminal hall.

The green-uniformed Information attendant, blowing on tea steaming in a clear glass embraced by a metal cup holder, pored over a newspaper and simultaneously sucked on a smelly Belomorkanal cigarette. She'd looked up with one apathetic eye as Vanesa approached to inquire about traveling into the city. Without putting down her cigarette or spilling a drop of tea, in a gesture as clearly practiced as blowing her nose or cupping her hands against the wind to light a cigarette, the attendant had reached up with one hand, slammed the office reception window down, and flipped the handwritten sign dangling on the frayed string from *Otevreno* — open — to *Zavreno* — closed. Vanesa's entreaties, first verbal and then increasingly percussive on the office window, had not even caused the woman to look up. If Vanesa had spontaneously self-combusted right there in front of the window, she felt sure that the attendant would have laconically and tiredly reached up and tripped the fire alarm, still cradling her tea cup in one hand, and then gone back to her newspaper.

If she'd noticed at all.

Passing by the night clerk, one part of her briefly wondered if he was even breathing. She ran up the two floors of steep and carpeted stairs to her room, and fumbled with her key, almost breaking it off in the lock. After entering the room, she threw herself into the white sterility of the bathroom, stripping clothes desperately off her body in layers, some already dried and crusted, others still wet and sticky. She left the reeking pile of clothes in a corner and climbed into the tub. She turned the water on full force, and didn't even wait for the shower to run hot before immersing herself in the cleansing, stinging stream.

And still no tears.

$$\longmapsto\!\!\!/$$

Terezin, 1941

Vanesa Sr.'s father toiled among the 300 Jewish workmen sent to prepare Terezin for its transformation into the "paradise ghetto." By January the following year, nearly 10,000 more Jews would join him, initially from Bohemia and Moravia but soon from all across Europe, eventually swelling the ghetto until its population density reached a staggering average of over 130,000 per square kilometer.

The notice had come in October of the previous year, a laconic, one-page form letter in German. Vanesa brought the envelope home from the post office, wrapped up against the autumn chill in her mother's long and thick woolen scarf. Her mother set down the tea she was drinking when Vanesa came in, and her hands trembled as she slit the envelope. Skimming the flimsy page, her mother pressed her knuckles to her lips, unable to answer her daughter's stream of questions.

Later, when her father came home, he explained that the paper said that they were going to move. He called it "relocation." They were going to live in a new *Judenwohnbezirk*, a Jewish residential district—the Nazis had forbidden the use of the term "ghetto." They were lucky, he said, using the same smile he used when convincing her to eat something that he himself despised. Since he was to be part of the "advance guard," they'd get their choice of where to live.

This, at least, turned out to be true.

On February 22, 1942, Vanesa, with her mother and younger brother Nicklas, arrived in Thereisenstadt on Transport Y from Kladno to join her father. The railroad spur extending into the walls of the Terezin ghetto would only be completed in June of the following year, built by some 300 Jewish slave laborers, including Vanesa's father. She and her family, along with tens of thousands of other Jews, had to walk three frigidly damp kilometers from the train terminus in Bohusovice. Their route took them through the village: past bored-looking Nazi guards posted every 100 meters along the treeless cobblestoned route; past countless eyes peeking from curtained windows, watching the macabre parade; past the more brazen villagers who congregated on street corners, shamelessly offering the marchers food at wildly inflated prices.

With heavy suitcases held by now-aching arms, they reached the thick, snow-covered, brick-vaulted ramparts of Theresienstadt after several hours. The barbed-wire barricade was moved, and they were marched into the ghetto that would be their home for the next three years. Nicklas whined feebly, his hand no longer sweaty in hers, as their mother prodded them on.

True to her Father's promise, they did enjoy "privileged" private quarters when they first arrived in Terezin, although the family was soon split up. The Nazis assigned them to a drafty attic apartment near the Dresden barracks, by the fortress's northernmost rampart, where her father worked. A narrow iron staircase twisted up from the back of the building's treeless courtyard to the low apartment door. The apartment was a dark, twenty-square-meter space divided in the middle by a rough shelving unit that held the family's meager wardrobe. Their carefully-packed, labeled, and weighed suitcases were immediately confiscated upon arrival, and never returned.

"We need to ask ourselves," my Vanesa once lectured me, "why the Germans would go to the trouble of making them pack according to such stringent restrictions, when they knew that their bags would be taken away immediately upon arrival in Thereisenstadt. The answer is simple: the power of hope. The very same reason the gas chambers at Auschwitz had hooks for people to hang their garments on prior to 'showering.' Hope, even when it is consciously or unconsciously known to be false hope, is the great normalizer. In its absence, we are adrift and unpredictable, and predictability was key to the Nazis' plans. They knew that people who had packed for relocation were far likelier to cooperate than people rounded up in the middle of the night, and that people who had to pay for their transport tickets to Auschwitz were more likely to get quietly on the train."

The apartment's small floor space was flanked with short sleeping bunks built into the walls. A small wood stove, not much bigger than a large soup pot, blossomed at the terminus of the winding chimney, whose harried window exit let in chilly air in the winter and mosquitoes in the spring.

And then... there was no more. Vanesa Sr. never spoke of the years between walking into the attic apartment in Terezin in 1942 and meeting her husband, Michael, in the Displaced Persons camp in Cyprus in 1946.

My Vanesa knew that her mother remained in Terezin until almost the end of the war, and was then sent to Auschwitz. She knew that neither her grandmother, grandfather, or Uncle Nicklas had survived the war. The rest she had to imagine, and later, piece by piece, to learn for herself.

Sometimes, she daydreamed that Vanesa Sr. had been a resistance fighter, hiding in the sewers, popping up at incongruous places, silently slitting the throats of unsuspecting Nazis. Or an intrepid *saboteur*, a factory worker who sabotaged munitions production by day and printed anti-Nazi literature by candlelight at night. Or even a nurse, caring for the sick, the elderly, the children of the ghetto. Anything, my Vanesa thought, anything but what Vanesa Sr. had most likely been after both her mother and father had been sent East on one of the countless transports from which no one ever returned: a scabby ghetto orphan, lice-infested, dressed in rags, scrabbling for blackened potatoes in the dirt, stealing from supply carts as they left the kitchens.

Later, as she learned more, my Vanesa imagined another scene. She dreamed that, nine months after her mother's arrival in Thereisenstadt, her interests in the surroundings not yet eclipsed by loneliness, hunger and rumors of the next transport, Vanesa Sr. might have looked out the dusty window of the sweltering third-floor barracks one day in July 1942. She might have seen a little boy almost her age struggling along the steamy rain-washed street behind his mother and father. She might have seen his arms straining at a child-sized leather-covered valise, which had been clearly labeled in white paint with his name, transport number, and destination. If Vanesa Sr. looked closer, she might have seen him pause, sitting carefully on the curbstone to avoid wetting his pants, as his father asked directions to the quarters the Nazis had assigned them. She might have seen her future husband Michael gaze around at the treeless streets, taking in the cracked plaster of the buildings and the uneven cobblestones over which the carts rattled in the morning, some bringing thin soup or moldy bread, others collecting the night's dead.

And maybe, just maybe, she saw him find a twig and scratch absent-mindedly into the dirt the symbol he'd only recently first encountered in Prague:

CHAPTER 4

PERSISTENCE

Prague, December 1991

She didn't call me. I've never gotten over this, even knowing how important Uncle Tomas was to her then, even knowing I was out that night, anyway. I allow myself the irrational luxury of indignation. I tell myself that I was her husband, damn it, she should have turned to me first, especially in light of what she was to discover. As if I was somehow derelict in my husbandly duties, as if I were the one so damaged as to lack the capacity to love.

She should have called me. But she didn't.

As petty revenge for her imposition on his late-night poetry writing, the indifferent night clerk made sure that getting through to Uncle Tomas in Israel was as difficult as possible.

She sat on the plush yet dusty bench in the hotel lobby's glass-walled international phone booth. She listened to many minutes of scratchy clicking—like thousands of kittens playing on sandpaper—and waited to speak to the one man capable of eliciting her tears.

Uncle Tomas picked up with a cross and sleepy hello, but recognized my Vanessa's distant gasp immediately. He said one word, *Kotě*—kitten—his pet name for her since time immemorial. Then, as he had since she was a girl, he waited for the flash flood to arrive and pass, simply listening and uttering occasional words of comfort. When her waters slowed to a muddy trickle, he spoke, asking in his soft, old man voice what had happened.

She blurted out the story, and imagined him nodding gravely, stroking his chin, considering what she said.

He always took her seriously, even when the entreaty was a simple childhood dispute. "And what do you think we should do about this, now, *Kotě*?" he would say after she finished, and then succinctly but flawlessly summarize the point of contention she related in his own words, to emphasize that he'd been listening.

Her own father would nod sagely and pretend to listen, but be hard-pressed to relate what she just said, at any age. Her mother would tear up at the first mention of anything even smacking of conflict.

But Uncle Tomas actually and truly listened.

And he listened now, despite the hour, despite the collect call, and despite Vanesa's long-distance snuffling. To her repeated entreaty, "What could they mean, I pissed people off?", he surmised that her Western clothes, her clearly non-native Czech, and even her Judaism could easily be an affront to some of the more bitter remnants of the recently-ended Communist era. They'd seen her leave her hotel, he guessed, perhaps spoken with the insouciant night clerk, and found out she was Israeli. She was lucky, he said, that it hadn't been worse.

"But what we need to do is learn from this, *Kotě*. Now will you come home? I worry about you. This trip, it was a bad idea. No good can come of this grubbing about in the past. Take it from an old man—look forward, not back."

He was not surprised when she flatly refused to even consider abandoning her quest. He knew that the stubborn little girl he'd once counseled had grown into a stubborn young woman—a young woman "as persistent as a kitten with a cockroach," he once joked, and the nickname had stuck. But he was right.

The persistence of a people that had not taken "no" for an answer from the world community on its path to nationhood seemed to have embodied itself in young Vanesa, who exceeded even Israeli standards of "devotion to mission," as the Israel Defense Forces liked to put it. From learning to ride her bike in one single day of scraped knees and bruised elbows, to using those very same elbows to make room for herself as a cub reporter in the competitive world of the IDF radio station, *Galey Zahal*, during her compulsory military service, to scrabbling her way to an MA *cum laude* in Modern History and a Ph.D. from Tel Aviv University—Vanesa was persistence incarnate.

This was a girl, he probably reminded himself as he hung up the phone, having vaguely promised her that he would contact his friend and find out what happened, who had grown up with parents she never really knew. Now she was willing to go to great lengths to finally know at least one of them.

>—/

My Vanesa's father, Michael Neuman, was born in Prague in 1931, a year in which still-young Czechoslovakia was experiencing the thrill that roller coaster riders feel at the peak of the largest hill, moments before plummeting into the unknown. Just prior to Hitler's 1933 rise in neighboring Germany, it was a time when the country, founded only thirteen years earlier on the ashes of the Austro-Hungarian Empire, was growing in commercial prowess, well on its way to becoming the tenth largest industrial economy in the world. Skoda automobiles, Prague ham, Pilsner beer—Czechoslovak products were in demand across Europe.

Even as Austrian and German banks failed in the wake of the worldwide depression that started in 1929 in the United States, the Czechoslovak economy remained stalwart... for the time being, at least. It was the age of prominence and almost universal esteem for the country's inveterate and seemingly eternal founding father and President, Tomas Masaryk. On the coattails of the country's prosperity, small businesses like that owned by Jakub Neuman, my Vanesa's grandfather, flourished.

The cramped, dank, and odious shop was tucked away in a courtyard just off Wencelas Square, only a block from the massive and stately National Museum building, wherein many of his works were displayed. Reached through a long dark passageway under the street-facing building, the entrance to which was bordered by a coffee shop on one side and a barber shop on the other, his store was a Mecca for Prague's elite hunting and naturalist community.

Unlike her mother's toxic memories, Michael's early childhood, he recalled to my Vanesa, was "pastoral." Pastoral. This was the exact word he used, she told me. Pastoral, in the heart of a burgeoning European capital, a mixture of horse-drawn wagons and cars choking the central square of the city. This was where her father had played, with the din of the streetcars clanging all hours of the day, living in a small flat above the shop.

"This is not my definition of pastorality," she said once, "and I always tried to imagine what he meant. Was it some kind of calm he found in the city? Was it the hunting trips he used to take with my grandfather? Or did he have some other, inner definition of pastoral in mind? Perhaps, in light of what was to come, he really meant simple, understandable, or just safe?"

She never asked him, and he never explained.

The more I think of this, the more I question Vanesa's ability to ever understand it. She too grew up in the heart of a city — a city, in which nature has been vanquished and humanity lives unafraid of feral competition, immersed in its own seething juices, self-absorbed, asking questions about and afraid only of its own kind. What could she know of pastorality?

Like Vanesa Sr., his future wife, Michael was nine years old when the German army marched into Prague. Like her, he could recall his parents' grim faces, the rumbling of the trucks and tanks, the tramp of leather-booted feet, and the outrage of the people around him, which was in short order locked tightly away, packed like Bohemian crystal under layers of cottony self-interest and let out only in private whisperings.

My Vanesa knew that Michael and his family were sent to Terezin in July 1942, as the Nazis stepped up relocations from within the Prague Jewish community. She knew that Jakub, like Vanesa's father in Kladno, received a letter one day instructing him to report with his family to the Prague's Hlavni Nadrazi — central train station — on the warm July morning, and informing what he could and could not take with him.

"How innocuously terrifying letters like that must have been," my Vanesa lectured me. "History can truly come alive if you try to imagine yourself in a given situation. Try to feel what my grandfather must have felt, as he held a flimsy piece of typewritten paper that was to change his entire life. Can you? Can you even imagine?"

She liked to challenge me, but her motives were rarely pedagogical. This particular challenge, like a thousand others of its kind, was designed to viscerally demonstrate how insensitive I was—how lacking in empathy, how unable to comprehend the vast gulf of sorrow that she traversed as she pieced together what little she knew of her father's trip to Terezin.

From her research, Vanesa knew when her father's family left Prague, and from what train station. She knew that Michael and Jakub returned to Prague shortly thereafter, which was a rarity, since not many Prague Jews sent to Terezin came back alive. She knew that her grandmother, Alena, stayed behind in Terezin, too sick to travel, according to Uncle Tomas. And Vanesa knew that neither her father nor grandfather ever saw Alena again.

"And that was all I ever knew," she said. As with her mother, Vanesa's father's life began in the 1930s and continued in the 1950s, but most of the years in between were blank, or at least blurred, like a charcoal sketch rubbed unrecognizable with the side of a hand. She had never pressed them for details, though.

"The biggest mystery of my life, and I could never bring myself to ask either of them about it. What if they thought I didn't care?" she asked me desolately, yet rhetorically, one evening after Michael's death. She was dry-eyed and remote, as if she mourned the loss of her father's story as much as the loss of the man himself.

She knew so little of Michael. He had tried sincerely to be kindly, fatherly, loving and involved in her life. He was always ready to try to assist her with homework, and tried to interest her in the art to which he was so intensely devoted. He created beauty, he said, and beauty was uncompromising. Yet like most of us, he excelled at spotting the flaws in what he created, while remaining blind to those within him.

"He was there, but not really there. It was like he went through the motions of life and played the part of the basically nice father really, really well. But it was still an act, a persona he assumed, and there were, of course, cracks in this persona. He never, ever, talked about the War. I tried a couple times, especially when we started to study about it in school. He was polite and smiling, but I got the message very early on, from both him and my mother, that this was not something we spoke of."

There was, however, a single revealing night, when she'd gotten a direct, if accidental, glimpse at the depths of her father's pain. "It was kind of like peeking in the window of a torture chamber. You know more or less the nature of what you're going to see, and one part of you just doesn't want to see it. On the other hand, there's no way you're not going to look in, if you can," she said.

She'd been sixteen, her mother's death four years previously still an open wound festering in the silence of the small, tidy flat above the shop, its rounded Bauhaus balcony overlooking Nahalat Binyamin Street's cramped intersection with Levinsky Street. It was late. She'd been out with friends. A winter rain lashed the windows, and she was chilled and wet, having forgotten her umbrella. Her sneakers were soaked and her toes cold. The lights in the flat were dimmed when she came upstairs. A scratchy Dvorak concerto played on the record player — cello now weeping, now imploring, now demanding, now breaking into radiant glory, as if all it had asked had been fulfilled.

Her father sat in the puddle of light that dripped from the single bulb over the scratched Formica kitchen table. The Kerosene "Fireside" heater glowed dimly nearby. He was almost incoherently drunk. "Like, one step short of alcohol poisoning," she told me. "Yet when I walked in, he noticed me right away."

He noticed her, and reacted quickly, but then he looked through her, as if she were transparent. It was as if she'd momentarily exited his awareness, and been replaced with something insubstantial yet infinitely more powerful. He stared with blank eyes, his voice a slurred whisper and his fists clenched as he spoke in Czech. "Goddamn you. Goddamn you! Preserving life. What kind of life did you preserve, Papa? And for whom? You? Me? Who?"

Vanesa asked him what he meant, but he didn't respond. He just put his head down on the table, muttering "goddamn you" over and over, hands still clutching the leather-bound diary with the yellowing pages, which he'd slammed closed when she came in. It was a book she'd seen twice in her life: once that night, and only again a decade later when it was given to her after Michael's death, some six months prior to her arrival in Prague.

CHAPTER 5

MOE

From the Diary of Michael Neuman, Prague, January 1943

We are limited only by that which we can't imagine. That's what Moe said when I told him that driving a tractor and taking care of farm animals was a funny job for a Jew. I asked him whether I could become an American soldier like him, if I just imagined it. He laughed and said in his funny American-accented Czech, which was always mixed with a little German, that he hoped by the time I was old enough, there'd be no need for the resistance.

His full name is Mojzis Jehlicka, and he was born in America. I came down to see him through the air duct, the one with the symbol in the grillwork. He liked to chat, said it helped pass the time while he was waiting to "ship out." His father, Petr, left the town of Most in the Sudetenland in 1920. Petr was always swimming against the tide, Moe said. If tens of thousands of expatriate Czechs were flocking from the US to newly-founded Czechoslovakia, his father would have been, without fail, the only one leaving.

Petr carried his small valise up the gangplank on the docks of Bremen, having no idea what was to come. He just needed to leave Most, to leave his father's tailor shop, to take matters into his own hands. He had no idea he would, that very evening, meet his future wife, Darina, in the third-class dining room. He had no idea they would be married only weeks after landing at Ellis Island, or that he'd shortly thereafter find himself traveling via train across vast Midwestern cornfields to stay with her cousins in South Bend, Indiana. And he certainly could not have guessed that only a year later, in the rickety white house on his and Darina's 40-acre farm just outside Wakarusa, Indiana, which was actually owned for the most part by the South Bend branch of Keybank, Moe would be born.

The name Wakarusa, Moe said, means "knee deep in mud" in some native American language. That's just how Moe grew up, he joked — knee deep in Indiana mud.

I said that at least in Indiana, there were no black leather boots clomping on cobblestones, like here — only black rubber boots sloshing in the mud.

He laughed and said that I had a point.

Moe never knew he was a Jew until after he was drafted into the US army in 1941. He was twenty-two years old, living in Chicago and working as a clerk at a meatpacking plant. The envelope from the US Selective Service Board came with the Order to Report for Induction inside, and he showed up on the appointed day for his physical. On the registration card, he checked White in the Race column, and Native Born in the Nationality column, and that was that. After basic training, he came home to Wakarusa for Christmas, being scheduled to ship out for Europe early in January.

Sitting by the radio, he and his father were listening to news of anti-Semitism in Germany — rumors of mass killings, roundups, deportations. Suddenly, his father began to cry. "And that was it," Moe said. "I was Jewish. They'd never told me, all that time. It just wasn't a part of their new American identity."

On Moe's farm, they raised cows and chickens, and even had a horse — a brown one with a white mark in the shape of a star on its forehead. In Indiana, Moe said, the sky never ends like it does here.

I tried to imagine a sky that just keeps going, out past the walls, over the barbed wire of the blockades, arching endlessly into the distance, but it's hard from in here.

In 1926, in the middle of winter and the middle of a snowstorm, Moe's younger brother Samuel was born. Moe still remembers his mother's screams, which he heard even from the barn, where his father told him to stay once he'd finished taking care of the midwife's horse, rubbing him down, hanging the rough wool blanket over his steaming back, feeding him a warm bran mash. They called him Sammy—the brother, not the horse.

Moe said I remind him of Sammy at my age, because I ask lots of questions, but usually don't wait for the answer to one question before I ask the next.

There wasn't much to the town of Wakarusa, built at the crossroads of Indiana State Road 40 and County Road 3, but the fact that the houses in town were so close—neighbors right next door, not two miles down the road—made it seem like a bustling city to Moe. Every day, as the grimy yellow school bus pulled into town, Moe would sit on his knees on the wooden bench seats and watch the houses go by with his nose pressed to the steamy glass of the sliding window. He'd watch the shops as the bus passed through the only intersection in town with enough traffic to warrant a stoplight, and think of how someday he'd see a city with real buildings.

The very same bus would take him, and later Sammy, too, down the gravel road on the long drive to the white farmhouse. Living so far from town, Moe and Sammy were instant playmates despite their age difference. It was a default arrangement, not one of choice, because Petr and Darina were far too occupied with running the farm to mind a little boy. That was a brother's job, they said. That was how it needed to be.

Some days, they would meet after school with Albert, who was Moe's age and lived on the neighboring farm. Albert would get off the yellow school bus with them, one stop early, and walk home whistling across the west field just as the sun was kissing it good evening with long orange lips. Over time they became a threesome—Moe and Albert, with Sammy tagging along. Sometimes they welcomed Sammy, but mostly they just put up with him. Occasionally, they were cruel in the intuitive, crushing way that only older brothers seem to know.

Albert Eberhardt spoke German better than Moe and Sammy. His last name meant "strong as a boar," but Moe always thought of it as "strong as a bear," since Albert was the most bearish boy Moe ever met. He was taller by a head than Moe, rounder by two feet, and had shocks of brown hair that seemed to have been glued to the top of his egg-shaped head. His parents had come from Germany less than five years before, and still hoped to return one day, "when things got better." That's why they spoke German at home, unlike Moe's mother and father, who insisted on communicating, even among themselves in the presence of the children, in clumsy English.

For a time, Moe, Albert and Sammy did everything together. They played hide-and-seek in the stalls and haylofts of the big red barn. They swam in the mud-bottomed pond—which was said to have leeches, although Moe never found any. They shot at squirrels and crows with homemade slingshots. They even rode the horse. And in the winter they'd go ice skating on the pond.

The pond was as big as half an American football field. A thick layer of green algae clung to its edges by the end of summer, and thick clouds of mosquitoes rose from it, so that even the horse wouldn't go near it. By mid-winter, the pond would freeze over, and once the snow had been cleared off with manure shovels, the surface was as smooth as glass. Skating on it was like flying. The frigid wind would bite at their cheeks, but could not disturb the warmth of their deep inner joy.

It was a crisp sunny Saturday, an early winter day when the air was so cold that Moe and Sammy's scarves turned white with frost from their breath, and they couldn't feel the tips of their fingers or ears after five minutes outside. Moe's father and mother were off in town, buying supplies, when Albert came by, dangling his skates over his shoulder and walking carefully as the tips of the blades poked him in the side with each step.

Petr had warned Moe and Sammy never to skate on the pond unless he personally checked the ice first.

"But it's a perfect skating day! What are you guys scared of?" Albert jeered when they refused to skate. The fog of his breath made him look like a locomotive pulling out of a railway station.

Moe and Sammy stood on the front porch, leaning against the peeling white porch columns. They were deeply bundled in solid color winter coats, polka-dotted mittens they'd received from some cousins, and striped knit hats, Sammy's with a pompom on top.

"I told you. We're not allowed to skate," Sammy insisted, "unless our dad checks the ice first."

"I'll check the ice," Albert said. "I'm almost twelve, and I'm very responsible. That's what my Ma says. I can do it. Come on!"

Moe didn't say anything. He knew what his father had said, but he thought that Albert was right, and that they were old enough to check the ice themselves. He couldn't say this out loud, though, in case Sammy told Dad later, so it was left to Sammy to decide. If he agreed not to tell, they could skate.

Sammy thought about the offer. His face screwed up in concentration as he considered the pros and cons, the costs and the benefits. Finally, he nodded enthusiastically. He wanted to skate. If somebody else could give permission, he was all for it.

Albert and Moe checked the ice carefully, prodding it with sticks at the pond's edge, and deliberating at length while Sammy waited on the porch. Finally, they turned to Sammy and nodded.

The older boys were fooling around in the center of the pond when they noticed that Sammy wasn't there. At first, they just figured he'd gone up to the house to pee, and continued playing. After twenty minutes, they finally got curious enough to take off their skates and check in the house.

Sammy wasn't there.

They called his name with increasing urgency, and Moe went to check in the barn.

Albert went back around the side of the house, towards the pond. That's when he saw the hole in the ice at the far end of the pond, and the back side of a blue parka hood bobbing gently in the center of the hole.

When they pulled him out, Sammy's face was bluish-white, the color of an old blueberry pie stain on a white shirt. His eyes were open and questioning, as if he couldn't quite figure out what had happened.

Moe told his father and mother that Sammy must have wandered down to the pond to skate without permission, while they were playing in the house. Yes, he was supposed to watch him. Yes, it was a brother's job. No, it wasn't too much to ask. Yes, he was so, so, so sorry. Yes, he knew they would never forgive him. And yes, he would go to his room.

The house fell silent after Sammy's death. Jobs were done, chores completed, meals eaten and dishes washed, but all in silence. Unable to successfully conceal the accusation in their eyes, Moe's parents looked away.

So did Moe.

About a week after Sammy's funeral, Moe and Albert met behind the barn after school one snowy afternoon.

As soon as they were out of earshot of the house, Moe opened the floodgates. "How could you tell us that the ice was safe?" he screamed, moving towards Albert until their faces almost touched. "We believed you. It's all your fault! You fucking Kraut, you killed Sammy! You killed my brother!"

Albert pushed Moe away. "I didn't hear you arguing with me. You wanted to skate! You could have stopped the whole thing. And besides...." Albert pushed Moe again and raised his fists, ready to strike. "You should have been watching your brother. It's your fault!"

Moe swung out blindly, missing Albert and falling to the ground, and sobbed. He stayed that way for a long time.

Finally, Albert turned to walk away. After he'd walked a few steps, he turned back and said simply, "Moe, I'm sorry... for Sammy. I liked him, too. He was a good kid. I'm... I'm sorry for Sammy."

Moe looked up, surprised, his tears frozen in winding tracks on his cheeks. His friend was trying to take a share of his guilt, trying to lighten the burden that he knew even then would weigh him down for the rest of his life. He nodded thanks to Albert, snuffled, and managed to croak, "For Sammy."

Albert turned to leave, and never came back.

Moe didn't see Albert after that, except at school, from afar. After a while, he didn't see Albert around at all. Kids said that he'd left. His family had sold their farm and moved back to Germany.

>—⫞

The sky was cloudy and as black as a midnight forest the night Moe dropped into the Protectorate of Bohemia and Moravia, the *Reichsprotektorat*, as the Germans now call this country, as if changing the name might somehow change how much they are despised. He was part of a small reconnaissance team, all Czech and German speakers. Their mission was top secret, and they needed to make contact with the Czech underground.

There was no hope for Moe to see where he was going to land, or even what was below him. As he floated down, trying to brace for the crunching impact but not knowing when it would come, a low-level gust of wind grabbed him. He was helpless in its grasp as it carried him farther and farther away from the silhouettes of his comrades' parachutes, which quickly dissolved into the inky sky.

Alone and without a radio, he had just his rifle, a map to the rendezvous, and his wits.

He managed to see the ground rising up to meet him just seconds before he landed hard in a plowed field. He rolled, and was immediately on his feet, weapon at the ready as he gathered the parachute into a puffy pile. He hid the chute in some bushes at the edge of the field, and checked his gear. He took a bearing on the stars, which were visible since the wind that had hijacked him had also blown away the cloud cover. He consulted his map, checked his compass, and set off across the field, ducking low to avoid being seen in profile against the stars.

The landscape around him lay completely silent, with no sign of life, animal or human, insect or bird. It was as if life had deserted that section of the world, except for Moe. He crept on, passing through a clump of trees, crossing a creek on slippery stepping stones, carefully going over a barbed-wire fence. He was tense; something was not right, but he had to get to the rendezvous—the mission depended on it, the very outcome of the war might depend on it, and his comrades were counting on him. He couldn't let them down.

After several hours, just as the sky in the East was turning to gray, he spotted the spire that marked the meeting point, in the cemetery next to the church. He crept to edge of the cemetery, now on his belly, each muscle under control as he inched forward like a snake stalking a mouse, his every movement calculated to avoid detection. As he raised himself above the rough stone wall, he saw several profiles in silhouette, all with the distinctive Allied helmet shape. He crept closer, over the wall, and then gravestone by gravestone until he was just behind the men. None of the other soldiers moved. They had not seen him. He couldn't see their faces, and he didn't like that, but he needed to make contact. There was no other way.

Slowly, he stood up.

The three German soldiers, who hadn't heard him coming, scrambled up so fast that the unstrapped Allied helmets fell from their heads to the ground. It was a trap!

Moe flopped to the ground, stomach first. He tasted dirt even as he cocked the carbine, just like he'd practiced a million times in basic training. He had cover behind the gravestones, and the Germans hadn't seen where he went. With his first shot, he took out one that came into his sights. He rolled gently to the next row of headstones and, upon hearing a crunch nearby, unstrapped the trench knife from his calf. As the German walked by him, he tripped him, pounced on him, and slit his throat, feeling the man's warm blood running over his fingers as he did so.

Only one German remained, and Moe had to get him before he alerted any other forces nearby. He heard a footstep, the snapping of a twig. The man moved toward the cemetery gate, several rows away from Moe. There was no time to lose, but Moe didn't have a clear shot. He engaged the carbine's safety and wiped his knife on his pants leg. It was better to handle this quietly, in any case, so as not to attract any other Germans.

The Nazi never saw him coming, but unlike the second soldier, this one put up a fight. Moe's carbine went flying as they struggled, his hand over the soldier's mouth to prevent him from yelling. The soldier went for his gun, but Moe knocked that away. Moe got the Nazi into a full nelson hold, but the soldier worked an arm free from his grip and went for his knife. Moe flipped him over before he could reach the knife, his own knife coming up to the German's throat, ready for the kill.

As the dawn turned orange, and the first rays of the new day fell on the graveyard, Moe looked down into the face of the German whose throat he was about to cut and....

Albert's eyes stared back at him.

Albert's mouth dropped open in mute shock as he recognized his old friend. "For Sammy!" he gasped, trying to move back away from Moe's now-hesitant hold. "For Sammy! For the love of God," he pleaded in a whisper.

Moe lowered the knife, and they stared at each other silently, as if carrying on a whole conversation with their eyes only. Moe nodded his head, and Albert got up to leave. He turned and looked back at Moe, and repeated "For Sammy!" one last time.

Albert left the cemetery, and Moe, behind, calling out in German as he ran. "An American paratrooper! After him, he's gone west! Follow me!"

Moe got up and headed off to the east.

After many other adventures, which he hasn't told me about yet, he ended up here with us in Prague.

CHAPTER 6

SOULESS

Wisconsin, 1982

The first time I kissed Vanesa Neuman was in the summer of 1982, and she tasted of peanut butter. It was the kiss of youth, hesitant at first—sheepish and smiling, stomach quivering like after a long drink of cold water in August heat—then increasingly eager, exploratory, and sensual. Finally, we surrendered to it with the breathless capacity for abandon that so inevitably dissipates with age.

Her being a counselor-in-training, a junior staff member, made her fair game for the returning senior staff, who were more than eager to try out what had until recently been off limits. She had convinced her father to allow her to return for the summer, I happily learned in one of the many tightly-packed aerogrammes she sent during the course of the year. I sent many letters myself, and our correspondence became the type of fluid, considered, and revealing written conversation now incongruous with the shoot-from-the-hip speed of emails and instant messages.

Even years later, as I looked over these letters in her loopy, girlish, gawkily endearing handwriting, they inevitably made me smile. Reading them alone in my dorm room at night all those years ago, I discovered the true power of a young man's yearning.

When I saw her again that summer, my yearning had not diminished.

Our first touches were hesitant, much like the way she'd revealed what she knew of her mother's life and history, to which she made only passing references. These were separated by interregnum banter, home updates, and — largely — news and politics.

As we became more familiar with each other, our hands sought out the right places intuitively, with an erotic fluidity that was — to my chagrin — chaste by strict definition. Her virginity was not one of the things Vanesa shared with me that summer. In our correspondence, however, she freely gave the details of her efforts to breach the gaps in her mother's life story.

"I could never ask my father about the war," she wrote to me in February of 1982. "It's just not something we talk about, something we could *ever* talk about. And my mother is gone, so it's too late to ask her. I could possibly ask Uncle Tomas, but... well, I've decided to take a different route. Don't tell my father — ha-ha — but I've been spending time in the Yad V'Shem archive in Jerusalem. I mean, he knows I go there, but he thinks it's for school. In fact, I'm researching my mother, and him, and Uncle Tomas."

My Vanesa had found her mother quite easily, and had reconstructed her story in the strictly historical sense. Yet people made up the stream of history — it burbled with their actions, flowed over the rocks of their emotions and fears, was sullied by their weaknesses, and rushed by their small triumphs.

No matter how many times she went back to Yad V'Shem, there were details my Vanesa could never find.

She could know that her mother, grandmother, and Uncle Niklas had arrived in Thereisenstadt on February 22, 1942 on Transport Y from Kladno. She could know that the train was owned and operated for the Nazis by the Bohmisch-Mahrische Bahnen company, and she could know the exact stops the train made on the way. She could know that her Uncle Niklas had died of typhus on December 13, 1942, several months after he was ripped from the care of his parents, who left Terezin on Transport Bk to Maly Trostenets on September 9, 1942 with 1000 other Jews, only two of whom survived, neither of them Vanesa Sr.'s parents.

She could know that Vanesa Sr. lived as an orphan, together with hundreds of other girls, in the building designated L410, next to the Catholic Church on Hauptstrasse, the ghetto's main street, for two terrible years after her parent's deportation. And she knew that Vanesa Sr. had been sent, together with 2498 other people, to Auschwitz on Transport Ek, which left Terezin on September 28, 1944. And she knew, of course, for certain that Vanesa Sr. was among the "lucky" 20% that were not sent immediately on arrival to the gas chambers, and that she was one of the only 51 people from Transport Ek that ultimately survived the war.

She could know these facts, but that left much more that she could never know.

"I'll never know how she felt, walking to Terezin in the cold from Buhosovice, being parted from my grandparents, hearing that her brother had died, getting on a train alone to Auschwitz," she wrote. "I can see the scenes like postcards in my head, accurate down to the most minute details, because I've learned all I can know. But the visceral depth of her horrors will always escape me. She carried them, and I'll never be able to share, never ease her suffering, never lighten her burden even just a little."

That regret only grew over time. It was regret satiated neither by meetings with Terezin survivors, nor by lengthy visits to the Beit Terezin Museum in Kibbutz Givat Haim. Her regret drove her, sometimes manically. It shaped her. It came to define her, and eventually surrounded and engulfed her. Her regret drove my Vanesa to subsume her very identity, to take her mother's name as her own—as if by carrying the name she could somehow assume at least some of her mother's pain, the pain she could never feel.

And so, when I kissed Vanesa Neuman that moonlit night on the dock where we'd sat platonically the previous year, I was attempting to approach the unapproachable. In retrospect, it marked the beginning of the end for us, or maybe the end which came at the beginning. It was the first of my infinite yet futile attempts to fix the unfixable.

But that night, she still tasted like the peanut butter she'd used—I found out later—as glue to stick chocolate chip cookies all over my just-washed white car, in response to some private joke that I can't for the life of me recall today. It seemed funny then. And her smug look, the way her mouth, still moist from our kiss, held a mock serious pose while her eyes silently laughed as I peeled the cookies one by one from my prize Ford—it was this memory of that summer of discovery that never left me, and likely never will.

>—/

Prague, December 1991

After the call with Uncle Tomas, Vanesa did not call me. Instead, she returned to her room, stopping briefly at the desk to request laundry service for her soiled clothes. The bespectacled clerk gave her his best tortured intellectual glare, resenting her imposition on his creative process, and jotted a note to himself. He then lowered his eyes to indicate the completion of their conversation, giving her mute leave to go.

Back in her room, the smell of urine still seeping under the crack in the bathroom door, Vanesa paced, trying to dispel thoughts best left unconsidered from her head. Yet they returned persistently, like little rivulets of water running under the door that prefaced the flood to come. She shouldn't have come. She didn't need to be here. She was, in the kindly yet crass words of her high school drama teacher, "pissing down her leg."

To my Vanesa, and to many Israeli children of survivors, Europe forever remained a dead world, a graveyard, a purgatory or nether-land whose inhabitants existed as if unaware of their undead status. They continued to eat, to breathe, to screw, and to love—but how could they be truly alive in a place that Vanesa's father had referred to, since she was a little girl, as "that desolate, soulless place"?

As a girl, this had conjured the frightening image of ghost cities. "Papa, how did they lose their souls?" she asked more than once.

"They didn't lose them, my sweet. They gave them away," he inevitably answered. "At least, many, many of them did."

Thus she had been on some level surprised to find so many souls in the streets of Prague, even under latently Communist-grey clouds, rusty scaffolding and neglect, two years after the Velvet Revolution that had brought the Iron Curtain down. She realized with surprise that the undead were very much alive, very much in possession of their souls, to all appearances. Had they regained them, she wondered, little girl-like, or had they actually never left?

After some generous assistance from the room's sparse mini-bar, my Vanesa slept fitfully, and dreamt a dream she'd had since she was a little girl.

It was not a good one.

>──/

It was a bright, beautiful morning. She was on her way to school. Allenby Street in downtown Tel Aviv buzzed with noise and chaos, everyone hurrying somewhere to do something important. The old Dan Cooperative bus pulled up to the concrete bus stop, belching black smoke from a sooty tailpipe. She climbed the grimy bus stairs and walked between the cracked plastic seats lining the dingy interior. Cigarette butts and crushed sunflower seed shells carpeted the floor. The dusty sliding windows let in only miserable slurps of tepid air in the summer, but behaved quite magnanimously when it came to winter rain.

A ticket seller at the rear-door entrance seemed to operate on auto-pilot, taking change and resignedly raising a pudgy eyebrow when a patron passed him a bill instead of exact change in coins. To passenger after passenger, he dispensed the flimsy paper tickets which, from Vanesa's experience, inevitably fell to the floor when it rained or flew out the window — and always just prior to the roaming conductor calling, "Tickets, please. Tickets!"

The door shut behind her, and as it closed the universe shifted perceptibly. Her sense of well-being, false in hindsight, evaporated. She was pulled, as if on an inexorable conveyor belt, into a new, terrifying yet amorphous world. Everywhere she looked, forms shifted malevolently. The ticket taker became a leering, pitchfork-bearing devil, and then a slathering, bristling monster. The old lady with the wheeled, plaid-basket shopping cart transformed into a green-faced, claw-handed witch. The hand straps dangling from the bar above became snakes looped around red-hot iron.

The imagery had changed as she grew older, but the feeling never did — abject, inexplicable terror, a sense of impending, unspeakable pain. Stomach-dropping fear that all was lost, that somehow she'd never get back to that bright day outside. Then came the paralysis, coming partly awake, only to find that she was trapped in the dream — unable to run, unable to wake. The terror pressed down, smothering her, blanketing her until finally, no longer caring that her mother or father would hear her, she screamed the primal scream of the tortured and damned, and awoke sweating — always to find that her scream, like her terror, remained internal and silent.

>──/

Using her newly-discovered research skills, Vanesa wrote me in March of 1982, she began also clandestinely researching her father and grandfather. Here, she confided, "Things got a little confusing." Although she had at least gained factual insight about her mother, records regarding her father were "less complete, to say the least."

She found a record of Michael Neuman arriving in Terezin with his mother and father on Transport AAt from Prague on July 23, 1942. She uncovered a record of her great-grandparents leaving Terezin for Auschwitz on Transport Dr, on December 12, 1943, and found proof of their deaths – both having been sent upon arrival to Auschwitz straight to the gas chambers with the other 2504 people on the transport. She also found a record of her grandmother Alena's death from Typhus, still in Terezin, shortly thereafter.

But my Vanesa uncovered only one record — a single instance in the masses of documents, testimonies, and personal accounts that she examined that year and in future years — as to what had happened to Michael and his father Jakub between their arrival in Terezin and the end of the war.

And this record made no sense.

"If nothing else, the Nazis were talented bureaucrats, especially in Terezin. Their record-keeping was meticulous, bordering on the obsessive. They kept records of the number of times each prisoner had been checked for lice, and how many lice, of what sizes, they found in each check. Very few of their victims actually fell through the cracks," Vanesa wrote me. "That's what makes it odd that, from the point of view of the Nazi records, my grandfather and father should not exist."

CHAPTER 7

BACKUP PLAN

Prague, December 1991

"A good historian always has a backup research plan," one of Vanesa's undergraduate history professors once said in a crowded lecture hall half-full of bored freshmen. Still a fresh-faced ex-army radio reporter, she'd chuckled internally at the man's audacity. After all, he was speaking of *history*. What Raiders of the Lost Ark had done for archaeologists, no one had yet imagined for historians.

He'd been right, in retrospect. Now that she was a historian, she'd made a backup plan before going to the trouble of getting a visa to Czechoslovakia, and before paying the widely-despised Foreign Travel Tax levied on Israelis traveling outside the borders of the small country at that time. She'd made a plan and now prepared to put it in motion.

It was a fitful night, passing slowly as Vanesa replayed over and over the events of the evening, including the oddly comforting conversation with Uncle Tomas, who had so adamantly opposed this trip. She had never seen him so upset, red-faced and literally blustering on the day before her departure. She had been frankly afraid for his heart, and tried to calm him with a little girl hug, which had always softened him up for whatever she intended to ask, laying her head on his broad chest so he could stroke her hair with his large hands.

He would have none of it. "Tell me why, *Kotě*. Explain to an old man so that I can understand. It makes no sense to me. We've always talked about things rationally. We've always thought out our courses of action, have we not? Why can you not now take a breath and explain to me what you hope to accomplish with this trip? Can you please try?"

So, she'd tried to explain that the diary was the key to something — something possibly good, something of which she'd never really even hoped to scratch the surface, and now found dangling enticingly in front of her face like the proverbial carrot in front of the donkey. Hungry for knowledge, how could she not pull the cart forward in an attempt to reach the carrot, no matter how heavy the load?

He was unswayed. "What is this 'know more about him' nonsense? What more do you need to know? I've told you everything you need to know. I knew your father from when he was eleven, remember?"

He had always been reservedly open with her, as if recognizing her sincere need to know, and sharing what he knew of her father's wartime experience despite the obvious discomfort it caused him. They'd been in Terezin, he said. He'd befriended Jakub, her grandfather, because they shared the same profession. He'd helped the man look out for Michael until they — Jakub and Michael, not himself — were sent to Auschwitz in 1944.

He'd told her, and she'd believed. In the world of silence in which she grew up, Uncle Tomas' sparse information was an earsplitting drum roll, a golden revelation of the past. It had been enough for her for many years, and even when it wasn't enough, she'd been unable to ask him. She told herself that it would be cruel, that the memories were clearly painful to the man, leaving him visibly relieved when her questions stopped. Allowing him his privacy seemed the only fair and humane thing to do.

She knew her reticence to push Uncle Tomas derived as much from fear — not just of what she might discover, but of the man himself — as from mercy. Whatever her true motive, she beat back the questions, locked them away, until the day that they just erupted out of her like a flock of hungry bats from an inky cave mouth. There were too many of them, and she had to find some matching answers.

That's when she started her trips to Yad V'Shem. Before long, she found the references to her father and grandfather. When she found no record of anyone named Tomas Marle with Uncle Tomas' birth date, having been either in the ghetto or in Auschwitz, it felt almost a relief—it meant that there *were* answers to be found, that there *was* more to know. The menace of eternal, blissless ignorance, at least, was lifted.

She wasn't angry—not at him, nor her father, nor her grandfather— that she had apparently been deceived about who Uncle Tomas really was. Nor would she ever confront either him or her father.

Yet she had decided to find out, that overcast day in Jerusalem, as she clutched the grey photostat of her grandfather's transport orders printed from microfiche.

She had decided to find out because, according to Terezin transport records, Jakub and Michael had been among the 18 deportees sent on October 27, 1944 from Prague to Theresienstadt on Transport Eu. This would have surprised her less, if not for a single historical discrepancy, as Professor Ben-Artzi would say, "of proportion that is historical itself."

It was clear that, if her grandfather and father had been transported from Prague to Theresienstadt in 1942, and then again from Prague in 1944, they must have returned to Prague in the interim. Of this, there was no record.

Yet even more importantly, the deportees of Transport Eu *never made it to Theresienstadt*. Their train car stood for a full day in Bohusovice, the rail station nearest Terezin. The next day, the Nazis coupled the car to another train, transport Ev. This transport—the very last to leave Terezin before the end of the war—went directly to Auschwitz-Birkenau. The eighteen members of Transport Eu, her father and grandfather listed among them, were all murdered immediately upon their arrival on October 29, 1944.

Yes, she had decided right then, smoking a cigarette on Yad V'Shem's Avenue of the Righteous among the Nations under an unforgiving Jerusalem winter sky. Yes, she decided that if notoriously accurate Nazi transport records negated her grandfather's, her father's, and by obvious extension her very own, existence, she would someday have to make her father's story, like she had made her mother's name, her own.

>—⫞

By the time the sunless morning's street sounds started to filter up to her room, Vanesa had safely locked the attack away, but she certainly hadn't forgotten. The reeking clothes that still graced the floor of the hotel bathroom, awaiting the morning's maid service, remained unimpeachable evidence. Yet Vanesa had grown up in a family where locking away bad things had been honed to an art. Her internal iron box bulged, strained its seals and leaked toxic fumes, as had her father's and mother's iron boxes before her.

But it held.

So she remained composed as she packed her research notes and the diary into her briefcase, then lugged it down to the dining room, where she picked unenthusiastically at a bland continental breakfast at least as grey as the morning sky.

"No one goes to Prague for the food, *Kotě*. The beer, yes, but not the food," Uncle Tomas had told her, and he was right.

She left the dining room and approached the desk clerk, a different but equally reticent young man—as if the hotel's human resources department had specified "standoffish" as a key hiring criterion. Vanesa extracted a phone number from her briefcase and asked the clerk to please connect her to the offices of the Jewish Museum of Prague.

He looked up at her with borderline malice, picked up the phone, and slowly dialed. He jerked his head in the direction of the same phone booth from which she'd spoken to Uncle Tomas the previous night, indicating that she should wait for the call there.

After being transferred with Soviet efficiency between four or five different departments, she finally reached the desk of Jonas Jakobovits, to whom she'd been introduced by the kindly Professor Ben-Artzi, her advisor in Tel Aviv University's Department of History. She'd written to Jakobovits only two weeks prior, when the details of her nascent trip were still vague, introducing herself and letting him know that she'd likely be visiting the museum in the coming months. She'd had no reply, and couldn't even be sure her letter had arrived.

"Ahoy, this is Jonas Jakobovits," a surprisingly young voice answered on the first ring, pronouncing the J's in his name as Y's in his soft Czech.

Upon hearing her own lightly-accented Czech, he quickly switched to thick-tongued English, but then politely reverted to Czech when she persisted. He sounded quite pleased to hear from her, and chatted as if he lacked frequent contact with anyone from the outside world.

"Yes, I received your letter, Dr. Neuman. Of course I would be pleased to assist you in any way I can. I'm actually free later this morning, if you would like to meet me at the museum's administrative offices on Jachymova Street. I can arrange for a cab, if you'd prefer. Where are you staying?"

She told him.

"Ah, then it's really only a block's walk, and the weather is thankfully clement, is it not? Oh... and how is Professor Ben-Artzi?"

She extricated herself gently from the eager young man's enquiries, promising to meet him within the hour. She gave a nod and a wave to the desk clerk as she walked toward the stairs, in faint hope of breaking the ice.

He glanced up at her briefly, wrinkled his nose as if smelling something vaguely unpleasant, and lowered his eyes to his book.

She headed up to her room, lugging the heavy briefcase.

Humans possess five senses, as a rule. From a strictly scientific point of view, Vanesa should have had no inkling of danger as she crested the stairs and turned down the narrow, dimly-lit hallway that led to her room. There was no physical reason that the hair on the back of her neck should have stood up even before she came to her door, which stood ajar. There was no actual cause for her to turn to look behind so rapidly that her long hair still swung backwards even as she returned her gaze to the front. There was no reason that the clomping footsteps receding down the stairs behind her should have even caught her attention, as there were, after all, other guests in the hotel. There were no reasons, she told me, yet she knew exactly in what state she'd find her room even before she swung the door open.

They had not been very thorough, she noticed, but then again, the spartan three-star room possessed few hiding places. They'd hit all the obvious nooks: under the mattress, behind the bureau, in her suitcase, in the desk drawers. They hadn't even made much of a mess, considering how Hollywood generally depicted such scenes.

Vanesa never spoke more about the incident. Did it scare her? How could it not have? At that point, she must have realized that her attack the night before had not been random. Did she even care? Was she so mission-focused that danger never occurred to her? Did she hope to irretrievably file the incident in her internal iron box, permanently archiving it?

>——/

The administrative headquarters of the Jewish Museum of Prague at 3 Jachymova Street was nondescript in the extreme by Prague standards, sandwiched as it was between two more distinctive buildings in the center of a narrow and short cobblestoned street. Vanesa recalled the words of museum historian Hana Volavkova, who spent most of the war years there and was the only surviving Jewish member of the museum staff. Volavkova described it as a strange, bland building. "Nowhere was there a tree or a bird, and even the highest floors of the building offered only a view of the neighboring roofs," she wrote.

Vanesa rang the bell of the wooden door set in a tall arched doorway and topped forebodingly by barred windows. She could see Volavkova's point. Waiting for someone to answer her ring, she recalled what she knew of the museum's rich history.

The Jewish Museum of Prague had been founded in 1906 to preserve the heritage of Prague's Old Jewish Town, called 'Josefov' after Joseph II, the Holy Roman Emperor who emancipated Jews with his Toleration Edict of 1781. The Josefov quarter was completely razed between 1893 and 1913, surprisingly not for reasons of punitive anti-Semitism, but for public health reasons—although there was certainly no shortage of anti-Semitism in the thousand years of Jewish history in Prague. The quarter was simply terribly unsanitary and unsafe, with a maze of winding alleys, no sewage system or adequate water supply, and wooden structures that housed more rats than people. After the razing, only six synagogues and the old Jewish Town Hall remained from the original Josefov quarter. Five of these structures formed the core of the museum, and six remained under its care until today.

The door opened abruptly, and Vanesa was soon following a reception-ist in a grey skirt, her hair pulled into a bun so severe that it resembled a helmet. As they wound through the narrow hallways, Vanesa mused on the museum's infamous wartime "notoriety." Closed to the public in 1939 by order of the Nazi occupiers, the Jewish Museum of Prague was re-commissioned in 1942 with a far darker mission.

When they arrived at the small, cramped office, Jonas Jakobovits rose to greet her. Vanesa's first thought was that Jonas was far better looking than a historian should be. His thoughtful eyes were utterly engaging, his brown pupils flecked with green. They drew listeners in, helping them make his passion for whatever he was discussing their own.

She accepted the folding chair he gracefully offered, and he squeezed back behind his cluttered desk. His tall frame, only partially visible over piles of books, manila folders, and binders, made the cheap wooden desk chair on which he sat again look flimsy. She sat, and mentioned her ruminations about the museum's wartime history.

His heavy brows momentarily furrowed. "We've never found any record of the museum actually being called 'The Museum of an Extinct Race,' as it became popularly known."

Vanesa looked cursorily around the high-ceilinged room. Her eyes lit on a group of paper-tagged candelabra on a dusty shelf. They caught the morning sun, which had finally emerged from behind thick clouds. Their tarnished silver threw sepia reflections haphazardly around the room.

"But, I must admit that I agree with you," Jakobovits continued decisively. "In retrospect, it's quite clear that the very preservation of the museum's facilities by the Nazis, not to mention the actual conservation and display work that they directed here during the occupation, indicate a greater plan. The directives for the preservation of tens of thousands of items of Judaica looted from Bohemia and Moravia, and the orders to create themed exhibitions — for example, Jewish life cycle events — all these came from the Nazis. It was an initiative of the head of what was originally called the *Zentralamt fur die Regelung der Judenfrage in Bohmen und Mahren,* The Central Office for the Settlement of the Jewish Question in Bohemia and Moravia. This office was headed by *SS Sturmbannfuhrer* Hans Guenther, who reported to none other than Adolf Eichmann — a name with which I'm sure you're familiar."

Vanesa found herself engaged, and not just by Jakobovits' deep and fiery eyes. She believed the "Museum of an Extinct Race" theory. To her mind, it perfectly suited the audacity of the Nazis, and was aligned with the malignant vision of Guenther's superiors, both his direct superior Eichmann and the senior Reich figure in Prague in the early war years, Reinhard Heydrich. Until his assassination, Heydrich had been Acting Reich Protector of the Protectorate of Bohemia and Moravia, and the architect of Hitler's Final Solution, which the Nazi leadership rubber-stamped at his behest in the infamous Wannsee Conference in 1942.

She nodded vigorously, silently agreeing with Jakobovits. How like Heydrich to create such a monument to his crowning achievement—the destruction of Czechoslovakian Jewry, perhaps of European Jewry at large. How like Heydrich to have Jews build this monument themselves, and then destroy them after its completion. How like Heydrich to ensure that the project was kept secret, even after his assassination in 1942. Despite the fact that it was fully staffed and active throughout most of the war, the Jewish Museum of Prague remained closed to the public even after the first exhibition was opened to Guenther and his staff in 1943.

As if reading her thoughts, Jakobovits nodded back at her so enthu-siastically that his glasses flew off their loose perch on his nose. They skittered off the desk and landed in a large wooden crate filled with hundreds of sets of black leather *tefilin*, phylacteries.

It was a mute testament to hundreds of fathers who had used them daily, thought Vanesa, and to hundreds of mothers and children that had likely followed them to their own nameless, numbered deaths. She wasn't sure how Jakobovits could work in the place, thinking it must be like coming to a cemetery every day.

Jakobovits retrieved his glasses, examined and polished the lenses, and continued excitedly. "What's more...." He leaned towards her with intended dramatic effect, but achieved more of a nerdy intensity. "I'm one of the 'radicals' here that believes that Heydrich and Eichmann had some plans up their sleeves that we still haven't discovered. Even our sleepy Prague Jewish historical community has its intrigues, you see."

CHAPTER 8

ZVI

From the Diary of Michael Neuman, Prague, March 1943

"You are such a product of your ghetto society. Look at you. You call yourself a Jew, yet you hide out in here like some skinny, sun-starved sewer rat. And here I am, stuck in here with you, instead of out there fighting and building a nation we can be proud of."

Zvi has angry storms like this, but they always pass, like the spring thunderstorms that show up so quickly over Prague. The black clouds appear suddenly from behind Prague Castle, and threaten the city with their voices of thunder. But the city always wins, and the storms, disappointed, slosh their buckets of water over the cobblestones, then race off to the east before the flow even makes it to the Vltava, as if hoping to catch the *next* city off guard.

Sometimes Zvi is just plain mean. I understand, since he, of all the friends I've met here, is least suited to life inside. I think he lacks the imagination you need to stay in the same room, day after day, night after night. When I sneak down to see him, quietly removing and replacing the grill with the symbol in it and then unlocking his door, he's usually pacing like a caged animal. It's like he's desperate to find a crack in the wall, just so he can satisfy his desire for action by scratching at it until his fingernails bleed. I admire this drive. It's like he needs to escape the ghosts of his past by either creating or destroying—it doesn't matter which.

Zvi is a powerful figure in his dark trousers and dirty white shirt, his sleeves rolled up past the elbow to reveal powerful arms, which still show the Mediterranean sun, even though he's been away from *Eretz Yisrael* for over three years. His curly hair is usually greasy, except after he bathes, when the dark ringlets stick to the sides of his head, making his heavy brows stand out even more.

"The Jew grew into the parasite that he is today because he is stateless, ungrounded, floating through the countries of the world like some untethered balloon. He is despised and subjugated because he lost what other nations take for granted: his land. Once we return to the soil, regain the land, *rebuild* the land — then and only then will we be able to stand eye-to-eye with our persecutors, and slap their filthy hand down before it strikes us. You see...."

He lowers his voice, points at me, looks me straight in the eye, and makes his point about personal sacrifice, the need to break free from the bonds imposed by society, or something equally likely to make me shiver with guilt and excitement. He embodies Zionist sacrifice, he says.

He left his childhood behind at sixteen, when he fled with his Dror Zionist youth movement friends, leaving his parents' poor home in Wraclow, Poland, for the fresh air of the "Kibbutz Kielce" Zionist training farm.

His eyes grow softer when he speaks of Kielce. He shows me a creased photograph of twenty men and women in their late teens or early twenties, posing in front of a whitewashed shack. Excitement shines from their smiling eyes, as if they know they're part of something greater than themselves. Zvi is holding a pitchfork, and not looking at the camera. His gaze is focused instead on one of the young women directly across from him.

"Sofia." He says her name softly, almost like a prayer. Then he turns back to me. "Do you know what it's like to be part of something so great? Can you know how it feels to have a real, personal, tangible role in *changing the world*?"

His rhetorical question hangs in the air, and then fades away, leaving an aftertaste of regret that I don't understand but can't escape.

"No," I tell him. "I cannot imagine."

He says he learned the true price of ideological commitment in Palestine. He and the ten members of his *garin* — that means "seed" in Hebrew, like the seed of a new settlement — were the lucky recipients of a "certificate" from the British Mandatory authorities. This gave them permission to emigrate to Palestine, which they did in early 1937. They joined their fellow Poles in Kibbutz Mishmar HaSharon, founded only three years earlier just south of the swamps of Wadi Iskandurah, which they call Nahal Alexander in Hebrew.

This was a turbulent time in Palestine, Zvi explained. The Arab revolt that had begun in 1936 grew worse in 1937. The violence that was initially directed against British forces now focused on Jewish settlements. Zvi had volunteered for the Haganah paramilitary organization almost immediately on his arrival. After a short basic training, he joined Yitzchak Sadeh's famous strike force, *Fosh*. They assigned him to a small settlement some thirty minutes south of Kibbutz Mishmar HaSharon, called Kadima.

>—⫯

"What's here to protect?" he asked Sofia, who had been assigned with him to organize the community's defense, as their donkeys trudged the sandy kilometers between the main road and the center of the poor settlement. Kadima had been founded only five years before on sandy land, purchased from the Arabs of the neighboring village of Kalansua by a Ukrainian land baron called Yehoshua Henkin. The Arabs were incredulous that someone would pay good money for such a place, but had been helpful and friendly to the new settlers. The early settlers bought their 15-dunam parcels in advance from Henkin, sight-unseen, and then showed up with their heavy German furniture, electrical appliances, and total lack of farming skills. What they found was a collection of widely-spaced wooden shacks standing in the middle of dry sand dunes, broken by swamps and scrub oak trees, far from the lovely European-style village they had imagined.

But they had not given up, these settlers. In half a decade, they built the beginnings of a community that *was* worth protecting, and it became Zvi's job to protect it.

He, Sofia, and their three Haganah compatriots quickly established themselves in a rough, sandbagged outpost on the roof of the Pomer family home. One of only two brick houses in Kadima at the time, it offered a clear view of the fields to the north, from where the raids had been coming. They fell into a "six-six" guard duty rotation—six hours on, six hours off. The late summer days quickly shortened into cool evenings, the gentle song of the breeze in the oaks broken only by the never-ending ear-buzz of mosquitoes.

"They are *not* coming from Kalansua, they are coming *through* Kalansua," insisted Nabil in pidgin Hebrew. He fell back into Arabic sometimes, especially when his dark eyes flashed with excitement. They sat together around the fire pit, the *finjan* in which they'd made their coffee already cooling on a nearby rock. "I know my village. We sold the land for Kadima. We have always helped the settlers. Why would we harm them now? The raiders are coming *through* Kalansua, from Tul Karem. I see them many evenings, groups of them, young *shabaab* sitting for hours in the coffee shop, waiting for full darkness to head south, towards Kadima. They are not *our* young men!"

Nabil, a young father just past his 24th birthday, had been appointed by the village council as liaison to the previous Haganah commander, and continued to work with Zvi. His large dark eyes were set across a flat nose, which gave him a look of wide-eyed sincerity. His thick lips, topped by a fine moustache, added just a hint of a lisp to his gentle speech.

"He may be lying through his teeth," Zvi told Sofia in bed, one rare evening when neither had drawn guard duty, "but he does it so sweetly that you can't help but believe him."

And, truth be told, Zvi did believe him. In fact, over the months that followed, into the chilly winter evenings, when they huddled close around the fire, they became friends.

Nabil taught Zvi Arabic, and told him about his daughter Aisha, a toddler just learning to walk. Zvi helped Nabil with his Hebrew, and told him of the cold Polish winters that made the Kadima winter seem like spring. Zvi watched Sofia's long dark hair and straight white teeth catch the firelight as she spoke to Nabil into the nights. They talked of the British, Nabil's wife, and cooking with the local ingredients that were so different from what she knew from her mother's Polish kitchen. She was curiosity incarnate, Zvi thought, his own beautiful and inquisitive little kitten.

With its endless cups of strong and sweet Turkish coffee, the fire pit in the Pomer yard became the community parliament. Each evening, the new settlers would seek Zvi's mediation with Nabil regarding problems of water rights and trade with Kalansua. Nabil and the new farmers would compare notes about working the rich sandy-red soil of the region, which after laying in swampy fallowness for centuries had been discovered ideal for citrus cultivation. They would share, angrily, news of the latest Arab attacks against neighboring Jewish settlements—news of property destroyed, of livestock killed, of fields burned, and of farmers slain with the reins of their plow donkeys still held in their calloused hands.

Nabil would listen gravely, nod sympathetically, and offer encouragement. He would remind them every evening, when he finally rose to make his way into the darkness to rejoin his own family, of the Kalansua village council's firm commitment to friendship with the settlers of Kadima.

Compared to the previous year, December 1937 was dry and cold in Kadima. That night, the moon was hiding behind thick rainless clouds, peeking out only every now and then, like a hesitant child behind a drawing room drapery. Both Zvi and Sofia had drawn guard duty on the graveyard watch, from midnight to six a.m.

The military outpost had an eerie magic that reached its peak just before sunrise. There was a deafening silence when gun metal reached its coldest, and breath fogged out most thickly. Senses were dulled from lack of sleep, yet heightened from growing fear. Zvi felt restless that evening, a bullet in the chamber of his Enfield rifle, his right forefinger caressing the trigger guard. There had been a major raid in Tel Mond the previous day—more like a minor battle. Two Hagannah fighters, whom Zvi knew from basic training, had been killed, and Nabil had brought news of more and more *shabaab* coming into Kalansua. Something big was afoot, and Nabil had promised to provide advance warning if at all possible.

Zvi blew on his chilled hands and hunkered lower behind the sand bags, while still keeping vigilant watch on the edge of the dark scrub forest just beyond the Pomer fields. He reached behind him to caress Sofia's shoulder, but she shrugged off his hand. She was too nervous for physical contact. The silence weighed heavy, and the air smelled of musty swamp. Their eyes adjusted to the cloud-cover darkness, and were momentarily blinded as the first rays of the sun broke through the clouds to the East. The light flooded the scene below, revealing a backlit shadow running rapidly toward them across the north field.

This was it! It had begun! Without hesitating, Zvi raised his rifle and fired a single shot. The shot split the silence of the dawn, the figure fell, and the quiet returned, covering Zvi and Sofia like a thick blanket.

Seconds later, they heard the voice. "Zvi... Sofia... my friends... Zvi...." It came from across the field, weak yet recognizable. It was Nabil.

Sofia hissed, "What did you *do*?" and hurried toward the rickety wooden ladder at the rear of the roof.

Zvi grabbed the arm of her wool khaki jacket. "Wait!" he commanded in a low voice. "Think for a moment. What if it's a trap? Why would Nabil have come now?"

"Zvi... Sofia...." Nabil's voice sounded lower now, but still clearly audible.

Sofia shrugged out of Zvi's grasp and turned back toward him. Her eyes flashed with anger. "He's *our* friend, and *you* shot him. If you're so worried about a trap, stay up here and cover me, because I'm going to help him!" She slung her carbine over her shoulder on its worn canvas strap, quickly descended the ladder, and silently made her way across the plowed field toward Nabil's now quiet figure, some 200 meters from the rooftop position.

>——/

"The sun was fully up, so I saw her going to him," Zvi told me. "I watched her walk away from me. Then the morning fog parted, and a whole line of figures emerged from the woods. I could see the long rifles, scythes, curved Turkish swords, and even picks in their hands. They were on her, a young woman clearly in a Hagannah uniform, before I could even begin firing. I watched as she fell and a wall of people closed in, blocking my view. The others had woken up, and we somehow held them off for the next several hours. They gave up just as our ammunition began to run low. As soon as the area was clear, I ran down to Sofia, but there... there wasn't much left to bury."

"And so you see," Zvi said, straightening up and trying his best to speak ideologically, which I knew masked his pain. "You see, there is a price to be paid for each and every decision you make, for each and every action you take. Never forget that what you *do* today in a very real sense determines what you will *be* tomorrow."

After the incident in Kadima, Zvi had volunteered to parachute into occupied Europe and help organize both emigration and resistance. After participating in the Vilna Conference, he made his way back into Poland, and was captured by the Nazis in Warsaw.

After many other adventures, about which I hope he'll soon tell me, he ended up here in Prague.

CHAPTER 9

SOMETHING BROKEN

Tel Aviv, 1973

My Vanesa was eight years old. Tel Aviv's summer heat came early that year, creeping up on a short spring in the night, the latter retreating as if ashamed of its inadequacy. To celebrate the gloriously hot weather, both her mother and father had spontaneously taken the day off for a family beach outing.

They'd taken the stuffy Dan Cooperative bus to the sparkling beaches of north Tel Aviv, ostensibly to ensure the outing was a true adventure. The truth was, Vanesa knew, her father preferred the urbane safety of the Gordon Pool, its salt water replaced nightly by powerful pumps that sucked the sea into a more controlled environment. While he swam in the nearby pool, she and her mother sat on the beach just south of the still-new Tel Aviv marina.

Vanesa loved the wildness of the sea, the way it licked at her toes with an unquenchable thirst for power, always demanding more of her than it would ever return. Her play at the water's edge was serious and concentrated. Her metal bucket and shovel created fortified structures of grave importance, then funneled quantities of water and sand to and fro with the urgent purpose of saving the people within from the evils without.

Her mother dozed gently in the shade of a faded beach umbrella, her body demurely covered by thin cotton pants and a long-sleeved shirt. She wore no bathing suit, nor had Vanesa ever seen her mother's naked body.

She wore long sleeves most of the year, and in all her years Vanesa had only seen passing glimpses of the mysterious number tattooed on the top of her mother's left forearm. The number was, she understood with a child's intuitive sagacity, not something to be discussed, not something to be shown, and certainly not something to be flaunted openly, like Uncle Tomas did. She'd seen the look of displeasure on her mother's face whenever Tomas appeared, sleeves rolled up, making no attempt to hide the shameful mark — indeed, apparently proud of his brand.

The jellyfish came early that year, too, as the waters warmed quickly. The clear blob looked like water floating within itself, inviting and intriguing to an eight-year-old eye as it bobbed in the waist-high surf. Looking back to ensure her mother was still there, Vanesa left her sand-encrusted bucket lolling half-in and half-out of the calm water, the already placid waves having been further tamed by Tel Aviv's rocky breakwaters.

She didn't scream. That task fell to her mother, who awoke to find Vanesa standing in front of her, fighting the tears that the red welts — running from her neck, across her bare chest, and down to below her waist like a crazed roadmap — struggled to elicit.

"It doesn't hurt much, Mama." She squinted in the sunshine, even as something feral burst from her mother's throat. It was a sound matched in Vanesa's young experience only by the air-raid sirens that screamed overhead during civil defense drills, which had begun that winter as rhetoric from Egypt began to echo more loudly across the region.

The screams brought the lifeguard running, as well as several off-duty soldiers, who charged up in bathing trunks, Uzis at the ready, sure that a team of Egyptian commandos had landed and begun wantonly slaughtering bathers.

The lifeguard pried her mother away and, along with the disappointed young soldiers, saw the true nature of the incident.

"My child! My child!" Her mother sobbed uncontrollably, attracting a crowd of onlookers even as Vanesa tried to calm her, embarrassment trumping the pain of the sting.

"It's okay, Mama," she said in an urgent whisper. She could take pain, she explained. She was strong. She could even hold her breath for a really long time, like she would have had to in the gas chambers. They played at this sometimes during recess, her and Zivit and Keren, and she never died because she was so strong.

Her mother's sobbing faded to mute, beseeching despair.

The lifeguard led Vanesa to the first aid hut, where the medic on duty applied a liberal dose of vinegar to lessen the pain.

Her father's silhouette appeared in the doorway of the hut. He ignored her mother's limp, weeping form slumped on the chair in the corner, and rushed past the startled medic. He quickly assessed Vanesa's condition and slapped her across the face so hard that her ear began to ring high and strong, and her face stung almost as much as her chest. Furious, he bent down until his face was only inches from hers. "What were you thinking? Look at you! How could you be so careless?"

He roared at her so loudly that the medic retreated, after a perfunctory attempt to explain that it was a common, and not at all life-threatening, injury. A passing policeman intervened, pulling her father out of the hut and past the gawking onlookers.

She sat on the rickety treatment table, ear ringing, face burning, her torso on fire, and guilt for causing her parents such suffering already creeping into the pit of her stomach.

The long walk home was permeated with the silence of something deep and unfixable. Her mother's eyes watched the ground while her father stared fixedly ahead, giving the appearance of a man deeply focused on the immediate, when in fact Vanesa knew he had left on another "Trip." It was not the first time he'd traveled this way. Her mother had explained that sometimes Father needed to go away in his head, and that she should just wait patiently for him to return.

And he always did return.

Where did he go on these Trips, she wondered. Did he visit the streets of his boyhood Prague? Could he peel away the layers of Tel Aviv asphalt and sand to reveal the rain-slick Bohemian cobblestones hidden just beneath the surface? Were the smells of sea salt replaced with wood smoke and roasting ham, when he went away like this?

Vanesa tried not to touch her chest, sticky with the salve they'd purchased at the pharmacy, and watched her father as they trudged across the city, wondering what it felt like to visit another place in your head while your body stayed where it was. Did you ever truly come back?

>—/

Tel Aviv, June 1991

When my Vanesa received the diary, after Michael died, she began to understand.

We'd only been married nine months and were living in a small flat on HaNevi'im Street, only a block away from Dizengoff Center. The gloriously nondescript old Tel Aviv apartment occupied a blandly-colored concrete building, featuring an elegant polished wood and glass entrance hidden from the street by concrete support pillars, and intricately-patterned ceramic tiles on the floors. Behind the heavy wood door of our whitewashed second-floor flat, floor-to-ceiling built-in wood closets lined both bedroom and kitchen, while a glass-enclosed kitchen porch created a bright yet cozy dining alcove. A balcony ran the length of the apartment, facing the Ficus trees that filled space between our building and the backs of the apartments on HaShoftim Street.

On Saturday mornings, we'd drink our coffee on the balcony, perching precariously on rickety chairs we'd rescued from the street, the source of much of our furniture those days. Vanesa would rest one heavy leg on my lap, her glass mug—never ceramic—steaming on the balcony wall, a Marlboro Light held loosely between her fingers, her face buried in Friday's *Yediot Ahronot*—never *Maariv*. The smoke would rise from her cigarette and dissipate along with the gentle sounds of Tel Aviv waking up.

The bedroom was so small that we'd pushed the bed against the wall, leaving one of us—her—access to the floor and one of us—me—stuck against the cold cement wall, head directly underneath the electrical outlet into which we'd plug the sickly sweet mosquito repellent device. Despite this innovation, our spring and summer nights in the screen-free apartment were plagued by the ear-buzz of mosquitoes, who had apparently never read the device manufacturer's marketing material.

The phone call came, as such calls inevitably do, in the middle of the night, on the morning of June 5, 1991. Our gas masks, which we'd dutifully carried on shoulders in flimsy cardboard boxes that had deteriorated at more or less the same rate as our fear of Saddam Hussein using chemical weapons, had been put away since the First Gulf War ended in March. Our nights still belonged to fear, however, even after the quiet radio station — which had broadcast white noise all night during the war, unless a missile attack was detected — ceased broadcasting. The freakishly alarming electronic bleep that had woken us so many nights during the Gulf War, followed by the twice-repeated Hebrew code *nachash tzefa* — referring to the *Vipera palaestinae*, a local venomous snake — was not quickly forgotten.

The phone call at four in the morning had us both out of bed in ten seconds, hands groping for gas masks, and me once again knocking my head on the highly-effective mosquito attraction device.

I got to the phone first. It was one of those fateful moments, like deciding not to step off the curb just before the unseen bus rushes by, or sleeping in a building on which an Iraqi Scud fell, but did not detonate. Except I wasn't saved by it, I was condemned. If only I'd tripped, or gotten tangled in something, and she'd reached the phone before me. If only she'd been the one to get the news directly from Uncle Tomas. Perhaps then she wouldn't have spent the rest of our time together blaming me for being the one who told her that her father had died of a heart attack while out on a late-night walk.

But I did get there first, and I did have to tell her, and she never forgave me.

"He was on a Trip," she said simply, after asking me to repeat the news twice. "He always comes back from his Trips. Always."

Since I had hung up the phone to break the news to her, she redialed Tomas, and the tears inevitably followed. She sat at the kitchen table the rest of the night, watching out the dusty glass windows for a dawn that came, but brought no comfort.

She did not speak to me that night, nor the day after. She did not allow herself to be comforted, at least not by me. I was extraneous to her grief, neither a contributor nor a detractor.

In accordance with Jewish tradition, they buried Michael later that day in a simple ceremony in the Yarkon cemetery, on the outskirts of the city. None of us had a car, including Uncle Tomas, who was too frail to drive in any case. The only one who didn't have to take two buses to get to the funeral was Michael himself. He arrived in a somber-colored van bearing the logo of *Hevra Kadisha*, the burial society. The driver doubled, economically, as the rabbi who officiated at the funeral.

A glorious, sunshine-soaked June morning meant funeral guests arrived in sunglasses and hats, clutching bottles of water as they wound their way through the vast Yarkon cemetery, behind the gurney carrying Michael's shroud-wrapped body. The countless thousands of boxy stone graves in the shadeless cemetery bobbed in the shimmering heat like a fleet of clunky sailboats, headstones straining upward in a vain attempt to catch and harness the light morning breeze.

At the graveside, I stood behind Vanesa, one hand protectively on her shoulder, and nodded gravely to the many well-wishers. As far as prayers go, the rabbi/driver's proved strictly of the form letter variety—"Insert Name of Deceased Here"—but he executed them convincingly. The man's polished *El Maley Rachamim*, a traditional funeral prayer, managed to sound appropriately nasal and imploring—even as he discretely glanced twice at the card in his hand to get Michael's name right. I wondered vaguely if any of the daily grief that surrounded this man rubbed off on him, or if he just passed through it with impunity.

Throughout the funeral, Vanesa remained stony-faced, deep inside herself, staring fixedly at the grave as they lowered Michael's shrouded body into it. I squeezed her shoulder in an attempt at comfort, and she shrugged my hand away.

Tomas stood directly across the grave from us, the traditional *kri'a* ripped in the collar of his shirt. He had an appropriately grave look on his wrinkled face most of the time. However, as Michael's body came to rest at the bottom of the grave and the eyes of all were on the first shovelfuls of sandy earth thrown over it—that moment when mortality slaps the face of even the most unexamined life—Tomas looked up, let out a long sigh, and allowed the corners of his mouth to gravitate momentarily upward. It did not seem a look of ironic memory, nor of maudlin wonder at the intricacies of life's ebb.

It was a look, unmistakable yet entirely inexplicable, of relief.

CHAPTER 10

THE GOLEM

Prague, December 1991

Jonas Jakobovits broke off his explanation mid-sentence, the wooden chair creaking ominously as he abruptly leaned his tall frame back, stretched his arms over his head, and leveled a penetrating gaze back in Vanesa's direction.

She noticed the muscles flexing under the thin fabric of his long-sleeve shirt, then quickly averted her gaze to yet another group of tarnished silver objects, this time a shelf of castle-shaped spice boxes, used in the *havdalah* ceremony at the end of the Sabbath.

"So, enough of my rambling," he blurted, poorly affecting shyness to disguise the suspicion in his narrowed eyes. "Let's hear what brings you to Prague, and how I can be of assistance." He leaned forward, resting his chin on one hand, and waited.

Vanesa had gathered her hair back into a single ponytail that morning, and it had already loosened. She removed the hair band from her hair, holding it in her mouth while she re-gathered the unruly mass into a new and tighter arrangement, and then started speaking.

She told her story succinctly and unemotionally, despite the flutter in her stomach and the tremor in her hands whenever she moved them. As she concluded her account, she retrieved the single sheet of paper from her briefcase and laid it on Jakobovits' desk, on top of some folders and in between the piles of books.

"This is why I've come to Prague, Dr. Jakobovits. This is why I need your help. And I do hope you can help me, because frankly...." She shook her head, smiled wanly and made a beseeching Princess Lea gesture with both hands. "You're my only hope."

On the paper she'd painstakingly copied the odd symbol she'd found in her father's diary. "It actually isn't just *in* the diary," she explained, "more like *all over* it."

Boldly emblazoned on the cover in thick black ink, doodled in the margins countless times in smeared pencil, carefully stylized in color inside the back cover — the symbol, whatever it was, had clearly occupied her father's thoughts to the point of obsession in the years he'd kept this diary.

"What's more," she further clarified, "I'm not sure the book actually *is* a diary, strictly speaking." In fact, the battered leather-bound volume she'd received after her father's death was a storybook, a collection of eighteen stories, each dated, each written in her father's even, serious, yet clearly boyish hand. The lines of text flowed perfectly straight across the pages, without erasure or correction, as if he'd copied them into the book from a separate draft. As a researcher and historian, Vanesa could clearly see that these texts had been lovingly and meticulously written. Did this speak to the significance of the stories themselves to young Michael, or to some pressing need to create beauty and perfection in the terribly flawed world in which the twelve-year-old lived?

She couldn't tell.

He'd created one story roughly every month during the period between February 1943 and October 1944, when — according to Nazi records — he'd been sent to his death in Auschwitz. The final total number of stories, eighteen, did not escape Vanesa's notice. Eighteen was the numerical value of the letters making up the Hebrew word *chai* — 'life.'

The stories themselves were clearly related from a twelve-year-old's *weltanschauung*. The language was simple, the plotlines linear and easy to follow, yet the content was nonetheless insightful, engaging, and moving. The stories revealed a sensitive and oratorical side of her young father that she'd never met in the silent, introverted adult version.

They told of Michael's imagined—or perhaps real—meetings with a set of characters, each with his or her unique story. All were told from Michael's perspective, first-person, as if he had heard them directly from their source. This is where it got confusing. The characters, Vanesa thought, were incredibly diverse, both in geography and culture, and their stories were amazingly detailed. Michael must have had limited access to research resources during his stay in... wherever he'd been during those almost two years. So how could he know the intimate details of the lives of a Zionist youth movement activist who emigrated to Palestine, a pubescent Moroccan girl about to be wedded to her second cousin, a Jewish American GI hiding in World War II Prague, a Polish *shtetl* housewife trying to deal with poverty and her husband's suspected infidelity, a Jewish Iraqi carpet merchant in debt to the local mafia, a Turkish moneylender struggling to hide his gambling addiction, and all the others?

Where had her father gotten the ideas for such stories? How had he learned the details of Moroccan cuisine, Iraqi carpet weaving, agricultural schools in Palestine, or daily life in a small American town? She had no answers to these or the hundreds of other questions that had flooded her historian's curiosity since she'd received the book many months ago.

She had no answers, but she did have hope.

She had hope not just because there were clearly answers to be found, because her father's story would not remain forever locked away in the iron box which he'd taken to his grave. She had hope because this diary, these stories, perhaps indicated the type of elusive heroic climax that she'd never found in her mother's story. Had her father actually met the people in his stories? Had he helped them? Was this symbol the key?

After she'd finished recounting the whole thing, Jakobovits looked at her, looked at the paper, looked back at her, and furrowed his brow.

The moment stretched out dramatically, and Vanesa exhaled loudly, suddenly aware that she had been holding her breath.

Finally, Jakobovits said, "I'm afraid I have no idea what this is, or what its exact relevance could be."

The flutter in Vanesa's stomach begin to turn into a lurch.

The young man continued eagerly, and started to get up. "However, I do see some familiar runic elements in this shape, which you have certainly already identified, correct? I have a colleague here in the museum who has made sort of a hobby of Nazi symbology. Shall we consult with him? It's just down the hall."

Vanesa vigorously nodded her assent, as the hope that had just fled so quickly began to cautiously creep back.

>——/

Tel Aviv, June 1991

After Michael's funeral, Vanesa deflated before my eyes. The air just slipped out of her.

She'd possessed an unswerving, yet unspoken, purpose since pre-adolescence, since she was old enough to function semi-independently in the world, since her mother had died when she was twelve. One mission had occupied her entire being, steered her course at every crossroad, hindered and blessed her in equal measure: take care of Michael, protect him, nurture him. Her mother's death had unleashed her own mothering instinct, but one so warped by tragedy that it lacked structural integrity, like a heat-twisted steel girder in a burnt-out building. Now this, her mission, her purpose — ineffectual as it may have been — remained unhappily and permanently fulfilled.

"I knew that my father had been through a terrible thing," she told me late one night, not long after Michael's death. We stood at the window watching passersby in the waning twilight. She held a sweating Goldstar beer in one hand, a Marlboro Light in the other. "I also knew that it was something not only beyond my comprehension, but beyond my consideration. It was not something I could consciously examine, certainly not something I could vocalize, but it was there, the elephant in the room, taking up space and sucking up the oxygen, making it difficult to move around, to even breathe. It was omnipresent, yet maddeningly invisible. And I knew — I *knew* — that I had to protect my father from it. He'd faced it once, and it had scarred him forever. I couldn't let that happen again, but I never knew how to prevent it. It would drive me nuts as a kid."

She smiled wistfully, took a drag from her cigarette, and let the smoke trail out of the corner of her mouth like Paul Simon's floating question mark.

We stayed in the flat over the shop on Nahalat Binyamin during the *shiva*, the traditional seven-day period of mourning. The warm weather forced us to leave the windows open day and night despite the chaotic south Tel Aviv street noise. The narrow street and squat buildings echoed the amalgam of voices, slamming doors, clattering carts, angry horns and grumbling engines. Friends, ours and Michael's, some that Vanesa didn't know, made the trek up the building's narrow and dusty staircase to sip sweet tea with mint from clear glass mugs, or cold water from plastic cups. Some came with pre-prepared platitudes, as flaccid and unappetizing as the desserts they brought. Many just came to sit, offering company, support, and the occasional sincere recollection of Michael from his forty-four years in Israel.

Tomas stayed with us there every day until late in the evening, drinking endless cups of tea, until shuffling back to his own flat two blocks over on Kfar Giladi Street. Vanesa found his presence comforting. He was the closest thing she now had to family.

I had my own opinions about Uncle Tomas, but had learned to keep them to myself.

The Jewish tradition of a near-immediate burial—often on the same day as the death, as in Michael's case—and the constrained seven-day mourn-ing period encouraged the bereaved not to dwell on the loss, nor negate its weight, but rather to use it as a springboard to the future. Toward the end of the week, Vanesa was beginning to heal, beginning to re-inflate herself, to look forward and start to imagine a future without her father.

Until, that is, the lawyer showed up and shook her world once again to its foundations.

We sat alone in the apartment on the sixth day of the *shiva*, low tide as far as visitors went. Those eager to come immediately had already come, and even returned more than once to reiterate their sympathy. Those for whom the tug of conscience had not yet overcome either laziness or shyness still had a day to vacillate or procrastinate.

Alone in the apartment, we were contemplating an afternoon nap when a knock sounded and a young noir figure opened the door. He wore a black suit, a straight black tie, black loafers, and heavy-rimmed black spectacles above which one black eyebrow crossed his lower forehead from side to side, like a hedge separating face from hairline. He let himself in, a black briefcase in hand, and bowed slightly and stiffly, his feigned deference inadequately concealing obvious self-importance. He introduced himself to Vanesa as Moshe Mizrahi, Esquire, her father's—and now her—lawyer.

I surreptitiously glanced toward Tomas, to gage his reaction. Unaware of my study, his eyebrows rose in momentary surprise, then furrowed deeply, along with his forehead, as he focused on the young man.

Mizrahi officiously conveyed his deepest sympathies to Vanesa, explaining that he'd only represented the family's interests for some five years, but had quickly come to appreciate her father's many good qualities, as well as his "prompt fiscal habits."

I took this to mean that Michael had paid him on time, a relative rarity in the south Tel Aviv business community, where already-lengthy "net plus sixty" payment terms often dragged out to "net plus *inshallah*"—'God willing.'

He also informed her that she was within her rights to discuss the matters he needed to address in private, with no one else present.

Afternoon torpor dispelled, Vanesa switched into full analytical mode. Uninterested in mundane formalities, she quickly introduced Tomas and myself, and dismissively told Mizrahi that he could speak freely.

"Very well." The lawyer looked gravely around the room, eyes piercing through the thick lenses of his glasses. "I am obligated to inform you that Mr. Michael Neuman left a last will and testament. I have already submitted an application for probate, and see no reason that this will, which was both signed in my presence and later notarized, should not be upheld in its entirety."

Vanesa remained silent, wide-eyed and intent, like a kitten mesmerized by a butterfly.

Mizrahi retrieved a small stapled document from his briefcase, the metal latches snapping alarmingly in the heavy afternoon silence, and continued. "The matter of inheritance is quite straightforward, as well. This apartment, the small commercial property on the first floor of this building, and all assets in the bank accounts detailed herein are bequeathed to Limor Neuman, also known as Vanesa Neuman."

Vanesa nodded sagely.

I could tell that she had not even considered that she would inherit property worth several hundreds of thousands of dollars. I had thought of this, not without a tinge of shame.

Mizrahi bent to his briefcase again, and extracted a large sealed manila envelope. He turned and handed it to Vanesa. "Mr. Neuman also requested that you be given this upon his death," he stated simply.

Vanesa opened the envelope and extracted the leather-bound diary. As she recognized the object she'd just received, her eyes went wide, and she almost dropped the heavy book. "I've seen this!" she gasped.

This time, I didn't need to look at Tomas, because I could clearly hear his audible intake of breath.

The diary was simply yet sturdily bound in scuffed brown leather. On the cover, the initials M.N. were embossed in fine calligraphy, as if the diary had been a present for a special occasion. A peeling leather thong tied it all together. Vanessa untied the thong to reveal the heavy cream pages inside, approximately half of which appeared to be filled with neat, flowing cursive writing. Each entry had been dated, the first being in February 1943, the last in October 1944.

Across the whole volume—in pencil, in pen, in charcoal, and even in faded crayon—appeared the symbol whose existence Vanesa would soon curse. The symbol that would play a life-altering role for her and everyone she loved. The symbol whose mystery would—had already, in fact—lead to pain, separation, injury, condemnation, forgiveness, and bitter and remorseless death.

>——/

Prague, December 1991

They worked their way down another high-ceilinged, narrow hallway, with dusty bare light bulbs hanging down every several meters on grimy, fabric-wrapped electrical wire. At regular lengths, wooden doors topped by small transom windows opened into rooms containing a virtual cornucopia of Judaica.

Vanesa momentarily smiled at the comically immense quantities of artifacts, but quickly sobered and reminded herself that these piles were, in a very real sense, mass graves.

They did not find the person Jakobovits was looking for, but an employee informed them that Marek Wolff had gone to lunch just around the corner. The hour being already past noon, they decided to join him at the iconic U Golema Restaurant, just next to the 400-year-old Maisel Synagogue on Maiselova Street.

More of a tourist trap than a local hangout, with its Prague Golem motif, the U Golema's Jewish owners nonetheless catered to a small but devoted lunch crowd from the museum staff, providing them higher-quality and lower-priced fare than that served to the tourists.

Jakobovits spotted Marek and a female colleague at a table in the rear of the restaurant, and waved.

Marek waved back, his arm whacking the life-size statue of the lovably monstrous Golem under which they were seated. The over-commercialized Prague Golem, Vanesa recalled, actually had a history deeper than its "Jewish Frankenstein" image. It had been so popular that a 1920 silent film told its tale to the world. According to legend, the Golem had been created by the renowned Rabbi Loew after he read in the stars that the Jews of Prague were in imminent danger. Made of clay, the Golem became animated when the Rabbi inserted a capsule containing the name of God and a magic formula into its mouth. The Golem lived until the Hebrew letter Aleph was removed from the word that adorned its chest, turning the word *emet*—'truth'—into *met*—'dead.'

The Golem's legendary protection from anti-Semitic attacks had, for centuries, comforted Prague's medieval Jewish community—at least its younger members. As a historian, however, Vanesa was more interested in the long-term atmosphere of fear that led to the creation and perpetuation of such a powerful, lasting, and extreme myth. It was testament to both the resilience of the Prague Jewish community and its fear of the pervasive hostility surrounding it.

Marek reached behind him to steady the Golem before it toppled, and stood when introduced to Vanesa, bumping and righting the monster a second time.

He was quite possibly the least Jewish-looking person Vanesa had ever encountered in a Jewish academic context—tall, blond, and Aryan enough to grace a Hitler Youth poster. His radiant smile, however, and flashing blue eyes could hide neither his intelligence nor his empathy. He stood a full head shorter than Jakobovits, but clearly outweighed him, and sported a ruddy Germanic flush on his roly-poly cheeks.

He greeted her in Czech, but quickly and obstinately switched to pidgin Hebrew when he heard she was from Israel.

She spent the next minutes creating mental parentheses that contained interpretive translations of what he actually meant to say.

He had lived in Israel for fifty years, he said (obviously meaning five). He stayed in a small boat (apartment) in Tel Aviv, where he liked to read (eat) falafel and have sex with the ocean (lie on the beach). What he missed most about Israel, he said, was the abhorrent (relaxed?) nature of the people. People were abhorrent all day long in Tel Aviv, he said, but also really knew how to live life in short (on the edge). He had been studying Philosophy at Tel Aviv University, where he had still had ongoing bushes (dialogs) with many tribe (faculty) members.

As tiring as the translation quickly became, Vanesa found herself nonetheless engaged by the enthusiastic young man.

He concluded his brief Hebrew monologue by explaining, "I only on museum tribe not Jew. But love I work here. My grandfather Nazi in Prague, hurt many Jews. I make justice now, help Jewish to learn."

At this, he thankfully reverted to Czech, apologizing for his Hebrew indulgence. He introduced Eva, his colleague, a bland-looking woman with short dark hair and eyes that radiated a mixture of boredom and cynicism.

Marek and Vanesa briefly traded enthusiastic stories of Tel Aviv University and life in Tel Aviv, until their conversation faded into an uncomfortable silence.

Marek turned to Jakobovits with a mildly questioning and expectant look, prompting the latter to abruptly remove the sheet of paper Vanesa had given him from an inside pocket and lay it on the table in front of Marek.

Seeing the symbol, Marek jumped up, violently jarring the small wooden table and tipping two glasses over. Twin streams of water and beer converged to drip directly into Vanesa's lap, despite her rapid placement of a paper napkin dam on the edge of the table. Backing away from the table, Marek bumped into the giant Golem again, which teetered for a moment and toppled towards the neighboring table, where an alert patron caught and rebalanced it.

Vanesa, instinctively retreating from the table flood in the opposite direction, rammed her chair into the diner behind her, who dropped his soup spoon, splashing his companion with hot soup and causing him to drop his water glass, which shattered on the hardwood floor.

As the Rube Goldberg chain reaction subsided, silence fell over the whole restaurant, and all eyes turned in their direction. Vanesa rubbed vigorously at her wet crotch, and Marek stared at the patron behind him, who held the Golem as if at the outset of a waltz.

"Where did you get this?" Marek said to Vanesa, his incredulous voice booming in the silent restaurant.

"So you've seen this before?" Vanesa's voice was suddenly hopeful.

Marek nodded, apologized to the patron behind him, and drew his chair back up to the table. He lowered his voice and looked into Vanesa's eyes as she, too, sat back down. "I've not only seen it, I have a collection of artifacts on which this symbol appears. The only thing I don't know is what the hell it means. Do you?"

CHAPTER 11

VALIDATION

Wisconsin, 1982

The first time I touched Vanesa Neuman intimately was under an immense Wisconsin sky, by the light of a campfire, with stars so close they were warmed by our heat.

I don't know how she got permission from her father to go camping with a senior counselor, in those days before Skype and cell phones, when physical distance was actually a factor in communications. I don't even know if she asked. All I know is that we took off in my peanut butter and cookie-free station wagon with a borrowed tent, some sandwiches, and a joint, and headed for the nearest state park with a level of determination and intensity that only young people eager to be alone can muster.

Revealing her body to me was not something that came easily to Vanesa. It was not a simple thing for her to reveal anything to me, or likely to anyone—ever. Every revelation was a partial, guarded step forward, followed by an inevitable retreat. This emotional trench warfare between us became, over time, a war of attrition—a war in which her forces, the most deeply entrenched by far, ultimately prevailed.

She sat by the firelight that second summer, a beguiling flower of softness and gentle scent. The challenge of unfolding her petals felt new and engaging. We smoked the joint, and as I turned to the serious business of getting as far as I could with her, she watched the stars and talked, her monologue punctuated only by my occasional arduous forays to her mouth, which tasted of honey and marijuana.

She loved the stars, claiming they were her most reliable companions. She even had what she considered a personal relationship with one constellation, Orion.

"He was the first man in my life," she purred.

I stopped kissing her nipple for a moment, looked up, and smiled mischievously. "You're just one person among billions who've shared the stars since the beginning of time. How close a relationship can you have with a constellation?" I teased.

She responded with a silence far deeper than words. She told me without ever opening her mouth of her solitude, her loneliness. She told me that people could not touch her. She told me that people were inherently bad. People betrayed you, she said wordlessly, as they had betrayed her parents, as they had betrayed Uncle Tomas, as they had betrayed the Jews of Prague, Kladno, and ten thousand other communities that were no more.

She told me.

If only I had known how to listen.

Orion, however remote and cold, would—could—never hurt Vanesa. Orion would never love her so desperately as to be unable to approach her, unable even to touch her. Orion would never hide things, terrible things, things that couldn't be shared anyway because they were so deep. Orion had no secrets, never cried for hours in a locked bathroom, never slapped her if she was so careless as to get hurt. Orion was just there, night after night, listening to a young woman's confessed fears—immutable, unperturbed, accepting.

>—⫟

Prague, December 1991

Marek made apologies to the waiter, to the patrons behind him, and to his colleague Eva. He led Vanesa and Jakobovits out of the restaurant and into the ominously grey Prague afternoon. The temperature had dropped, and the heavy sky had begun to cough up bits of snow mixed with rain, making the cobblestones slick and mucosal.

They hurried around the corner to the museum, and soon entered Marek's cramped but warm third-floor office. He gestured for Vanesa and Jonas to sit on the two folding chairs in front of his desk. While they were removing their coats, Marek picked up the phone on his desk and ordered tea for all. He sat down heavily in his own rickety wooden office chair, which appeared standard issue for museum researchers. The chair buckled under his bulk, but held.

Vanesa remained silent, expectant and eager, but slightly hesitant—as if about to learn something she was not entirely sure she wanted to know.

Without further comment, Marek reached under the desk and removed a battered cardboard box. He placed it on his cluttered desk, pushing several bound sheaves of paper aside to make room on the small wooden table. He removed the worn cover, and a burnt smell escaped. It filled the room with the odor of a campfire pit after a rain.

Vanesa glanced past Marek's right shoulder to the grimy window-panes. Outside, the day's first snowflakes silently snaked their way to oblivion on the wet street.

"These were found in an incinerator in the basement of a building near the Hlavni Nadrazi, the central train station here in Prague," Marek began.

A knock sounded on the door, and he accepted the tea tray with thanks from the grey-smocked woman, who glared with politely subtle malevolence as she handed it to him. He closed the door, turned, and proffered the tray. They each took a glass cup. He put the tray on the bureau behind his desk and took the last remaining cup for himself. For a long moment he blew on the tea to cool it, the steam fogging his glasses. Finally, he set the cup down and began to deliberately remove plastic-encased items from the box.

The first item was the crumbling remnants of a grey-green SS uniform shirt, burnt from the waist up, with only the shoulders intact. The right collar bore the standard SS double *sig* rune insignia, but the left side bore a tarnished silver version of Michael's symbol. Next emerged a blackened lapel pin—or perhaps a tie tack—in the same shape. Following this, Marek produced a wooden-handled stamp of the type used by bureaucrats to stamp papers. The charred wooden handle had a heat-warped rubber pad, on which the symbol could still be discerned. More and more items came out of the box in quick succession: a piece of a metal comb, a twisted wristwatch with flaps of a charred leather strap still attached, a silver letter opener, a broken glass paperweight, the delicate remnants of cream-colored stationery — all embossed with the symbol.

Marek looked at the items spread out on his desk with the mixture of mundane familiarity and wonder usually reserved for parents watching their children. He must have seen these things a thousand times, yet still seemed to marvel at them, to puzzle over where they might lead him. He looked at Vanesa intently, his small blue eyes seeking hers with eagerness.

She met his gaze, but could offer no answers, only more questions.

His disappointment evident, Marek took a calm sip of tea, winced as the hot liquid burned his tongue, and began to speak.

The friendly collegial tone from the restaurant had vanished, the incredulity of the discovery of Vanesa's version of the symbol along with it. Marek lapsed instead into that pedagogical tone that academics adopt in lectures, meetings, or any encounter whatsoever when they feel the imperative of demonstrating the knowledge they've accrued.

"Dr. Neuman, I have a BA and Masters from Charles University here in Prague, and I did my Ph.D. and post-doctoral work at Oxford, specializing in the history of the Nazi period. I wrote my doctorate on the Nazi handling of Jewish artifacts looted from Bohemia and Moravia. As I told you, my grandfather was an active member of the Nazi party. I make no secret of this, nor am I proud of it. It's simply a fact that I've learned to live with. I have devoted my entire life — literally, since I was old enough to understand — to learning about the Nazi movement, its leaders, its symbols, the logic and meaning behind its terrible deeds. I have visited most major Nazi-era sites, from concentration camps across Europe, through Nazi headquarters in most capitals, and most recently bunkers in former East Germany."

He paused and leaned forward across his desk, interlocking the fingers of both hands, his gaze intense. "I have encountered this symbol only three times in all my years of research, the third time being today in the restaurant with you. And, I'm sorry to tell you, I am no closer today to understanding its meaning than I was when the items you see here were presented to me some ten years ago by the janitor of the building in which they were found."

Vanesa nodded gravely. She felt neither crushed, defeated, nor even disappointed. Rather, she sat on the edge of her seat practically afire. Here was her first taste of validation, the trailhead of the path that would, she had no doubt, lead her to the answers she sought. True, it remained only a nibble, but she was hungry for more.

She looked eagerly to Marek, and he continued.

"So, let me tell you what I do know about this symbol. First off, it is clearly runic in origin. As you know, the runic alphabet was used to write Germanic languages prior to the wide scale adoption of the Latin alphabet by around 1100 CE. The Nazis held the runic alphabet in a mystical awe, if you will, and many key Nazi symbols were comprised of various combinations or versions of runes. Henrich Himmler, the head of the *Schutzstaffel*, the SS, from 1925 to the end of the war, was a self-proclaimed runic scholar and quite passionate about Germanic mysticism. He actively promoted the adoption of Armanen runes for the SS—most notably, of course, being the double *sig* rune which became the symbol of the organization itself. This symbol was so prevalent that it was actually added to typewriters during the heyday of the Nazi movement."

He took another sip of tea, and settled back into his chair, visibly enjoying Vanesa's rapt attention. He again interlaced his pudgy fingers thoughtfully, the neatly-manicured and buffed nails momentarily catching the hazy light from the window, and continued.

"Our mystery symbol, as you've no doubt ascertained, clearly has one *sig* rune. This rune, according to Guido von List's interpretation, which the Nazis adopted, stands simply for victory. The other part is either a *leben* rune, which stands for life, or a *tod* rune, which stands for death. It's difficult to tell, since the presentation of both the *leben* and *tod* runes, which are mirror images of each other, is generally vertical, whereas ours appears horizontally. The fact that the *sig* rune is connected to the *leben* or *tod* rune in our symbol is also significant, but only in the absence of other examples. Runes were truly believed to carry mystical power, and although they appeared in combination on various SS decorations, like Himmler's famous *Ehrenrings*—'award rings'—they were not generally touching or connected. There's really no precedent for this type of usage, at least not one that I've found, and I can only wonder at the significance."

Marek paused again to sip his now lukewarm tea. He leaned forward, elbows coming to rest lightly on the desk, and nodded towards Vanesa's and Jonas's tea, which they had barely touched.

Jonas took an apologetic sip of his tea, cleared his throat, and spoke. "What about the combination of the rune meanings, and their relation to the physical position of their appearance. For example, runes were read left to right, correct? So our symbol could be taken to mean victory from death, no?"

Marek nodded. "Yes, I've considered this, but it might be a bit of a stretch. It could just as easily mean victory from life, could it not? Or maybe both, victory from life and death. We can't know. The key problem is that we don't know the exact context of the symbol's usage."

As he continued, a hint of optimism crept into his voice. "What I can say, with some degree of certainty, is that this symbol represented an organizational unit, most likely in the SS. Just take a look at the diversity of the artifacts the janitor recovered. The Nazis loved their trinkets, and took pride in displaying their group affiliation. Even if the actual nature of the group they belonged to wasn't clear to outsiders, the very fact of their belonging to it would have been enough to motivate this display of symbols. They would only create 'toys' like tie tacks and letter openers, not to mention stationery and stamps, if they represented some sort of operational group. However, if this was the case, then we're talking about a unit that was either very secret, was dissolved very quickly after its creation, or was very, very small. There's no record of it in any of the archives I've visited, including the Berlin Document Center."

The room fell into a ponderous silence.

Vanesa stood, as she often did when about to fire off a barrage of questions, and paced the office like a murder detective interrogating a prime suspect. She walked behind Marek's desk and placed her empty tea cup on the tray. "What about the proportional size of the symbol, in its various applications? Is the *sig* rune always the same relative distance from the *tod* or *leben* rune, independent of the size of the symbol? And...." She stopped pacing and turned abruptly to face Marek. "What about the third instance you mentioned, the other time you encountered the symbol in use?"

Marek also stood, their figures together taking up over half of the available floor space in the cramped office. He nodded vigorously. "Yes, I've examined the size issue quite thoroughly, and this is an interesting point: the figure is exactly proportionate in all its applications. The connecting line is always exactly the same length relative to the figure's overall size. However...." He sat back down. "I have yet to understand the relevance of this in discovering the meaning of the symbol."

Vanesa frowned. "And the third instance you found?"

He removed his glasses, untucked a shirt tail, and began polishing them fastidiously. Satisfied, he turned toward the light from the window to check for smudges, and mumbled half to himself, "Oh yes, of course, the third instance. I found it while conducting a survey of an abandoned ghetto dormitory — purely by chance, really. It was the oddest luck. It had been carved into the supporting beam of a triple-decker bunk, in a dormitory that had housed men and older boys. These bunks, it turns out, were only built in the autumn of 1942, so it was obviously not carved before this date."

"But where did you find it?" Vanesa grew impatient, and moved to stand over Marek, who retreated somewhat from the intensity of her questioning.

"In what ghetto?" Vanesa insisted.

He cleared his throat, "Ah, terribly sorry. I found it in the Hanover Barracks, in Terezin — Thereisenstadt, that is, only about an hour from this very office."

CHAPTER 12

TEREZIN

Prague, December 1991

The eyes that watched Vanesa and Marek through the heavy snow falling from the slate-grey Prague sky were, by contrast, starkly blue.

The eyes scowled below the homeless man's snow-topped knitted hat as Vanesa and Marek bought their tickets at Prague's Nadrazi Holesovice terminus. The slouching body in which the eyes resided trudged out of the station, leaving slushy footsteps in the snow, half-walking, half-staggering toward the double row of open-air bus stops on the station's west side. He watched the two of them as they huddled under a flimsy corrugated roof—scarves drawn, collars upturned, waiting for the 8:40 a.m. bus to Litomerice, with a stop in Terezin.

The homeless man glanced up and took in what he could see of Nadrazi Holesovice through the lacy snow curtain. Opened with Orwellian irony in 1984, when Ronald Reagan had just begun referring to the Soviet Union as "the evil empire," the station was a monument to the monolithic Soviet architecture that still scarred much of Prague. From afar the structure made a bid for stern, if humble, elegance. Its black-glassed office façade disdainfully assessed the mundane tools of human mobility from above. From up close, however, the impression dissipated. Low ceilings, dark waiting areas, worn wooden benches, overflowing trash cans, the omnipresent odor of urine—all gave mute yet undeniable testimony to the building's true, seedy character.

As the travelers shook the snow off their coats and boarded the grey bus, the watcher turned away, seeking and finding a payphone.

He dialed with chilled fingers, and finally glanced cautiously from side to side as he reported, "They're on their way," then hung up.

>——/

As they settled back into the worn seats of the aging but comfortably-heated bus, Vanesa puzzled at the man sitting next to her. He'd hardly spoken in the slippery, thankfully short taxi ride from the Jewish Museum, a fact she'd attributed to simple morning fogginess. Yet Marek had continued providing polite, curt but empathetic answers to her enquiries throughout their trek through the filthy bus terminal, as they waited for the bus, and now, in their warm seats.

She began to see that the true source of Marek's silence was discomfort.

As the landscape turned slowly from asphalt-bound urban to white-cloaked, clay-fielded rural, the driver turned the radio up, and a serious voice talked of heavy accumulations and a ground travel advisory.

She turned to Marek. "Do I make you uncomfortable in some way?" Her Israeli directness was calculated to so overwhelm the European stolidity behind which Marek was hiding as to elicit an actual, sincere answer.

The look of a hunted soldier watching lines of enemy troops approach his trench momentarily crossed Marek's face. Then he smiled, the assault repelled, and took a deep breath as he turned to her.

"Yes, in a way, but it's not your fault. I just... know what you're in store for today." His voice was grave, but his eyes remained compassionate. "You... lost family in Terezin, correct? And you've never visited before? Nor any other Holocaust-era sites?"

At Vanesa's puzzled nod, he continued, his tone softening, his voice low and familiar. "You work in academia, Dr. Neuman, so you are familiar with our colleagues who shun field studies in favor of 'scholarly' textual research. To my taste, these scholars do their audience a disservice, because they relate their subject matter based solely on other peoples' experiences. I believe that there is no substitute for actually touching evidence, viewing artifacts, visiting a site. Things that carry deep significance, personal or professional, should be experienced in person. However, I have also learned that no academic preparation is sufficient to mitigate the power of one's emotional response to such experiences. I have visited many such places.... I remind you of the past issues that I, too, face. Do you understand what I'm saying?"

She nodded, her eyes momentarily moistening at his warning that a visit to Terezin would be difficult for her. She had, of course, thought of this. Terezin, where her mother had starved for much of the war. Terezin, from whence her father had disappeared off the face of the earth, or at least off the face of Nazi records, between 1943 and the end of the war. Terezin, where her grandmother and uncle had died, alone and feverish, cared for by the overloaded hands of strangers. Terezin, from whence two of her grandparents had been shipped off in freezing cattle cars to be murdered.

Terezin. She had a sudden impulse to scream at the driver to stop the bus, to turn around, to go away from Terezin, not toward it.

Her stomach lurched as the bus slid, scrabbling for control on the snow-slick freeway onramp. She stared out the window for many long minutes, until the whitening landscape was abruptly broken by Mount Rip, the rounded volcanic mountain where, according to legend, Praotec Cech, the first Czech, had looked over the rich heart of the Bohemian flatlands — a spot of seminal significance, the symbolic birthplace of the Czech people in their homeland.

Significant enough that a plaque on the mountain's side read boldly, "What Mecca is to a Muslim, Rip should be to a Czech."

Had her mother watched Mount Rip go by from the window of the train from Prague? Her father? Had they still felt themselves Czech, even with yellow stars so carefully sewn to their coats? Had they wondered at their fellow Czechs, whose collaboration — with many, many notable exceptions, Vanesa reminded herself — facilitated their deportation and imprisonment?

She tried again, for the millionth time, to pick at the emotional scabs covering the raw fear, the grief, the putrescence below. She was unsuccessful, her mind still firmly rooted in analytical safety.

She turned back to Marek. "Thank you for your concern. I'm sure it will be difficult, as many of your travels must have been for you. You have done significant research in and about Terezin, I gather?"

He confirmed that he had, and clutched suddenly at the seat's armrest as the bus slid again and then righted itself.

The driver appeared unperturbed by the increasingly dangerous road conditions, showing no signs of sacrificing expediency for mere safety's sake.

Marek seemed relieved to return to the emotionally-neutral safe haven of his research. So relieved, that he asked perfunctorily whether Vanesa was familiar with Terezin's history, and then, ignoring her positive response, launched into a lengthy monologue that was only interrupted by Vanesa's gasp as the ramparts of Terezin came into view.

"As you know, Terezin is actually a fortress constructed between 1780 and 1790, under the rule of the Hapsburg monarchy. It was constructed at the confluence of the Elbe and Eger rivers, to defend the important route between Dresden and Prague, and named after Hapsburg Empress Maria Theresa, who died the year construction began. The large fortress, which became the Jewish ghetto known as Theresienstadt, covers almost four square kilometers, and was designed to comfortably accommodate some 11,000 soldiers. It's basically a town with massive fortifications surrounding it."

Moving into full lecture mode and with increased animation, Marek spoke at length until, perhaps sensing he'd lost his audience, he paused to look at Vanesa.

She'd been staring out the window, eyes unfocused and glistening, facing the white landscape. Now she turned toward him and nodded vaguely to show that she actually was listening.

He continued. "The perimeter fortifications stretch over three kilometers, are up to thirty meters thick and thirteen meters high, designed in the tradition of the Marquis de Vauban, the most famous military engineer of the age. When you stand in front of these brick-faced ramparts, when you look up at the enormous bulwarks and ravelins from the moat—which could be flooded thanks to a system of floodgates built on bridges crossing the neighboring rivers—you really have to marvel at the enormity of effort required to build something like this. Ironically, the fortress was never attacked."

Vanesa again nodded vaguely, which was all the encouragement Marek required.

"Fast-forwarding to modern times, the Terezin Jewish ghetto was a pet project of Reinhard Heydrich, who initiated the ghetto in 1941 when he became Acting Protector of Bohemia and Moravia."

Vanesa turned toward him as he continued to speak—of Wannsee, of the removal of the town's small non-Jewish population, of barracks, of transports—and as she watched his mouth, she imagined she could actually see the streams of words coming out, the letters flowing into the air above his head, bouncing off the luggage rack, being sucked out of the window, and dissipating like smoke into the bus's snowy slipstream.

They turned off the divided highway onto a two-lane road by the town of Lovosice, and the bus went into a full slide, careening alarmingly as the driver counter-steered. Several luggage items fell from the overhead rack.

Vanesa, intending to grab the seat's armrest, instead gripped Marek's hand tightly. She did not let go, even after realizing her mistake.

After regaining control, the driver came over the intercom and apologized. He then succinctly announced that the bus would only go as far as Terezin, with no return service guaranteed until the weather improved.

A collective groan rose from the passengers.

Marek seemed to take the news in stride. Pausing to let the driver finish, and still holding Vanesa's hand, he continued his monologue.

His fingers were pudgy, his palms sweaty, but the hand was warm and solid. She held on as he spoke of population density, of daily caloric intake, of the governing council, of epidemics, of cultural events, of children's drawings, of musical events. She held on as the white-frosted sign said Terezin 5km, and still Marek spoke. His words began to swirl in her mind, mixing with the grey sky, the windshield slush, and the white landscape to form a toxic sludge that slowly coated her brain from back to front.

Her brain grasped, just before the sludge flowed over the front, that she was going to a place beyond words. *Transports, barracks, crematoria* — there was no need for these words there. The toxic sludge spread to the backs of her eyes, tickling the back of her nose as the very air around her swelled with its stench.

The bus slid around a bend, passing a snow-covered tourist billboard with the picture of a stony-faced Hapsburg soldier in a blue waistcoat and white stockings, standing under the words "Visit the Amazing Fortress of Terezin!"

Because that's where they were going, wasn't it? A historical monument; an actual Hapsburg fortress that had existed for over 200 years; a tourist attraction; a town with churches and shops and restaurants, where people lived and children played. And the town was growing, she knew, with younger people moving in and new houses being built outside the ramparts. A whole new generation had rediscovered Terezin, and the municipality invested in a large rampart renovation project to draw more tourists.

The sludge got thicker, spreading down her throat now, threatening to choke her. Still the bus lurched and slid forward.

Marek's words—*guard towers, processing center, delousing*—continued to pour from his mouth as a small white sign with the Star of David pointed right and said simply, "Krematoria." Her eyes locked on this sign. How could it be so small, so unimposing?

The bus slid madly, relentlessly forward, and the railroad tracks of the spur from Bohusovice came up on her right—*slave labor, transports, raw potatoes*—meeting with the road in a blaze of rusted steel, cracked asphalt, and frozen filth.

The bus jogged left, passing a cheery white bed-and-breakfast with smoke rising from a tubular metal chimney. As it skidded across the railroad tracks through the ramparts of Terezin, the daughter of Vanesa Neuman, Auschwitz inmate number A-25034, felt she could see vivid details that were half-hallucination, half-memory, yet no less emotionally intense for their fleetingness. She saw the lines of people trudging from the direction of Bohusovice. She saw her grandfather and grandmother, and her mother, one hand clutching the sweaty hand of her toddler uncle, the other clasping the handle of the small brown valise with the white lettering. She saw not in the black and white of photographs but in living, three-dimensional color. It had been real. It had been here, and not only could she see, but at long last, she could *feel*.

She felt the little girl's fear, masked by fatigue but still tangible. She felt the sweaty hand clasping so tightly, seeking comfort and trying in vain to shut out the terrible things outside. And she could smell, even in the frozen December air, the wood smoke from the barracks chimneys, the steam of potatoes boiling in the kitchens, the crisp disinfectant from the delousing sheds, the gun oil from the guards' rifles, the loamy smell of razor wire barricades dragged aside in the dirt.

Marek was pointing alternately right and left now, speaking unintelligible words like Bahnhoffstrasse, Hamburg Barracks, Ghetto Guard, supply carts.

Vanesa remained deep in her reverie, seeing and now hearing. She heard not the squeak of rubber bus tires on snowy pavement, but the muffled rattle of wooden wheels on snow-padded cobblestones — carts carrying steaming vats, pushed toward the ghetto center by women in filthy rags; carts carrying bodies, pushed by emaciated men in the opposite direction; children running alongside the food carts, begging the women for scraps.

Then, as the reverie waned, she felt not the gentle, sliding deceleration of the bus as it pulled up to Terezin's broad central square, but the same sinking sensation that must have been in the little girl's tummy as she stopped, lowered her heavy suitcase, and looked around the square at the cheerily-painted, uniform buildings, and the imposing façade of the Church of the Resurrection. In her mind's eye, Vanesa met her grandmother's gaze, as her mother must have done in that very spot fifty years previously, desperately seeking but finding neither reassurance nor hope.

And as Vanesa Neuman stepped down from the bus, a single tear made its way from her eye to her chin, then to space, landing in the impassive Theresienstadt snow like so many millions of tears before it.

>——/

Another pair of eyes squinted through the blue smoke that rose from a cigarette dangling loosely from their owner's lips. He watched Marek and a red-faced Vanesa alight from the bus on the north side of Terezin's frozen central square. Then, he glanced across the square, through the heavy snow, to yet another watcher. A head was nodded, a glance thrown, a wink acknowledged, and the eyes turned away.

CHAPTER 13

THE LIE

Tel Aviv, 1986

The first time Vanesa Neuman and I made love was in 1986, on a narrow Tel Aviv University dormitory bed. Topped by a thin foam mattress, one side touching the peeling whitewashed cement walls — which were delightfully cool in the summer but ass-chilling in the winter — the rock-solid bed couldn't have made a noise even if it had wanted to. A good thing, because our lovemaking was unplanned, silent, and a bit tacky given that her roommate was snoring only meters away in the room's other bed.

It was glorious. I'd never wanted anyone more than I wanted her that night.

She didn't face me when we made love, not that night or ever. I never touched her breasts amorously again; nor would she ever, once we'd made love that first time, kiss me again, beyond a perfunctory lips-only exchange. Physical intimacy with Vanesa Neuman was a one way escalator, each level trumping and invalidating the previous. By her unspoken logic, once we'd reached the coital level, previous levels were simply unnecessary.

When I landed in Israel that year, on my junior year abroad, it had been almost two years since I'd last seen Vanesa. Our letter writing had waned, understandably, as her workload in the university grew, but I wasn't worried. We had never been closer, despite the distance and despite her sporadic letters. I believed this, and had spent the months preceding my trip mentally constructing an airport meeting scene that would have dignified a big-budget Hollywood melodrama:

> *After collecting my luggage from the crowded carousel in the Ben Gurion Airport arrivals hall, I push past overloaded luggage carts, wheelchairs, and old women waddling so slowly that I want to scream at them that I need to see Vanesa now. Can't they understand? I need her. I make my way outside, where hundreds of people crowd the walkway's waist-high metal rails, waiting to meet loved ones or colleagues. She's not there, or so I think at first, scanning the crowd eagerly, disoriented by the noise. Then the footage switches to black-and-white. The men in their open-necked dress shirts, some holding signs with foreign-sounding names scrawled in magic marker, the mothers navigating prams expertly through groups of matching-hatted tourists, the children with eager faces looking up at me, first with joy, then with obvious distaste as my identity disappoints – all these fade to slow motion and out-of-focus anonymity as the camera finds Vanesa. She is glorious in tight jeans, white Keds, and a blue-striped untucked t-shirt. She is also the sole island of crystal-clear Technicolor in this sea of stark grey. She, too, looks disoriented. She doesn't see me. Her brow is furrowed, her lips are set in a pout of concentration. I call her name, she turns, and the scene is reanimated in full living color as her smile dissipates the grey fog.*

This meeting was so clear in my mind, and so occupied my imagination, that I walked right past Vanesa as I exited Passport Control. I was yanked out of my reverie by the sound of my name, but even after turning toward the source, I still didn't recognize her. The next moments whirled in confusion. My brain simply refused to align the image of Vanesa waiting after I passed through Customs and exited the airport, with the image of this young woman, the temporary security pass clipped to her belt, who was staring so expectantly at me.

Finally, it clicked, and I blurted out incredulously, "What are you doing here?"

"That's what you've got to say to me? 'What are you doing here'?" Her eyes probed mine angrily, but my eyes were already downcast in quick response to her berating.

Every relationship has defining moments, some as dramatic as a sunset proposal, some as mundane as the shrug of a bare shoulder. These moments fade in intensity, but never in latent significance. For Vanesa and I, this airport meeting — so carefully planned on her part, since obtaining an airport security pass at that time was nearly impossible, and so minutely scripted on my part — was such a moment.

Every smile, every embrace, every kiss and caress thereafter were tainted by it, whether overtly or subtly. It was a wake-up call from the front desk of reality to our private suite of penpal bliss.

>——/

Tel Aviv, June 1991

The day after Vanesa received Michael's diary from the noir lawyer was the last day of the *shiva*. Several stragglers came by, in a hurry to get on with their business, the *shiva* call being just another line item clogging their weekly to-do list. Vanesa received them graciously despite having been up the entire night.

She'd sat at the Formica-topped table, the very table where she'd first seen the book on that rainy night so many years before. By the light of the single bulb, hung low above the table on the same dusty cord, she read and re-read Michael's stories, all the time tracing the outlines of the symbol, which appeared on page after page.

On the eighth day following Michael's death, Vanesa left the flat on Nahalat Binyamin for the last time. She walked out the apartment that Sunday morning, the diary tucked safely into her bulging briefcase, and went straight — as straight as the circuitous routes of the Tel Aviv bus system allowed — to her singular source of answers, a place where all made sense, and what didn't make sense could be slowly, methodically unraveled.

She arrived an hour later at the boat-like concrete edifice of Tel Aviv University's central library.

>——⫫

Over the next several months, throughout that long hot summer and well into the fall, I saw my wife only occasionally. She holed up either in the university library, or in the Yad V'Shem archives in Jerusalem, or with the survivors and researchers that staffed the Theresienstadt Martyrs Remembrance Association, on kibbutz Givat Haim, or in any number of the countless Holocaust remembrance and research institutes that sadly dotted our tiny country.

She took a two-pronged research approach. On one hand, she tried to work out the symbol's meaning. She had quickly identified its runic origins, and had worked out the same possible interpretations that Jonas Jakobovits and Marek Wolff would later offer. The key, she believed, lay in the symbol's context: where it had appeared, and how her father had come into contact with it.

To determine this context, she attempted to identify the individuals described, and thankfully named, in her father's stories. She believed Michael's stories must have been based on actual encounters with real subjects. The primary question was: how could a twelve-year-old Jewish boy living in occupied Czechoslovakia have come into contact with such a diverse group of Jews, whose origins ranged from North Africa, Europe, America, and elsewhere? Did he encounter them during his short time in Terezin, or thereafter? She struggled, unsuccessfully, to establish some correlation between the little she knew of her father's and grandfather's activities from 1942 onwards, and the detail-deficient stories her father had written.

Her first breakthrough came late that summer. She'd been working in the recently computerized Yad V'Shem archives in Jerusalem, cross-referencing the eighteen names in the stories against various search terms. She'd first tried her father's and grandfathers' names, with no relevant results. She'd tried "Terezin," "Theresienstadt," "Buhosovice," "Prague," and a long list of other terms, all with similar negative findings. For "Praha," however, the Anglicized Czech spelling of Prague, she found two very significant results.

There were a number of characters in her father's stories for whom he had noted, in passing, years of birth. For two of these names, corroborated by the birth years, she found references to similar, albeit fragmentary, Nazi travel documents, which turned out to be partially burned but still legible on the microfiche viewer. The travel papers had allowed the named bearer to travel via train from Prag Hauptbahnhof, what the Germans called the central Prague train station, to Istanbul, Turkey, which was outside of Nazi-controlled territory.

"You do realize what this means, don't you?" She tossed the question out to me while she was once again changing clothes, eating, and showering simultaneously, knowing full well that I did not. Without waiting for an answer, she excitedly continued through the shower curtain. "It means not only that these people actually existed, but also that they may have made it out of Nazi hands. It means that they could actually still be alive, and it means that I might be able to find them."

>——*

Terezin, December 1991

On the bus radio, the announcer still talked of blizzard-like conditions as the vehicle's door closed. It glided away from the bus stop, the crunching of tires on packed snow the only audible sign of departure. Other passengers hefted bags of various sizes and, quickly engulfed by white, scattered and disappeared into the snowstorm.

Vanesa nodded briefly to Marek, who had been questioning with his eyes the wisdom of their walking four blocks to the Hanover Barracks in the storm. She clearly had no intention of delaying for mere weather, he grudgingly accepted.

Violent gusts of wind grabbed at their coats, unwrapped scarves, and clawed at hats. As that wind screamed in their ears and their rapidly-whitening scarves chapped their chilled noses, Vanesa and Marek made their way across the utterly deserted Marktplatz, Terezin's central plaza. They traversed gravel paths whose white dusting lent them neither grace nor mystery, in Vanesa's eyes. Even through the cold, she felt clearly the weight of the evil that had transpired here, as if it had seeped into the earth, coated the buildings, and infused the very air itself—inescapable, suffocating.

They crossed to the south side of the square.

In 1944, the Nazis had built a music pavilion there, facing the coffee shop that opened in 1942, which offered comfortable chairs and steaming ersatz coffee or tea. Around the corner, a small shop sold items of clothing and other indispensables, all of which could be purchased by the Jewish residents using specially-issued Kronen from the Theresienstadt Bank of Jewish Autonomy, opened in May of 1943. The bank's 50 staff members used state-of-the-art adding machines to keep detailed records of deposits and withdrawals for its 50,000 registered customers.

The healthy, happy Theresienstadt residents could return after concerts in the pavilion to their airy, well-apportioned barracks or cozy apartments, and rest on sheets freshly starched in the local laundry. After a nourishing meal cooked in the central kitchen, the evening air fresh and cool, they could attend lectures on literature or philosophy, or view exhibitions of paintings created by Theresienstadt's numerous artists. For Theresienstadt was, as the Nazis went to such astounding lengths to prove to the outside world, definitively not a concentration camp, nor even a ghetto. It was, rather, an actual city, given to the Jews by the Fuhrer himself, and well-documented in the 1944 film titled *Der Fuhrer schenkt den Juden eine Stadt*—'The Fuhrer Grants the Jews a City.'

Over the years since she initiated her quest, Vanesa had watched the remnants of the 90-minute propaganda film numerous times in the Yad V'Shem archives, hoping anew with each viewing to gain some small insight. The film had been directed by a noted Jewish actor, who was forced into the task in exchange for his life, and later gassed along with the rest of the Jewish cast and crew. The odd project was initiated on the heels of an overwhelmingly successful—from the Nazi perspective—and tightly-orchestrated visit by representatives of the Danish and International Red Cross to the Theresienstadt ghetto in June of 1944. Having convinced these representatives of the international community of the favorable conditions in Theresienstadt, and by extension successfully whitewashed the tremendous industry that comprised the Final Solution, the film was to be the coup de grace of the well-oiled Nazi propaganda machine.

Kurt Gerron, the film's director, had done his job well, crafting a cunningly well-planned piece conceived to project exactly the image that the international community so blindly wanted to believe about the Nazis' treatment of the Jews. He gave them well-narrated scenes of cleanly-dressed, clearly well-fed residents enjoying a classical music concert; men working in metal workshops, playing soccer, or working in communal gardens; old people enjoying the sunshine on park benches. He even gave them children frolicking and eating to their hearts' content in an orchard. What more could the public ask for, than black-and-white proof dispelling the rumors of starvation, disease, and persecution?

What Gerron simply couldn't, or perhaps didn't want to, control was the minute expressions on his actors' faces. It wasn't something anyone picked up on in a single viewing, but when one watched the footage over and over, it became clear that none of the adults were really smiling. The children were sincerely happy, at least some of the time, but the adults were deathly serious. It was in their eyes. They knew. They understood.

Marek and Vanesa passed the former ghetto coffee shop, now an antiques store, and continued south with heads lowered against the wind and biting cold. Marek obviously knew the town well, guiding Vanesa confidently towards the Hanover Barracks, just across from the fortresses' southern rampart.

A lone Trabant glided by them over the snow, fishtailing on balding tires as it turned the corner. Vanesa followed Marek blindly, imagining each step she took crushed a lie.

Step: the lie of happy well-fed residents. Theresienstadt inmates subsisted on less than 1000 calories a day, and the film's famous orchard snack scene had to be shot several times, as the children at first wolfed down the food they received so ravenously as to clearly betray their starvation.

Step: the lie of a thriving ghetto economy. The 50,000 registered customers whose transactions the bank staff recorded never existed, and items for sale in the ghetto shop had been looted from the confiscated luggage of the inmates themselves.

As she trudged on, Vanesa ground her heels ever deeper into the unyielding cobblestones, her rising anger finding vent as she strove to ground out the most heinous lie of all.

Step, *step*. She stamped each foot hard enough to jar her backbone, pulverizing the lie that the world didn't really know the truth about Theresienstadt or the other camps. She crushed the lie that the Red Cross delegation did not realize that their six-hour, minutely scripted, carefully choreographed tour was a farce; the lie that the various passing groups of freshly scrubbed, healthy children encountered during their tour was in fact the same group, herded surreptitiously by camp guards from one "chance" encounter point to the next; the lie that the camp was not overcrowded during the visit, because almost 20,000 inmates had been shipped to their deaths in the months preceding it to make room.

As they took their final steps towards whatever awaited them within the Hanover Barracks, Vanesa mentally crushed the final lie: the lie that today's residents of Terezin could live, could work, could raise their children in this city of ghosts, without knowledge of or regard for the evil that infused the place. Did they not know that their home would forever be Theresienstadt, could never again be Terezin? She looked at a snow-dusted, flowerbox-adorned window, its lace curtains demurely hiding the residence inside. Did they know but not really understand? Did they not grasp the significance? Were they unaware of the scope? Or, she thought, slamming a final heel viciously down on the snow-free cobblestones in the building's main entrance, was it that they simply didn't care?

CHAPTER 14

THE BARRACKS

Terezin, December 1991

The anger that had now replaced Vanesa's initial shock at being in Theresienstadt warmed and refocused her, much like the sudden escape from the relentless and biting wind. She passed through the arched, tunnel-like passage that ran under the building and into the courtyard of the Hanover Barracks. The courtyard held a small collection of old cars, some on cinder blocks, and a larger collection of tall weeds, everything dusted with snow. From beneath crumbling plaster, patches of the building's original brickwork leered malevolently. Rows of windows — some broken, some boarded-up — glowered from above. On either side of the passage, glass-enclosed guard stations stood open to the elements, their doors missing or ajar. Beyond the broken glass and rubbish littering the floor of the station, to her left, a staircase led up into darkness.

Without hesitation, Marek entered the guard station, picking his way among the debris, and headed for this staircase. Turning impatiently, yet not unkindly, he gestured for Vanesa to follow.

Silence and a heavy smell of decay permeated the stairwell. Paint peeled like rotting flesh in long strips from the walls. Light filtered with difficulty from the first-floor landing ahead.

Marek stepped cautiously, keeping to the side of the narrow staircase and testing each step before placing his weight on it.

Vanesa followed closely behind, her anger diluted with an irrational yet tangible fear. She was suddenly aware that she was not just entering an abandoned building, but a torture chamber in which thousands of people, some of them *her* people, had languished in the not-so-distant past. How many tens of thousands of feet, shod in tattered leather shoes—if they were lucky—had trod this very staircase on their way down to forced labor or up to bedbug-infested and hungry sleep? How many emaciated bodies had been carried or dragged down, destined for the crematoria, their ashes dumped unceremoniously into the Elbe?

The intangible held no allure for Vanesa; the inexplicable was only the precursor of explanation. And yet, as she drew breath after breath of Theresienstadt-tainted air, she herself succumbed to the weak irrationality she so despised. She saw a river of tears running down these stairs, flowing over her feet as she conjured the ghosts that lurked in these walls, their continued crying the source of the torrent. She froze upon entering this tomb, a place where living, healthy, well-fed bodies did not belong. Her fear intensified, becoming palpable as her breath shortened and the greyness of the faded walls around her became more pronounced. She looked up to Marek, who had already breached the top stair.

After leaving the stairwell and entering the broad first floor hallway, he turned and again beckoned to her gently.

Regaining mobility, she looked behind her to the looming blackness of the stairwell, and stepped forward.

>——⫞

Tel Aviv, November 1991

"Look, it's quite simple. I don't know why you and Uncle Tomas refuse to understand." Vanesa answered my protests to her impending trip while stuffing warm clothes haphazardly into a suitcase.

For once, Tomas' and my own positions were completely aligned.

"There's no possible way for me to confirm my theory from here. I've been at it for six months, as you've seen. I've exhausted every resource here, and I've come up with a plausible theory backed up by solid evidence. Now it's time to move to the clinical trial stage, to borrow a medical reference. Field research. There's no other way."

I wasn't prepared to concede yet, although I had recognized from the outset the futility of argument. "But this theory, I still don't understand what interest this secret SS group would have had in helping Jews escape. I mean, you said yourself that this would have been in direct contradiction to Nazi policy after October 1941, right? So, how could a group that reported directly to Himmler himself do something so clearly against Himmler's own policy? And on such a large scale? It doesn't make sense." My last sentence came out somewhere between a whine and an appeal.

Vanesa softened, put out her hand and stroked my hair, canine-like. "It does make sense, my poor boy," she cooed. Then her tone darkened. "It makes perfect sense. *Money.* Live Jews brought in money, dead Jews cost money. Shipping Jews to Terezin cost money. Keeping them there cost money. Shipping them East cost money. Letting them leave brought in money. Don't forget that any Jewish family that wanted to leave had to give up essentially all they owned. They'd have to pay a slew of quasi 'taxes,' in addition to the full value of any goods they wanted to take with them. They also had to hand over deeds to real estate and give the Nazis blanket Power of Attorney covering any other property. The voluntary cooperation of these people would have been more valuable to the Reich than their enforced removal—more property recovered, less effort expended. So yes, it was Himmler's 'official' policy to ship Jews East and kill them. Eichmann did a bang-up job of it, as we know, but Himmler was nothing if not pragmatic. This would have been win-win for him and those under him: he could partially fund the Final Solution—not a cheap endeavor—and any number of side projects by milking a relatively few Jews dry, and still get rid of them. Not to mention," she added sagely, "that he and the members of this group could probably line their own Swiss bank accounts, to boot."

I sat down on the bed next to the rapidly-filling suitcase, moving aside a pile of bras, socks and underwear large enough to stock a used lingerie store, and tried again. "Fine, that makes sense. You're right. I can buy the existence of the SS group, and I can see the logic in getting Jews to voluntarily give up their assets. So let's say this group existed, and the symbol you found in the diary was theirs—that still doesn't explain your grandfather's involvement. What could he have possibly offered this group that would be sufficient to justify his, and your father's, release from Terezin?"

She stuffed in the pile of underwear, threw a pair of boots on top, and took a quick assessing look around our bedroom — the discussion was drawing to a close. She secured the zipper on the now-bulging suitcase, silently righted the bag with effort, and set it by the door.

Her forehead wrinkled pensively as she turned to me, and after a long pause she said, "It's complicated. She touched my forearm and looked straight into my eyes. "You're going to have to trust me. I have a plausible theory, but I'm not quite ready to share it. I will tell you, I promise, but let me just convince myself first. Okay?"

>——/

Terezin, December 1991

Crack! The stair under her right foot buckled, then snapped. She pulled back in time to avoid an immediate fall, reaching for the rough bannister to her left. It broke off in her hand. She stared in amazement at the piece of wood she was now holding, and teetered backwards. A scream rose in her throat as she grasped the inevitability of a fall. Nothing remained to grab onto.

The hand that grabbed her wrist just before she fell was the same warm and pudgy-fingered hand she'd held onto as the bus slid into Terezin. It steadied and calmed her, pulling her up the remaining stairs, through the narrow doorway, and into the hall.

Marek took her by both shoulders, and bent slightly to look directly into her eyes. "It's okay. You're fine. I've got you. Nothing will hurt you here. Do you understand?"

Vanesa nodded dumbly and looked past Marek at the dim hallway, unbelieving, still fighting back the panic.

The high-ceilinged hallway reminded her at first glance of the aisle of a medieval cathedral. A mixture of diffuse grey light and snowflakes flowed in through the broken windows that lined the upper southern wall, high out of reach. Strips of peeled paint, dead leaves, and an inordinate amount of grey feathers littered the floor, partially covered by the snow that had already begun to form small drifts. On the right, solid-looking wooden doors, most open, were set in the wall at regular intervals like a row of toothless, hungry mouths.

Marek worked his way down the hallway, staying next to the outside wall, where the 200-year-old floor timbers were less likely to have rotted. Near the fourth door, he stopped and turned back to Vanesa. "This is the room. Come." He entered without another word, the darkness swallowing him.

Shaking off the ghosts and ignoring the hair on the back of her neck, which had begun to prickle as if stimulated by an unseen static-charged hand, Vanesa stepped lightly across the littered floor and entered the dormitory.

>——/

Tel Aviv, November 1991

"So, you're going all the way to Prague based on a theory that's so poorly formed, you can't even share it with your husband?" I knew this was pulling the argument in a completely different direction, and that I would likely pay dearly in that intangible marital currency in which Vanesa and I traded like back-alley stockbrokers. I also knew how sensitive the issue was to Vanesa, how hard she'd worked to discover what she had already learned, what it meant to her to learn anything about her father, what he had been, *who* he had been, and what he had done. She was much more qualified than me to assess and analyze historical evidence, and I still trusted her judgment.

Nonetheless, since I'd already stepped in the steaming mound of marital dog shit, I decided to keep walking. "I can buy the SS group theory, like I said, but your grandfather helping these people escape? How? What could he have contributed to the endeavor? Why couldn't the Nazis just ship the emigrants off without help? And, and...." I was grasping at straws. "...wouldn't that have made him, if it's true, some kind of *collaborator*?"

I regretted it even as it crossed my lips. I always had a unique talent for saying the wrong thing at the wrong time to Vanesa. Was this a result of *my* lack of tact or *her* oversensitivity? Less the former than the latter, perhaps, but in any case, my deeply offensive words ripped the first irreparable tear in our fabric of trust.

She dropped the cup of coffee she was sipping, and it smashed on the hard ceramic tiled floor. Hot coffee and shards of glass spattered the legs of my jeans. She turned to me with a look of fury that would have put Medusa herself to shame.

"Collaborator?" she spat before I could apologize. "He was saving lives, you asshole. I don't call this collaboration, I call it heroism. He left behind his wife in Terezin, remember? He took his twelve-year-old son away from his mother to Prague to help Jews escape the Reich. That's selfless. That's goddamn near saintly. What do you know about this, anyhow? Where is your family? Safe in America? Where were they in the war? *Collaborator!* If you're too blinded by your own ignorance to understand the difference between collaboration and self-sacrifice, I don't see that there's anything further to discuss."

And with this, my wife, my first love, the epicenter of my universe — for good or for bad — threw her long wool coat over one arm, grabbed her giant suitcase, and headed out the door on her way to the airport.

>——<

Terezin, December 1991

The small room had low ceilings and was completely dark. From somewhere above, a host of pigeons cooed. Vanesa found the sound, which seemed to increase in intensity as she ventured deeper into the room, deceptively comforting — like a lullaby, soothing and relaxing, distracting her from the fear that had settled in her throat along with the choking dust her footsteps raised.

In the dim light from the doorway, she could make out four rows of three-tiered bunks, each row subdivided into six sleeping sections that would have held three people each, sleeping side-by-side. She quickly did the math, and shook her head. A total of 72 people had lived in this small space — people who had not been allowed to bathe regularly, people who were more often than not sick with contagious diseases, people who had the bowel afflictions of the chronically undernourished. There was no lavatory on the entire floor, Vanesa knew from the survivor accounts she'd read. There would have been only a communal bucket in a corner of the room. The windows, which faced the courtyard, were boarded closed, as they would have been then to discourage suicide attempts. Surprisingly, of the roughly 150,000 people that came through Theresienstadt, only 500 attempted suicide, and less than half of those were successful.

Vanesa shuddered and looked around the cramped space, which must have been an inferno in the summer and miserable in any weather. *Could I have lived like this?* she wondered. *Would I have had the strength to get out of my bunk, infested or not, every day?* Perhaps the true test of strength would have been to willfully *not* get out of bed, to *not* succumb to false hope, to *not* play a part in the giant and twisted ruse that was Theresienstadt.

Marek's flashlight beam shone from the far side of the room.

She headed in that direction, stepping around partially disassembled bunks, discarded suitcases, and stalagmite-like piles of pigeon droppings. The noise of the pigeons increased, as if they resented the imposition on their previously quiet haven.

Marek turned when she arrived, handed her a small flashlight, and indicated that she should start searching the next row of bunks. "I recall the room for sure, but not the exact bunk." He shrugged apologetically. "When I surveyed this barracks, I was not yet aware that this symbol had any significance. It is, I recall, somewhere on the second tier of bunks, more or less at eye-level."

Vanesa carefully made her way to the adjacent row of bunks, and stopped, suddenly struck by the recollection that her grandfather Hayim, her mother's father, had been among those brought to Terezin in early 1942 to prepare the camp's infrastructure. She hadn't thought of it until now. She caressed the bunk's rough wooden vertical supports with her flashlight beam, then ran her free hand over the wood, smoothed and oily from the thousands of hands that had grasped them since, she imagined, her grandfather had built them.

What must it have been like to build your own prison? Would there have been any satisfaction in having a personal stake in such a hell?

She recalled her mother's occasional memories of Hayim, which would simply pop out at the most incongruous times—in line at the neighborhood *makolet*—'mini-market'—at the sink washing dishes, walking together back from school. These recollections were so few and far between that each had left a lifelong impression on the girl so starved for answers.

Her mother's eyes would grow distant, and her hands would stop whatever they were doing, as if the power of the memory had completely seized control of her body. She'd tell stories of how Hayim would pick her up and swing her around when he came home in the evening, until she was so dizzy that she'd beg him to stop, not actually wanting him to. Or how he'd bring her metal shavings from the factory in Kladno, beautiful and in interesting shapes but razor-sharp, and how she'd kept them, over her mother's strenuous objections, in a small metal tea box by her bed. Or of the handmade dollhouse, complete with miniature furniture that he'd worked on every night for months prior to her sixth birthday. Her mother always punctuated these stories with, "But that was before." Then, inevitably, her mother would end with a session of closed-door crying that left young Vanesa alone in the apartment's small living room, head swimming, wondering what she'd done wrong, overcome with guilt at having made her mother so sad.

These memories, despite their impact, had never made Vanesa feel any closer to the grandfather she'd never met. Now, walking down the row of bunks he may have built with his own hands, she felt an intimacy she'd never imagined grow between her and Hayim. He had been here, she thought, and he would have been glad she'd come to see this place, a monument to the powerful, calloused hands her mother had remembered. A monument to his love, forever denied her.

From across the room came a sudden shuffling, an audibly sharp intake of breath, and a faint gurgle. The pigeons stopped cooing their lullaby. There was a flapping of wings. A palpable silence fell over the dark and fetid dormitory room.

>—⊀

Tel Aviv, November 1991

My wife stormed out the door, but turned back to get in the last word.

I let her, still reeling from guilt, and smart enough to know when to keep my mouth shut.

"Take your baseless collaboration theories, and go fuck yourself."

With that, she slammed the door to our flat, leaving me behind in the silence I'd come to know so well. I berated myself for being so crass and thoughtless, yet at the same time I doubted the veracity of her theory, whatever it was. What connection could there have been? It was far more likely, I reasoned internally, that there had been a paperwork mess-up, that her father and grandfather had been in Prague, but not on the transport to Auschwitz. It was reasonable to assume that Michael had simply seen this symbol, whatever it was, and become enamored with it, as young boys would.

I should have known better than to use the word "collaborator," though. When the new evidence had come to light earlier that year about John Demanjuk, the Ukrainian Treblinka guard who'd been tried and convicted in Israel, we'd had a long argument over the usage of the term.

"Now, *he* is a collaborator in the true sense of the term," she had said. "But the word has been vastly misused as regards the Nazis, especially in Israel. It has been applied far too loosely, in my opinion."

I settled back on our hard couch to listen as she continued her lecture.

"There were no shortage of Jews who worked with or for the Nazis, but were they all collaborators? I don't buy into the theories of Hannah Arendt and Raul Hilberg, who claimed that without the cooperation of Jews, the extent of the genocide would have been measurably diminished. Did Jews in any sense facilitate the tragedy of the Holocaust? Undeniably. Would alternatives to this assistance have been found by the Nazis? Absolutely. And would these alternatives have resulted in even greater suffering and losses? I truly think so."

Because the *Judenrat*, the Jewish Councils who oversaw the ghettos, the members of the ghetto police force, even the Jewish kapos in the concentration camps—most of them, Vanesa believed with all her heart, were not collaborators in any sense of the word. These people had chosen or been forced to carry the burden of responsibility in impossible circumstances. They acted either out of pure self-preservation or out of a sense of duty, not necessarily for personal gain, and not necessarily from cowardice. They bore the derision of the Nazi masters and the hatred of their fellow Jews. They made difficult decisions that often saved lives, even as they shouldered the massive guilt for lives that would likely have been lost in any case.

Theirs was the "grey zone," as Auschwitz survivor Primo Levi called it—a place in which black-and-white morality, in the absence of the social contract, faded to uniform grey. Who was more guilty, the "collaborating" kapo that ensured all prisoners in a barracks received equal portions of food, even if this involved beating prisoners to keep them from stealing, or the individual prisoner, who stole food from his weaker companions? Who caused, and who prevented, more suffering?

In any case, Vanesa contended, these "collaborators" paid dearly for their choices, or for the simple misfortune of having been chosen. Many were killed by their fellow prisoners, and many eventually committed suicide, some long after the war had ended. In Israel, a handful were tried in the 1950's and 60's in the so-called Kapo Trials, although they were based on populist legislation, designed more to placate the 200,000-strong survivor community in the fledgling state than to seek true justice.

The grey zone was, Vanesa concluded, as devoid of justice as it was of clear-cut morality.

>—/

Terezin, December 1991

"Marek?" Vanesa called softly toward the light from Marek's flashlight, which was now shining up from the floor in the direction of the room's outer wall. Perhaps he was looking under the bunk for the symbol, she thought. She lowered her voice now. "Marek?"

She started to move toward the light, still keeping an eye on the beams of the bunks she passed. As she rounded the end of the row, with anticlimactic banality, she saw it. It was right above the spot where she'd placed a steadying hand to step over a fallen board—the symbol, partially obscured by net-like cobwebs, but clearly carved into the soft wood. She brushed a hand across the beam to remove the remaining dust. The symbol was colored in black—perhaps pencil, perhaps soot—and directly below it, in letters no taller than her thumb, Vanesa uncovered the validation she'd come to Terezin to find.

"*Zachrana zivota*," the words read, carved and colored such that their connection to the proximate symbol was unquestionable. She exhaled, suddenly realizing that she'd been holding her breath, and read the words again, as if finding them difficult to comprehend. "Preserving life," they read, in Czech.

So it was true. Rather than wait for the hope he knew would never materialize, her grandfather Jakub had opted to facilitate the lesser of two evils. He had chosen to work with the Nazis, but did so with the clear motivation of saving Jewish lives. And he had taken Michael with him. Michael, who in his impressionable youth had raised the symbol of the Nazi unit they'd worked with to iconic status, carving it into the wood of what had briefly been his bunk, before leaving for Prague. He would have been proud of it, would he not? They were, after all, preserving life. This would have been something to celebrate, a clear moral lifeline in the maelstrom of their day-to-day hell that even a twelve-year-old could understand.

Thus it was also true that her father had met the people in his stories. They'd passed through on their way to Istanbul and new lives—lives made possible by her grandfather's dedication, sacrifice, and altruism.

A surge of pride rose in her chest, and her cheeks flushed with excitement. With joy in her voice, she called out, this time with no hesitation or fear. "Marek? I found it. Over here!"

She smiled and swung her flashlight toward where he had been standing, but the narrow beam of light revealed only empty space. Perhaps he'd left the room, she thought, or decided that this wasn't the right dormitory, after all, and moved on.

Her excitement suddenly retreated before uncertainty. Fear crept back in, and the hairs on the back of her neck again prickled. She forced her fear down, relaxing her shoulders and furrowing her brow analytically.

"Marek?" she again called, now with growing annoyance. She had no time for this. There was still so much work to be done.

The sound of footsteps echoed about her. She turned rapidly back in the direction from which she had come, then swung around again, confused as to the actual source of the noise.

"Look," she called out, exasperated, "we need to get out of here, okay? Let's go."

Now she was truly focused. There really was no time. She'd tasted the elixir of discovery, and intensely wanted to drink more. In fact, this thirst so consumed her, the questions flooding her mind so captivated her, and so intent was she on sharing her discovery with a fellow scholar, that when she slipped in the pool of blood spreading from the inert form wearing Marek's clothes, she had no time to process what or whom she was seeing.

She had no time before the hand clamped over her mouth. She had no time to puzzle at the motivation for this attack or its connection to the incidents in Prague and the secret she'd just uncovered. She had no time to consider her grandfather's decision, her father's stories, her mother's anguish, Uncle Tomas' long silence. She had no time for moral quandaries, no time to debate the borders of collaboration and self-preservation. She had no time before she felt the knife pierce her back once, twice, three times — red hot pinpricks that quickly faded to dull throbbing. She had no time as her questions, like the moral conundrums of her grandfather before her, were engulfed by Terezin's darkness.

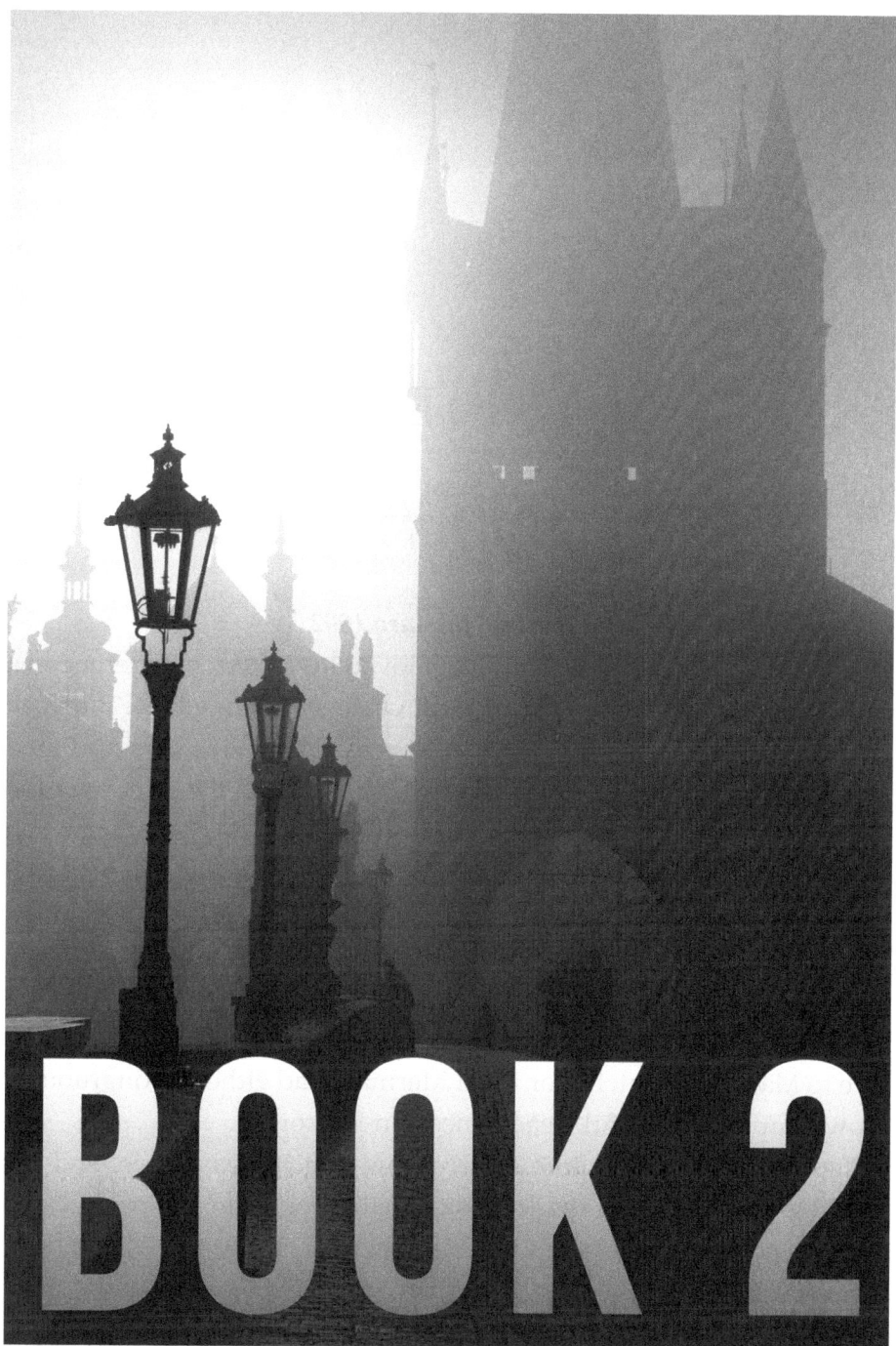

BOOK 2

CHAPTER 15

FLOODGATES

Tel Aviv, January 1992

The first time I told Vanesa Neuman I loved her, we were barefoot on a grassy hill at a Grateful Dead concert. Or so she claimed. We'd driven the hour or so to the show, a group of eager young counselors crammed into my station wagon, Vanesa warm against me in the middle of the front bench seat. We'd shared a joint on the way, then another when we arrived, then another when we found a spot on the hill, next to a group of acid-heads convinced that I was Jesus and Vanesa was Mary. We didn't argue with them, making the most of our temporary deific notoriety.

In my pot-induced stupor, I might just as easily have professed my love to Margaret Thatcher or Ethel Merman, had either incongruously showed up at a Grateful Dead concert in Wisconsin.

Yet Vanesa recalled quite clearly slow-dancing to Ripple, and me bending down to push the long dark hair back from her perfect ear-lobe so I could whisper the words into her ear. These words had been in my soul from the moment I met her, so they may have found their way to my mouth in such an uninhibited context. I don't remember it, but I believe her. Why would she lie?

>—<

The call from the Foreign Ministry came the morning after the stabbing. Awoken from a deep sleep, and then quickly overwhelmed by the news, I comprehended only keywords, like some Cliff Notes version of a traumatic notification phone call: Terezin... stabbed... critical condition... medical airlift... lucky....

She was unconscious for three weeks, and in and out of hospitals for three months. Although she was never again the same Vanesa I'd loved, at least we were still together. And together, we deteriorated during those first grinding weeks, both regressing to a lean and feral state.

Her curves fell away, the fertile rolling hills of her body turning to craggy mountain peaks and valleys. Her cheeks sunk and bags grew under her eyes.

My body, too rebelled — against endless hours in a plastic chair next to her bed, against sporadically consumed cafeteria food, against sleepless hours of angst.

She'd been lucky, the Foreign Ministry representative that visited the hospital told me. One of the workshop owners had seen her and her colleague go into the barracks, and had reported the trespassers to the local police. The doctors echoed this assessment. She'd been lucky that the knife had missed the Abdominal Aorta, hadn't even nicked the Inferior Vena Cava, had only damaged the liver, only destroyed one kidney. She'd been lucky the ambulance had arrived quickly despite the snowstorm, lucky that Uncle Tomas had arranged for the flying medical transport to retrieve her from Prague, lucky that he'd managed to arrange this on such short notice, and lucky that she was a tough and stubborn young woman.

Lucky.

I sat in that chair, all day and every night, for those first weeks. The world moved around me, and winter deepened outside as I internalized the ICU's noisy routine: the beeping, the gurgling, the intubated groans, the nurses who were noisy and the nurses who were quiet and respectful. The sun rose and set outside, and I learned which doctors would spare five minutes to give me a thoughtful assessment, and which were too harried or self-absorbed to bother; which orderlies would set aside a plate of hospital food for me, and which would more strictly obey the rules against feeding visitors. I got used to sleeping sitting up, in snatches of two or three hours, to changing Vanesa's diapers, clearing her surgical drains, giving her a sponge bath, adjusting her feeding tube, emptying the bag from her catheter. I got used to the sterile hallway floor which always shone horseshit green, reflecting walls painted a complimentary shade of vomit. I wondered countless times who chose the color schemes for public hospitals. Was there a special design academy that taught the unique ability to disregard aesthetics, common sense ergonomics, and good taste?

The enforced intimacy of caring for her, though certainly one-sided, made me feel close to Vanesa, a feeling I'd missed since we parted so badly when she'd left for Prague. I savored it in my own perverse way, as if I already knew that she'd never again need me.

Then one day, it evaporated. As I returned from the shower the nurses let me use—against regulations but most likely out of self-interest—Vanesa opened her eyes and looked at me. Or looked past me. She blinked, scanned the room, recognized me, and vaguely smiled. It was like our meeting in the airport when I first arrived in Israel—surprisingly expected, disappointing, defining, devastatingly banal.

She had no idea what had happened, no clue as to how she'd come all the way from Terezin to Tel Aviv in an instant. I started to explain, but had gotten no farther than the word "attacked" when she gripped my wrist roughly, blurting urgently in a voice still scratchy from intubation and lack of use, "What about Marek? What happened to Marek?"

I told her about Jonas Jakobovits, who called every couple days to enquire about her condition in his thick English, and who had applied for a visa to come visit. I told her about his updates of Marek, who'd been less lucky than Vanesa. Although he was alive, I told Vanesa gently, the knife had severed his spinal cord, and he was paralyzed from the neck down. He was lucid, however, and Jonas said he'd been asking about her incessantly. She could call him, if she liked, as soon as she was up to it.

She turned away from me, her lips compressed together to suppress the sob or the scream welling in her, and nodded mutely.

Then I told her the rest of the story: the police investigation turned up nothing; the authorities baffled at the seemingly random act of violence perpetrated in such a sleepy village as Terezin; the helpfulness of the Israeli consul; the swift airlift thanks to Uncle Tomas.

Something in my voice gave me away, because she gripped my wrist again at the mention of his name. "Where *is* Uncle Tomas? Why isn't he here?"

I took her hands, summoned empathy as a substitute for actual regret or sadness, and told her about the stroke.

It had happened several days after she'd been flown back, when it had still been touch-and-go as to whether she'd live. They'd found him in his apartment, alive, but partially paralyzed and unable to speak. He had quickly stabilized, but remained unable to walk, write or communicate. He was also, it turned out, destitute. This made it fairly easy for the courts, which had quickly released the low-rent "key money" apartment he'd lived in for some 30 years to its original owners, and ordered Tomas moved to a state-run hostel for Holocaust survivors near Pardesiya, where he could get the round-the-clock care he required.

I'd been in the courtroom when the judge made his decision. I simply couldn't resist my *yetzer hara* — 'evil impulse' — to see this man's demise in person. I was confident in my dislike — to put it mildly — of the man, but still didn't know why.

As the judge spoke, it was clear that Tomas was quite lucid. He understood, and was strenuously upset by the events taking place.

I recognized but couldn't understand the horror in his eyes as his "sentence" was pronounced, his hands jerking against the wheelchair armrests, drool flying from his mouth as he shook his head violently, ineffectually, from side to side. He was wheeled out of the courtroom, and I went back to the hospital. I hadn't seen him since.

I held Vanesa's hand tightly as I told her she could visit him when she was well enough. "The facility in Pardesiya is supposed to nice, and the staff has kept Tomas informed of your progress. He seems to understand, although he can't communicate. I haven't been to see him," I admitted, squeezing her hand, "because I've been more concerned with you." I didn't mention the vicious argument I'd had with Tomas the evening before his stroke — an argument that had almost come to blows.

I'd spent a good part of that first horrific week, while Vanesa hung between life and death, reading with Tomas the long pages of crumpled legal pad notes that were in the briefcase found by her side in Terezin. Amazingly, what appeared at first glance to be just cramped, handwritten scribbles turned out to encompass all the findings of her decade-long research into her family, methodically written and exactingly cross-referenced.

>——/

Tomas and I said our cold but cordial good evenings, and he walked stiffly out the door of the ICU room, sliding the heavy glass partition shut behind him.

The knowledge that Vanesa was here because of what he had done, or not done, or said, or not said, had been simmering in me for days. The pot inevitably came to a boil, and steam forced its way dangerously from beneath the lid.

I followed him out into the hallway. "I hope you're happy. You know she wouldn't have been over there if it weren't for you, don't you?" My calm voice belied the adrenalin shakes traveling from my spine to my shoulders, down my arms, and back up my neck. "Whatever it was, I hope to hell it was worth it to you, because you did this, as sure as if you'd stabbed her yourself. And you know it. I can see it in your eyes. So don't bother to explain yourself to me, because I could give a shit whether or not you were with Vanesa's grandfather in Theresienstadt—which apparently you weren't. I could care less about your exact connection to Michael, or why he put up with your presence for all these years when he so clearly despised you. But Vanesa cares. She *does* want to know, and you clearly have answers she was—still is, likely—so desperate to find. But you let her go look in Prague instead of just giving them to her. What the fuck are you hiding? What the fuck did you do? And was keeping it secret really worth what it did to her?"

Tomas remained silent throughout my whispered tirade, backing away unconsciously as the extent of what Vanesa had known about him, and what I now knew, became clear. Panic flashed across his eyes, giving him the brief appearance of a cornered alley cat. Then his stoic veil of charm slithered icily down. He turned silently, his back straight, and walked slowly, deliberately away from me.

The vestiges of my love for Vanesa, the flames of angst over her uncertain future, and the burning outrage that had always scorched my bowels whenever I encountered blatant injustice, combined explosively.

"You bastard! You fucking bastard!" I heard myself yelling, giving up any pretense of trying to maintain the silence of the hospital corridor. "She loves you like a father! Do you hear me, you piece of shit? What is wrong with you? What did you *do*?"

A kind-faced orderly, hearing the fracas from a nearby room, restrained me from running after him.

His footsteps echoed for several seconds, and as the other patients' family members shuffled tiredly back from their rubber-necking to the bedsides of mothers, fathers, and wives, the only sound remaining in the hallway was that of my sobs.

>——✝

The winter of 1992 was the wettest in Israel since 1968. The Sea of Galilee, having sadly withered in the preceding years, swelled to bursting like an overripe gourd. Thousands of Israelis flocked to its shores as the lake's caretakers opened the floodgates of the Degania Dam for the first time since its construction, to avoid imminent flooding in Tiberias and other lakeside communities. After years of drought, thousands cheered the sheer ostentation of countless cubes of excess water rushing down the lower Jordan River to the stillness and evaporative mortality of the Dead Sea.

In Tomas' absence, Vanesa's own floodgates remained closed throughout the weeks of her Ichilov Hospital stay, and for the agonizing months spent in the Beit Levinstein rehabilitation hospital in Ra'anana. Amazingly, she channeled the immense pressure building up behind her personal Degania Dam into secondary, productive channels, whose water wheels of inquisition began to spin furiously right after she awoke.

Two days after she opened her eyes to look past me—something she really never stopped doing—she was already on the phone to Marek. It was a lengthy and clearly emotionally-charged conversation in Czech, of which I understood nothing, but her manner was as intensely businesslike as her hospital gown, peaked visage, and weak voice would allow.

She had not yet shared with me the details of the trip to Terezin, which were of course missing from her meticulous notes. She'd already written, in an astonishingly matter-of-fact style and repugnant detail—as if she had been a mere observer—about her attack in Prague. She'd also covered the ransacking of her hotel room, the contents of which had been collected and returned to Israel by the helpful Israeli consul.

Thus, I knew what her theory had been going into Terezin, but knew nothing of her findings leading up to the stabbing. I patiently waited to speak to her about this, my own floodgates barely containing the torrents of anguish that had been swelling inside me at the obvious, yet still unvocalized, change that had occurred between us. Something had changed, and the extent of the transformation grew clearer daily, as I settled again into the hospital routine. Still, I reasoned, she needed to focus on healing. I could rise above, and do what needed to be done. There was time. There was no cause to burden her. I was strong enough.

I stayed in the hospital every day with her, and most nights. I wheeled her up to physical therapy and down to x-ray, helped her to the plastic chair in the shower, and waited patiently outside the door as she demurely washed a scarred body to whose nakedness I was no longer privy. I held her elbow as she painfully and determinedly walked the hallways of the ward for hours a day. I watched, silent and strong, as the simple and calorie-rich hospital fare began to reconstruct the curves that had faded away, curves that were now, in my new role as chaste caregiver, relevant only on the convalescent, rather than carnal, level.

Three times a day, the stainless steel cart rolled into the room on squeaky wheels, bearing the Kosher color-coded plastic plates and squat coffee cups ubiquitous in the Israeli army and other government institutions—blue for dairy breakfasts and dinners, and orange-tan for meat lunches. She ate with relish, cleaned her plate, and often requested seconds. She knew what her body needed, and was determined to get past the pesky physical limitations that were keeping her from satisfying the more pressing demands of her soul.

She spent hours scribbling notes, which she did not share with me, and even longer hours lost in thought, eyes fixed on the parking lot below the window next to the bed she now occupied in the three-person room. She liked watching the Subarus, Peugeots, and Fords jockey for the few parking spaces, and smiled at the frequent parking spot battles that usually involved enough light-flashing, hand-waving, and horn-honking to make them clearly identifiable, even from five stories up.

I read, searched for nurses in the halls when it was time for her pain medication, chased down rehabilitation specialists for consultations, and tried to avoid thinking about what would happen when she got out of the hospital.

CHAPTER 16

RESPECT

Tel Aviv, February 1992

On a sunny afternoon some three weeks after she awoke, Vanesa and I had 'the talk.' It had rained that morning, and we walked slowly to the solarium at the end of the hallway. The sun sparkled sorrowfully on the raindrops clinging to the windows, from which you could see, between two buildings and through the thin winter foliage of a tree, the distant slice of blue that was the Mediterranean. I longed to be on the shore, watching the bruised purple sky of the next storm front skipping merrily across the whitecaps—immune to consequences, ignorant of fear.

Breathing hard, Vanesa plunked down on the faux-wood Formica bench and turned to me. Her eyes narrowed in concern or sympathy, she took a deep breath, and said simply, "I'm sorry you're unhappy. You deserve to be loved. I truly appreciate everything you're doing for me. We should talk about what's next."

It could have been a seminal moment, a scene of Hollywood intensity. It could have been the opportunity to smash both our floodgates and cling to each other in the violence of the deluge.

Instead, I nodded a polite acknowledgement of her gesture, and retorted flatly, "I read your notes while you were unconscious. Tell me what happened in Terezin, and what you're planning to do when you're released?"

She nodded back, as if in professional courtesy, as if I were a colleague whose skill at emotional sublimation she recognized and appreciated. Then, she told me everything, up to and including her current thoughts.

"...so, now, we just don't know. Why would anyone want to hide this underground railroad for Jews, almost 50 years after it stopped functioning? Are they protecting hidden money or stolen property? It's obviously something worth killing over, to whoever's responsible. What was my grandfather's exact role, and Uncle Tomas', for that matter? Marek has some ideas, and would like to help me find out once he's settled in a permanent living arrangement. So, after I'm done with all this...." She gestured to the hospital hallway and the IV still running into her arm. "I'm going to see Uncle Tomas, then I'm going to sell the store, take a leave of absence from the university, and go back to Prague to find out."

I nodded, unsurprised, and then countered, letting my well-contained belligerence peek out just a bit. "And what if it's not what you think it is? What if you're wrong about this mysterious Nazi organization and your grandfather's part in it? What if you're wrong about the people in your father's stories? What if it's something bigger, something far less well-intentioned or, for that matter, nothing at all? What if the next time whoever attacks you doesn't fuck it up?"

She looked me directly in the eyes, the corners of her mouth upturned in the hint of an ironic smile, sunlight catching and holding the shine of her just-washed hair. "Honey," she said, condescendingly yet without rancor, "some questions are simply worth pursuing to whatever end they may lead."

>——/

Pardesiya, June 1992

Vanesa slowly alighted the faded and dusty Egged bus at the Pardesiya Junction, after a 45-minute crawl from Tel Aviv in choked traffic. The one-kilometer walk from the bus stop to the government-run Holocaust Survivors Hostel took significantly less time than it had the first time she'd come here by herself. Once she'd reestablished the lost trust in the stability of her own legs, the walk had measurably shortened. Now, she walked with a non-specific limping gait, the pace of determined recovery, far from the cane-reliant shuffle with which she moved out the doors of the Beit Levinstein Rehabilitation Hospital just two months earlier.

The highway noise faded as she walked, further muted by a loving June sun which caressed the red-soiled fields with one hand and the back of her neck with the other. Raucous green Rose-Ringed Parakeets screamed as she entered the cool shade of a row of majestic Eucalyptus trees, their calls a patterned curtain that fluttered lightly in the breeze, dancing with the branches and leaves.

When she'd first ridden there with me, she had been shocked at the entrance to the Lev HaSharon Holocaust Survivors Hostel. As we approached the gates, she'd given voice to her thoughts in an awestruck whisper. "God help me for even thinking this, but this looks like the entrance to a goddamn labor camp."

Now, just starting to sweat in the early summer heat, she noted only that the place actually looked more like part of a dilapidated British Mandate-era army base, which it once was, than the "advanced mental health facility" touted in the Ministry of Health literature.

From the broad gate that dissected the rusting metal mesh fence surrounding the property, she could see the collection of squat white buildings, some wooden and topped with roofs of faded corrugated metal, and some concrete with roofs sagging under slate tiles that had once been a warm red. The residential portion of the compound was a tidy, recently whitewashed quadrangle of concrete buildings, garnished with ample greenery and peppered with peeling yet serviceable wooden benches.

The wings of the building huddled around a central hub with a white-framed glass door that seemed welcoming, if institutionally bland, until she was actually standing before it. That's when the smell hit her, seeping out from the unsealed crack between the doorjamb and the door. The sad, sickening smell of bleach struggled valiantly but in vain to conceal the reek of unwashed bodies, excrement, damp mold, and unacknowledged yet unforgiving despair.

The entrance door stuck on the uneven floor tiles, its aluminum frame giving out a metal-on-stone screech that made Vanesa cringe. She closed the door behind her, eliciting a companion screech. The grey Formica-covered reception desk sat empty, its fiberboard showing through at floor level, where decades of washing had swelled the wood and split the covering. A wheelchair moped forlornly in the center of the entrance-way, its blue seat cover asserting with ineffectual dignity that it was the "Property of Sorroca Hospital, Beer Sheva."

A voice scratchy with age reverberated through the hallway, repeating "Don't want! Don't want! Don't want!" in a never-ending loop, until it was cut off with, "Then what *do* you want? Shut up!" in heavily Russian-accented Hebrew.

Vanesa made her slow way to the three-person room where Tomas lay in a low and rusting metal bed, situated farthest from the door near a window that opened onto a bare courtyard. The bed sagged in the center from his weight. His eyes were open, and as she moved into his field of view, he clearly recognized her, although the expression on his face — permanently frozen in a look somewhere between heavy-lidded boredom and bemusement — did not change. She nodded to the patient in the bed closest to the door, who looked up from his rocking back and forth, stopped mumbling momentarily, then looked back at his blue-veined feet and resumed rocking.

She took a rickety plastic chair from the empty bedside next to Tomas, dragged it close, and sat down heavily with a light grunt and a tired sigh. From a room down the hall, a voice called out in Polish, an insistent and loud matronly bellow, "Moishe! Moishe! Dinner time! Come home! Come home now!" One of the staff had translated this recurring call for Vanesa, explaining that Henya was calling her son, who had been murdered in Sobibor.

She waited for the voice to quiet, and smiled at Tomas warmly, genuinely happy to see him. "That walk should be getting shorter, but instead I seem to be more tired every time. And how are you today, Uncle? I see your roommate is out. Has he been a little quieter this week?"

Tomas blinked once, their signal for "yes," a primitive but effective system, and necessary given his continued paralysis.

She continued to chat lightly, speaking of the weather, the university, and politics as she looked him over, her eyes running from his greasy unwashed hair, to the wrinkled linen on his bed, to the bulging deep yellow catheter bag tied to the bed rail with a scrap of bandage. The sour smell of inert sweat emanated from him. She rose with difficulty, still chatting, and went to the room door.

Henya's voice rose again, echoing in the hall, "Mooooiiiishee! Come home this instant! Your dinner is getting cold!"

No staff were in sight. She shuffled back, and resumed her place beside Tomas.

"I'll go find someone to straighten you up, but first I want to tell you something, okay?"

Tomas responded with a blink and a barely-perceptible narrowing of the eyes.

She took a breath, exhaled at length, and began. "Do you remember Mitsy, the cat? The white one?"

A blink.

"Do you remember what you told me the day she was run over? I was ten years old and I'd found her near the entrance to the store, where she usually waited for me to come home from school. But she wouldn't wake up. I wasn't heartbroken, even though she was the first living thing that I ever loved and lost. I remember lying on my bed, just... empty. I wasn't overcome by feelings; I was overcome by the absence of feelings. Father was down in the shop. He hadn't known what to say beyond a mumbled 'sorry,' and mother was in the bathroom, crying alone, like she always did when anything bad happened. You came in and sat down next to me, and then I cried, because then, in your presence, I felt. You let me cry, and when I was finished, you dried my tears and said, '*Kotě*, many things in your life will leave you, but we never really lose anything as long as we remember. Your memories, the good and the bad, will never abandon you.'"

Vanesa smiled and wiped away a tear that had trickled down one cheek.

Tomas stared impassively as Henya's voice, now angry, again bounded into the room, accompanied by a rhythmic metallic banging of bedpan-on-bedrail. "Moishe, if you're not back in one minute, there will be HELL to pay!"

"I know you were comforting me, but I also know now that you were talking about yourself, about your memories. I never asked you, or

Father, about the past. When I was little, I pretended that one day, when I was old enough, you would both share your stories with me. When I was older, I tried to pretend that it wasn't important. I thought that I shouldn't care, that I should respect your right to silence, and that what we had today was more than sufficient. I should be grateful to have a real mother and father—and you—when so many of my friends had no one. But it didn't work, because the knowledge of the memories you wouldn't share with me became to me a persistent memory itself."

The metal-on-metal banging increased in intensity and urgency.

Vanesa raised her voice and leaned in to ensure that Tomas could hear. She had prepared this speech, and refused to be interrupted.

"It was like nausea, a bad, long-term case of nausea—needing to throw up but never getting the relief of actually doing so. I was emotionally obsessed. I could recognize it—still can—like nausea, but there is no controlling it. There is no magic milk of magnesia I can take to eliminate this feeling. I wish there were."

Tomas gazed impassively, without emotion, not yet comprehending.

The metal banging trailed off, as if Henya had tired or despaired of ever receiving an answer from her lost son, then renewed furiously. This time, it was not accompanied by a motherly holler, but by a deep and resonating wail, a gut-wrenching cry that launched fifty years of pent-up despair out into the hallway, "Mooooiiiisssssshhhheeee, why? Why? *Why!*"

Vanesa shifted in her chair and continued in a tremulous voice, which grew in both volume and intensity now. "This is why I went to Prague, Uncle. This is why it was worth it. This is what I have to make you understand. I know you know about my research, the details of what I discovered about you, Father, and Grandfather. And I know you know the answers to my questions, but I will not ask you to share your memories. They are yours, and I respect your right to keep them in the dark. At the same time, they are mine, too, and I need to bring them out into the light. I need to touch them, even if they're dusty, or razor sharp, or rotten. I need to feel them because, as you said to me when I was ten, they will never desert me, even if I try."

A scratchy male voice sounded now, rising coarsely above the din of clanging and wailing, confronting the wall of sound emanating from

Henya's room. "He's never coming to dinner, you old bitch. He's *dead*. He's smoke. He's ashes. So shut the fuck up!"

Vanesa took a breath, and took Tomas' hand. As she held his palm, so soft and smooth, his grey pajama sleeve slid back to reveal the faded number tattooed on his forearm: A-25379. She touched it with a tentative index finger, then covered it with her palm and squeezed his arm firmly.

"And that's why I'm going back to Prague, Uncle. I sold the store, but I'm keeping the apartment. I took a leave of absence from the university. My physical therapist says I'm ready, and my trauma counselor says it may actually be an important psychological step, going back. As for my husband, well, we...." She registered the sudden alarm that had appeared in Tomas' wide eyes.

They were watery, and he was blinking urgently, emphatic double blinks, over and over, separated by a pause. *No, no, no, no....* His chest rose and fell rapidly, and a fresh trickle of saliva ran from his mouth as he strained to speak, managing to produce only a grotesque bark that slid from the back of his throat, wet and incomprehensible.

From the hallway, Henya's voice began again, this time with pleading. "Moishe, please come home to Mommy. Please come back to me, my sweet, sweet boy. I'm waiting for you. Pleeeeeaaassseeee...." The banging resumed with increasing urgency.

Vanesa squeezed Tomas' arm more firmly, perhaps a bit too firmly, but the effect was immediate, as his breathing slowed and his eyes refocused. She again traced the number with her finger.

She looked into Tomas' eyes when she spoke, her voice not accusing, perhaps even kind, yet resolute. "The numbers in the A series in Auschwitz stopped at 25378, Uncle. They were supposed to stop at 20000, then restart in the B series, but some clerk overlooked this, and the last 5378 of these were issued to a trainload of women that had arrived from Hungary. A-25379 is not a number that was ever issued at Auschwitz, nor at any other camp that used tattoos for prisoner identification, as far as I could find."

Henya's voice now changed. Insistence had failed. Anger had failed. Pleading had failed. Her voice now rang flat, tired and hungry, as unemotional as a frayed gray-striped camp uniform. "I'll come find you, Moishe. I'll find you, and we'll eat together. We will."

Vanesa dropped her voice a notch lower and squeezed Tomas' hand lovingly. "Whatever I discover, Uncle—about you, about Father, about Grandfather—none of that can change this. This is real, and no past can change it. I have respected your silence over the years, and I still respect it. I understand that you can't tell me what you know, that for whatever reason this is not a story you can share, but now you have to respect my need to know. Regardless of the outcome, regardless of the nature of the truth, regardless of the cost—I must know."

CHAPTER 17

STICKY SILENCE

Tel Aviv, 1976

Vanesa was eleven years old, and the silence in the flat slid from one room to the next with snail-like viscosity, broken only by the honking of the truck horn, which still burst through the evening quiet at occasional intervals from afar. The silence in the living room stifled, flowing from under the now-unlocked bathroom door, palpable, sticky. It would never wash off—not with words, not with detergent, not even with hope.

Tonight's silence hung heavier than usual, however, much heavier. It had been her fault—her fault that Father had been at his desk, head bowed as if praying over the small leather album with the collection of black-and-white photographs that had clearly once been crumpled and re-smoothed. She'd been confused because he browsed the album from the end, not opening it in the direction her Hebrew readers opened.

He explained patiently that this book worked in a different direction, a direction not of this place, not of this time. Then he turned back to the album, and the silence had resumed.

It was her fault—her fault that Mother had been silently crying in the bathroom, again, and her fault that.... The thoughts ran through her head as she sat absently rubbing her sticky hands on her dress. She'd made two terrible, terrible mistakes, and now they were all paying for her thoughtlessness, her insensitivity, her stupidity. What had she been thinking?

The first mistake was not cleaning her plate.

———

She knew food was sacred, something to be hoarded in bulk bags that strained pantry shelves, overflowed into storeroom cabinets, expanded refrigerator capacity to extremes that defied the laws of physics. Only spoiled children left food on their plates, and as she pushed her chair back, deep in thought about what she'd heard that day, she left the trimmings of the tough beef roast bleeding watery gravy from the high side of her plate.

Her father glared; her mother lowered her gaze.

Father set down his fork and knife with deliberate purpose, and started to raise his voice in the tense tones of his there-are-starving-children-blah-blah-blah lecture, which inevitably spiraled into a tirade about spoiled *sabra* children, who never wanted for anything. The brats. Did they not realize? Did they not understand?

The honking outside, previously sporadic, grew more insistent as the driver's annoyance grew. Her father turned with brief but feral animosity towards the open window, silently mouthing the word "barbarians" as he turned back to the table.

His lecture had not had time to grow beyond its initial outrage before she cocked her head, the thought that had been whirling inside finally ready to move from brain to mouth, and said, "I have a question. What are *sabonim*? Are you *sabonim*? Does that make me a *sabon*, too?"

Her father jumped to his feet, knocking the chair over behind him, and rushed at her, the lecture forgotten, the horn—which was blowing ever more urgently—forgotten.

She froze, staring at the bulk of his onrushing figure until he was upon her, his strong, calloused hands closing on her shoulders. She saw his fingernails were only half grown back since they'd last loosened and dropped—a result of the constant exposure to the arsenic he used in the shop. She went limp as he shook her, demanding to know where she'd heard this?

"Who said this? Who *could* say this? What kind of people live in this godforsaken place, who can say things like that? What do they think, that we were on vacation over there?"

The intensity of his interrogation abated only when the horn from below turned into a long single blast, at whose sound he dropped her like a child's forgotten toy, flew to the window, and screamed curses in Czech at the driver below.

She fell to the floor, hitting her head on the chair on the way, and lay there dazed, her father's curses mixing not unpleasantly with the horn's whine into a sickly-sweet cacophony, on which she drifted until the slam of the bathroom door shook from her reverie. She scrambled to her feet, but the door was already locked.

The driver's voice from below, answering her father with equal belligerence and rancor, forced its way into the flat. The harsh voice partially drowned out the determined rustlings she could hear through the door, and muffled her ineffectual pounding on it, but could not completely mask the echoes of her mother's harried murmuring. Then a car door slammed, an engine raced, tires squealed, and a throw rug of silence fell over the room.

Her mother's voice, clearly addressing no one, grew clearer. "Preserving life, he said. Preserving life. What kind of life was he preserving? Who's? For what reason? For *sabonim*? For *soap*?" Her voice grew fainter as she mumbled on, but the desperate tone, so familiar to young Vanesa, hung in the air.

Her father walked wearily to his desk, opened the album, and hung his head.

She remained sitting with her back against the door of the silent bathroom, calling weakly every now and again for her mother to answer, telling her that she was sorry, that she hadn't meant it, that she didn't even know what the word meant. Suddenly, her hands grew damp, as the sticky silence flowing out from under the bathroom door corporealized, turning from frozen white into warm red. She lifted her sanguine hands in disbelief, smelling the rusty odor of blood, and screamed.

Her father kicked down the door, and the sounds of his moans, the edge of hysteria in his voice on the phone, the ambulance's siren wailing from the street, the heavy footfalls of the ambulance crew coming up the stairs — these sounds all faded into a vague mishmash. But the look in her father's eyes as he followed the gurney out the door — a look of accusation, of silently vicious condemnation — seared into her mind.

Then she was alone, again, with just the silence for a companion, until Uncle Tomas arrived. She asked him, crying hysterically, utterly lost, what those kids had meant, taunting her by calling her parents *sabonim*.

"Soaps," she said. "What's so bad about soaps? It's funny, no?"

Uncle Tomas explained, "It isn't funny at all. It's the worst kind of crass *sabra* slang. Some, and only the most insensitive," he said, "called Holocaust survivors *sabonim*."

>——/

Tel Aviv, 1991

"He didn't say why," she told me in her usual lecture tone, slightly deflated by the memories of the story she had just recounted. "Only years later did I learn what this referenced. It referred to the soap that the Nazis had allegedly produced from the body fat of murdered Jews."

She sighed. "You see, not everyone in the newly-declared State of Israel, and even prior to the official declaration of independence, was happy about receiving over 200,000 refugees from Europe. They were not universally welcomed here with the warmth and compassion that popular history would have us believe. In fact, Holocaust survivors were largely resented by the population that had made *aliyah* before the war, some of them generations before. Survivors were, of course, resented for the simple reason that they added a tremendous economic and social burden to an already overburdened population.

"But the resentment went far, far deeper. Survivors were not resented solely for practical reasons. They were resented, in fact despised and frequently derided, both behind closed doors and sometimes quite openly—as in the *sabonim* slang—because of what they represented. They were perceived as victims, old-world Jews, sheep who had been led to slaughter without fighting back. Victims didn't sync with the mask of the new self-sufficient Jew that Zionism had crafted, the self-reliant, tough and prickly *sabras* that were to populate this new country. They were, and still are, referred to collectively as *she'erit haplita*—'the remnants of expulsion'—an idiom that suggests useless, ineffectual leftovers regurgitated from some lost world.

"In the post-war collective Israeli consciousness, survivors were not even afforded a distinct identity, like the Oriental Jews expelled from the Arab countries. These people who had lost so much, who had been exposed to unimaginable physical and mental trauma, were lumped together and perceived as soft, often crazy. They were a burden that had to be borne, surely, but not happily. *Grudgingly.* They were, in a very real sense, a source of shame."

Vanesa paused for oratorical effect, leaned forward as if to better engage her audience of one, and lowered her voice to ensure maximum attention. "I believe that what the historian sees, and what the layman does not, is that human nature can be cloaked in ideology. It can have its face painted with the colors of culture, and it can don pluralistic plumage, but in times of trial, in times when the people fight over who gets to strip the last shred of meat from the bone, our true face is revealed, glorious and degenerate in equal measure. This happened in wartime Europe, and this happened in post-war Israel. It still happens every day, everywhere. Personally, this is what draws me to history, because the only recourse we have is to look back and understand our history, accept our nature, and unabashedly look our true selves in the eyes. This, I believe, is the only way to gain a realistic perspective on our future."

>——/

Prague, June 1992

The trip from Ruzyne International Airport to the house where Marek was staying in Prague's plush Stresovice neighborhood took only twenty minutes in Jonas Jakobovits' red Skoda Favorit. A clear June sky smiled down on them, blue with just a smattering of fluffy white clouds, making the open-windowed trip pleasant, if somewhat noisy. The Skoda, lacking air conditioning and with pieces of plastic interior already dangling loosely despite its relative newness, was not the best venue for conversation, even with the windows closed. Vanesa contented herself with a smile for Jonas when he looked over at her, and gazed out the window at the city going by.

He seemed happy to see her, although the trauma and stress of the past six months were clearly etched in the bags under his eyes and streak of grey at his temple, which she hadn't noticed the last time she'd seen him. These small chinks in his aesthetic armor, however, seemed to have no effect on the overall power of his presence. He remained the tall, well-built, intensely intelligent and handsomely dark-eyed man that she'd met last winter.

When he wrapped his arms around her at the airport with an intimacy borne of six months of near-daily overseas phone calls, she'd felt momentarily safe and protected, a rarity for her since the Terezin attack.

As they drove east on the wide green Evropska parkway, they passed a billboard for the recent Guns-n-Roses concert at the Strahov Stadium, and Jonas gave a thumbs-up, indicating that he'd been at the packed concert. He took his hands off the wheel momentarily, attempting an electric guitar solo pose—à la Slash, the group's iconic guitarist—that was as ineffective as it was hysterical, and smiled broadly.

She returned his smile, and turned her face back to the window. She tipped her head back and let the wind stream through her hair as she watched the overhead wires of the city's electric tram lines, which now ran down the center of the broad street, fly by overhead. She felt Jonas's glancing yet appreciative gaze as she did so.

She struggled to understand her feelings upon this return to Prague. Was it triumph to have returned alive, determined to find and confront her attackers? Was it resignation, understanding that the key to her destiny had long ago been interred somewhere under Prague's rough cobblestones, waiting for her along with the answers she so desperately sought? Or was it less romantic, a simple, tooth-gritting determination, that Israeli let's-get-it-done-and-move-on force of will which is both glorious and reckless in its unwillingness to stop and consider the personal consequences of failure?

In addition to his duties at the museum, Jonas had explained in one of their many phone calls, he'd taken on the role of research assistant, academic liaison, logistics manager, and errand boy for Marek, since they'd moved him into the converted bedroom in his Aunt Agata's small flat four months previously. It was not an easy role, Vanesa knew, but having introduced Marek to her, triggering the chain of events which led to his injury, Jonas felt both morally obligated and at least as curious as

Marek and Vanesa as to the motives behind the attack and its connection to Vanesa's original mission. Over the past months, he'd spent nearly every evening with Marek, reviewing shreds of evidence from obscure historical records and passing references in testimonies obtained via mail from Yad V'Shem—anything that could help them find the meaning of the symbol that decorated Michael's diary, Marek's eclectic collection of Nazi-era paraphernalia, and the bunk in Theresienstadt.

It had finally happened, Jonas had told her excitedly after their embrace at the airport that morning, taking her elbow to steer her towards the baggage claim. Marek, with Aunt Agata's help, had called him late last night, said that he'd found something incredible, but wouldn't say what. Marek just kept repeating "it's in the map, it's in the map, how did we not see it before?" Jonas couldn't get anything else out of him, so he and Vanesa would be surprised together.

They stopped at an intersection, and Vanesa watched pedestrians clad in short pants pass under a huge billboard that dwarfed them from above, displaying a giant map of Czechoslovakia, split in two, with the words "Dissolution Now!" emblazoned in bold red letters. The summer of 1992 was hotter than usual, by Prague's cool standards, resulting in the ubiquitous short clothing that showed off legions of ivory arms and legs, which contrasted sharply in Vanesa's mind with the tanned limbs of Tel Aviv's masses.

The heat's effect on the sweaty citizens of Prague was cooled by the shadow of the dramatic events shaking the country. The Velvet Divorce, the voluntary and peaceful dissolution of Czechoslovakia into Slovakia and the Czech Republic, was finally at hand.

"The vote," Jonas yelled over the roar of traffic, "will likely come sometime next month." They accelerated away from the intersection, racing one of Prague's omnipresent red and white trams. "I'm in favor," he yelled again, "even though the majority of citizens, at least according to the polls, are not."

The landscape was becoming more and more urban now, low-slung office buildings giving way to high-rise apartment buildings, until Jonas finally turned right off the parkway into a pleasant residential street. They drove for several more minutes before turning left onto U Laboratore Street.

Vanesa started at the street name. She hadn't realized where exactly Aunt Agata lived, and looked to Jonas with an inquisitiveness that bordered on alarm.

He smiled ironically, wordlessly reassuring her, understanding completely the source of her angst.

They both knew well the story of another young woman, only several years older than Vanesa was now when she arrived to this very street in Prague 53 years earlier, almost to the day. This young woman, too, had come at a time of great change in the city, a time of great promise for some, of great tragedy for others. She too had arrived with hopes and aspirations, expectations and dreams no less real than Vanesa's.

Round-faced and pretty, Veronika Eichmann, née Liebl—Vera to her friends and husband—must have been pleased with quiet U Laboratore Street, Vanesa thought, looking down the wide, shady lane. She must have been overjoyed at the lovely house her husband, *SS-Obersturmfuhrer* Adolf Eichmann, had procured at number 22 U Laboratore—the former residence of a wealthy Jewish family.

She'd married him late, a slim twenty-six to his twenty-nine years, when he was an *SS-Scharfuhrer*, just a corporal. He'd just taken the first significant step in what was to be a meteoric career, when he transferred into the Jewish Department of the SD, the Security Service of the SS. Four years later, they lived in Berlin, and Adolf continued to climb the ladder. In short order, he earned the prestigious posting to Vienna, heading the *Zentralstelle fur judische Auswanderung in Wien*—'the Central Agency for Jewish Emigration in Vienna'. This posting had proven a challenge for Eichmann, but he'd risen to it grandly, earning the respect of his superiors. Vanesa recalled that Eichmann had actually considered the posting to Prague a step back—fewer Jews, less capital involved.

Vancsa wondered whether Veronika Eichmann ever thought, even in passing, of the family into whose home she moved. As Jonas parked the car on the street in front of number 18, Vanesa doubted she had. It would simply have been a given, something as unquestioned as tap water. After all, did one ponder the organisms that ceased to exist during the water purification process?

As Vanesa climbed out of the car, the familiar pain from the now-healed wounds on her back came in a quick flash, as it always did when she'd been sedentary for too long. They left her luggage in the trunk, as she would be staying in Jonas's spare bedroom, near the museum in the Josefov quarter.

They stood in front of the large brick house, perhaps considered a mansion in its grander days, which were now long past. It had been crudely chopped up into apartments, each with a separate entrance. Jonas pressed the intercom button next to the door labelled Wolff, and waited for an answer. When none came, he pushed on the entryway door, and it swung open.

"They often leave it unlocked," he said over his shoulder, leading her inside the entranceway.

They followed a narrow hall that had been built against the house's external wall, and climbed a rickety metal- and plastic-enclosed staircase that hung precariously from the same wall. Their feet left deep impressions in the pile carpet that covered the stairs, each step detonating mushroom clouds of dust, clearly visible in the afternoon sunshine that slanted through the opaque roof.

Vanesa smiled, basking in the sun's warmth, which was magnified by the intimacy of the enclosed space. She watched the dust as it whirled in patterns that would bring a chaos theorist to orgasm, before it fell in graceful slow motion back to the carpet. She felt as light as the brightly-lit stairs, as carefree as the dust mites swimming in the air around her. Her euphoria was born of relief, as if she'd made it nearly across a dilapidated footbridge over a deep chasm, with terra firma just steps away.

She hadn't forgotten the deep sorrow of Marek's injury, but she'd had months of late-night overseas calls with him, and these had truly tempered her sense of the tragedy. Marek had been surprisingly upbeat even from their very first call—probably putting on a stoic mask for her benefit, she thought at first. Yet their almost daily chats had revealed that Marek's stolidity was not affected.

He had truly and wholly accepted the radical change in his life, the upheaval of his personal and professional plans for the future. "I've always been a fan of Epictetus," he'd told her simply one late night.

She'd been sitting on the couch, her smooth legs curled under her nightgown, her hair still pillow-mussed, unable to sleep owing to the nagging pain in her back.

"We have no real control over what happens to us," he'd continued. "We can influence events, but overall, humans suffer far more from their pointless attempts to obtain the illusion of control, than from actual events themselves. So I accept what happened to me. What else can I do? Besides," he finished with a chuckle, "I'm the portly son of a prominent Czech Nazi, who works in a Jewish Museum cataloging items stolen by the Nazis from the Jews. How else could this tragicomedy have possibly turned out?"

Vanesa had laughed out loud at this, for in the face of such logic, was laughter not preferable to tears?

She did not dwell on Marek's physical condition as she alighted the stairs behind Jonas. Rather, she was wholly focused on what she'd heard from him about Marek's discovery. It had always been about the symbol, she believed — the key to unlocking her father and grandfather's wartime experiences. If he'd truly solved it, it would be more than just a revelation, it would be a victory over the secrets that had polluted her childhood, a victory over the silence that had contaminated her relationship with Michael, the silence that always lay just below the surface, a ravenous alligator waiting to drag unsuspecting prey down into its mute realm. She resented, had always resented, his silence, but now she was going to prevail.

It had cost her, and it had certainly cost Marek, but she would prevail.

Thus, it was with the triumph of conquerors and anticipation of ardent lovers that they let themselves into the small apartment, each calling "Agata!" or "Marek!" excitedly in turn. This sense of achievement made her discovery of Agata — slumped in the corner of the dining room, a small trickle of dried blood meandering from the single hole in her forehead to the bridge of her nose, flies silently crawling over her eyes and lips, sticky grey matter clinging to the wallpaper behind her — that much more terrifying and incongruous.

Vanesa screamed and backed out of the room, tripping over one of the many objects she now noticed scattered on the floor. She looked around wildly at furniture overturned, contents hanging lifelessly from half-opened drawers, pictures askew on walls. Still retreating mindlessly from the horror in the dining room, she ran butt-first into Jonas. She turned and, upon seeing his own wide eyes, quickly understood that a similar terror awaited in Marek's bedroom.

She pushed past him and found Marek in his bed, face purple and eyes wide open, as if staring at the ceiling in wonder of God himself.

CHAPTER 18

WIN-WIN

Prague, July 1942

The *SS-Sturmbannfuhrer* considered Irena Dodalova an undeniably attractive woman for her age. He stared at her in the seat next to him, his cold assessment that of a horse trader examining a mare, as his motorcade swept through the streets of Prague with the reckless speed afforded those for whom the police closed off streets. The rushing air from the partially-opened windows of the Grober Mercedes cooled the car somewhat, but the heat remained oppressive even at this hour.

If only I could travel in the convertible, he thought. He shifted uncomfortably on the leather seat, adjusting his collar while trying to maintain dignity in front of the Jewess and mentally cursing the new security regulations, Reinhard Heydrich's recklessness, Prague summers, and his superior officer, whose pedantic management style necessitated this trip. *At least I – and history – stand to gain something measureable from it. And no great progress was ever achieved without some small sacrifice.*

He composed himself and resumed his assessment of the Jewess. Her eyes remained downcast in fear, respect, and perhaps a hint of... defiance? *Most likely fear.* He cared little. He had nothing to prove. He held her small life in his hands, but that power had ceased to excite him long ago. She was a lovely specimen, however, if a bit old for his tastes, and clearly underfed. They kept them lean in Thereisenstadt, he'd give them that, but she had those long lashes, those dark luscious eyes. *Once she gets rid of the rash on her hands from the Mica processing, and those legs are fattened up a bit....*

He thought in passing that if things were different, he'd have the driver pull over and sample the merchandise right now. But there were plenty of local girls that were all too willing, so why bother? And it was too damn hot. To top it off, he reminded himself, one did not become the head of the Central Office for Jewish Emigration by acting crassly and impulsively. Leave that to the troops.

He mentally closed the subject. He would appreciate that she was a striking Semitic morsel, and leave it at that. He smiled inwardly, for most importantly, she was a *talented* Semitic morsel, which is why he was bringing her to his boss this morning.

The four-vehicle motorcade stopped smoothly on the empty street in front of the imposing cream-colored mansion perched at the corner of U Laboratore and Delostrelecka Street. Built close to the street, the house loomed as clean-cut and unencumbered as a freshly-shaven cheek, dominating anyone approaching by car or foot. Two armed guards flanked the low gates of the property entrance.

SS-Sturmbannfuhrer Hans Guenther waited for the head of his security detail to open the car door, the sign that he could safely exit the stifling armored vehicle. Security had been tightened since Reinhard Heydrich's assassination two months previous — *riding in an open car with no escort, the stupid schwachkopf.* In fact, travel had become so tedious that he tried to avoid leaving the office unless absolutely necessary. He motioned impatiently for the Jewess to exit the automobile first, just in case of a sniper, and then instructed the driver to keep her in the entrance hall until he was ready for her.

They entered the house's cool interior, and Guenther turned to Irena briefly, addressing her directly for the first time since she'd been brought to him that morning. "Short answers, be positive, no requests whatsoever, agree with whatever he says. He is to be addressed as Herr Obersturmbannfuhrer. Are we clear?"

She nodded. Thankfully, her German was excellent. More importantly, she seemed to understand what would serve her own best interests.

The servant showed him in, and Veronika Eichmann met him with a bright smile, looking like the oversized subject of an Adolf Wissel image in her peasant-styled circus tent of a maternity dress. She was enormously pregnant, moving with difficulty but still convivial and chatty.

Guenther greeted her with a smile. She turned to lead him to the west side of the house, where her husband awaited, and he shuddered inwardly at the sight of her swollen calves and prodigious backside. *Revolting. It's no wonder Eichmann comes to Prague as infrequently as possible.*

She announced his presence to Karl—she always called him Karl—and excused herself to go look in on her sister, gesturing that he should go ahead and enter the airy porch where *SS-Obersturmbannfuhrer* Karl Adolf Eichmann was sitting in a padded wrought iron chair in front of a glass-topped table, sipping his coffee.

The porch windows were thrown wide, and the shrill chirps of a group of Blue Tits added to the pastoral ambience of the breezy, pleasantly apportioned room. *Either Frau Eichmann or the previous residents of this home had a reasonable eye for décor*, Guenther thought, standing at attention and waiting for Eichmann to acknowledge his existence.

"So, what have you and Siedl come up with that couldn't wait until I got back from Berlin?" Eichmann finally looked up briefly from the previous afternoon's edition of *Der Angriff,* which he had flown in daily.

That permanent squint in his left eye makes the Austrian shit look far shrewder than he actually is, Guenther thought. Still standing at attention, Guenther smiled obsequiously—a gesture Eichmann did not notice as his gaze had returned to the newspaper—and cleared his throat.

"*Herr Obersturmbannfuhrer*, I have identified a talented Jewish film director who was recently sent to Theresienstadt. At my request, *Obersturmfuhrer* Siedl, the commandant of Theresienstadt, transported her to Prague. I have brought her here for your inspection this morning." *That ought to get the squinty bastard's attention.*

And so it did. Eichmann folded the paper neatly and laid it aside. His coffee cup clattered lightly as he replaced it in its saucer. "So, you have brought me a Jewess for breakfast? And what am I to do with her? Is she to film my morning culinary habits?"

Guenther forced a self-deprecating smile at the inane joke, and continued. "*Herr Obersturmbannfuhrer*, I would like to task the Jewess with making a film about Theresienstadt. I believe that such a film, properly made, could be a most effective tool to assist *Reichsfuhrer-SS* Himmler in showing Germany and the world the excellent conditions we have provided the Jews there."

As Guenther had expected, Eichmann was intrigued. Himmler, the head of SS, was itching to show Goebbels at the Reich Ministry of Public Enlightenment and Propaganda that the SS could face the world without outside assistance. Eichmann, who thought the posting to Prague a step down from Vienna, needed to demonstrate initiative and vision, rather than simply languishing here once he'd gotten rid of the Jews. Guenther had proposed a win-win situation: Himmler would get the prestige of an independently produced SS film, Eichmann would show proactivity and his grasp of the bigger picture, and Guenther... well, he had something to ask of Eichmann in return.

"*Herr Obersturmbannfuhrer*, the Jewess and her husband, who we believe was a spy for the United States and now resides there, owned a small studio in Prague. She has been widely recognized in her field, and is quite capable of creating the script, directing, and overseeing the production of our film. Perhaps the *Obersturmbannfuhrer* would like to meet her? *Herr Obersturmbannfuhrer?*"

Eichmann started. He had been lost in thought, no doubt already preparing his triumphant introductory speech at the film's first showing — perhaps in Prague's grand Rudolfinium hall, perhaps with the attendance of the Fuehrer himself.

Guenther again donned his best subservient smile and waited patiently for Eichmann's answer.

><del>—</del>/

The interview went well. The Jewess had answered Eichmann's questions succinctly and professionally. She would produce a fine film, Guenther believed. It would complement his own documentary efforts in the museum, which were much farther-reaching, of course.

Since June that year, his assistant Karl Rahm had been ordered to have all libraries and objects of historical importance that were "collected" from the Jewish communities of Bohemia and Moravia shipped directly to Prague. There, his staff of Jews, headed by the former museum director — Jakobovits was his last name, but he could never recall the Jew's given name—was cataloging and organizing the mountains of objects no longer needed by their former owners. Tens of thousands of intricately embroidered tablecloths, prayer shawls, Torah covers, velvet phylactery bags, and Torah ark curtains were arriving by train and truck from the far corners of the Protectorate. They were stored in piles, along with heaps of silver Torah pointers, filigreed *kiddush* cups, spice boxes, menorahs, *etrog* dishes, *seder* plates, *mezuzot*, alms boxes, ritual *tahara* nail files and combs for preparing the dead, and thousands of other fascinating and curious items that had apparently facilitated the ritual life of the Protectorate's former Jewish residents.

His great idea had been born, as so many great ideas were, while drinking beer. Fortunately, these particular beers had been consumed with Reinhard Heydrich, who had just been appointed as acting Reich Protector of the Protectorate of Bohemia and Moravia, replacing in practice, if not in name, the incompetent Konstantin von Neurath. He was the most powerful man in Prague, arguably in the whole of Europe.

>——⊀

"*Herr Reichsprotektor,*" he said, speaking boldly, warmed by the informal camaraderie born of several rounds of excellent Bohemian Pilsner. "Do you agree that it is the responsibility of the destroyer, the master, to preserve a taste of what he has destroyed? To leave a legacy that is a record of his triumph, so that future generations will realize that the utopia in which they live came at a price, and will never take it for granted?"

Heydrich looked surprised at the young officer's brashness, but nodded his encouragement for Guenther to continue.

And so he did, for some time. He spoke of destiny, legacy, mastery and rightful places in the order of human society, and he spoke of the wonders he'd seen in New York.

Heydrich agreed.

>——⊀

With Heydrich's support, Guenther brought his vision to fruition. The first exhibit of his museum—this Museum of an Extinct Race, as he thought of it to himself—was set to open in just months.

But Heydrich was dead now, and the unsentimental Eichmann could either take or leave the museum. He lacked the vision to grasp its significance and importance.

Thus, Guenther had brought Eichmann a present, a chance to shine in front of the Reich's *crème de la crème*. This is how the game was played. The museum, he had no doubts, would continue to grow, but he wanted more, for his vision stretched far beyond Jewish *objets d'art*.

A dull ache had begun in his lower back from standing at attention for so long, but this type of opportunity did not present itself every day.

"*Herr Obersturmbannfuhrer*," he began, and Eichmann again looked up, as if surprised to find his junior officer still standing in front of him. "I am happy you are pleased with the film project, *Herr Obersturmbannfuhrer*. I believe it will be of great benefit to the Reich, and to the SS. If I may, *Herr Obersturmbannfuhrer*, I would like to suggest another idea. It is a small addition to the late *Reichsprotektor* Heydrich's ongoing museum project, but one that I'm sure you'll agree will add both depth and a powerful realism to this monument to your — that is, the Reich's — efforts in the resolution of the Jewish Problem in Europe...."

Eichmann now again looked intrigued, and as Guenther proceeded to explain, his trademark crooked smile spread into a broad satisfied grin.

>—/

Prague, June 1992

The warm summer night enveloped them like a soft duvet when they finally left the arctic climate of the over-air-conditioned police station. Almost midnight, the physical and emotional exhaustion hung between them on the short drive to Jonas's flat, dividing the Skoda into two self-contained sides between which interaction, beyond an occasional reassuring sad smile, was impossible.

Prague's streetlights flashed by one-by-one. Vanesa leaned her head against the plastic headrest and closed her eyes, but re-opened them each time the visions of that morning's sights revisited her. She feared this silent slideshow would remain with her forever, the imaginary slide projector clicking remorselessly during long wakeful nights. *Click!* The flies crawling on Agata's lips, some entering her mouth. *Click!* Marek's limp hand dangling from the bed, his manicured nails a light shade of purple. *Click!* Agata's feet, toes turned inward, one shoe missing, a hole in the heel of the stocking through which a rounded callous peeked out. *Click!* Marek's clouded eyes, their look of puzzlement, focusing upward. *Click! Click!* Repeat.

She'd had lots of time to absorb these images in the long minutes between their discovery of the bodies, the gulping hysteria of their futile calls for help, Jonas's shaking hand dialing 156 to reach the police, and the actual arrival of the officers to the flat. She'd tried to look away from the horrors, look at anything but the two bodies, which drew her gaze inexorably to them in mortality-driven curiosity, ensuring that no detail would be lost in her never-ending mental slideshow. She'd had plenty of time to absorb other details in the flat, too, before the police officers tromped up the stairs of the apartment with weapons drawn, their voices tense and commanding. Most notably, she'd had a long look at the map on the ceiling of Marek's bedroom, which Jonas pointed out to her after hanging up with the police, momentarily overcoming his shock as if realizing they must examine it now or forever lose this opportunity.

The two police detectives that questioned them in the flat, and later in the sparse yet freezing interrogation room, were both middle-aged and both wearing ill-fitting shirts with their neckties somewhat askew. One had some kind of sauce stain near the collar of his shirt, the other was unshaven, his comb-over flopping loose to reveal an expanse of pasty white scalp whenever he looked down. Vanesa had mentally dubbed them Abbot and Costello, since sauce stain was tall and slim, and comb-over short and rotund. They'd been at first suspicious, all the more so when they quickly deduced the connection between Vanesa and Marek—information which she and Jonas, by unspoken agreement, had not volunteered.

Luckily, airport personnel had reliably identified them, placing them together around Marek's estimated time of death, sufficiently far away from the crime scene as to eliminate any suspicion. Despite this, Abbot and Costello had half-heartedly tried the "good cop, bad cop" routine, until they'd realized that neither she nor Jonas was trying to hide anything.

Thus the long afternoon, evening, and night of questions focused on the details of her attack in Prague—notably why she hadn't reported it—the attack in Terezin, Jonas and Marek's ongoing research, and the reason for Vanesa's current visit.

She'd been forthcoming with details of her research, of the attacks, of the symbol, of her suspicions. Abbot and Costello had been unimpressed by her contention that there might be a connection between her research, the attacks, and the murders. She'd seen Abbot look at Costello knowingly when she'd brought that up. It was a look that clearly said "Yea, right. Can you believe the imagination on this one?"

The jerk of the Skoda pulling up next to an empty parking space on the cobblestone street woke her from what must have been a light sleep.

Jonas's quick and deft parallel parking was clear testament to years of urban driving. He opened the car's hatchback and took her suitcase for her, leading her to the heavy iron and glass entrance door just two buildings down.

They walked up two flights of narrow wooden stairs, Jonas lugging the suitcase uncomfortably but stoically. As they entered his flat, they were greeted by a large grey Persian cat that was either ecstatic to see her beloved master, ravenously hungry, or both. Gently sidestepping the cat, he showed Vanesa her room, deposited the suitcase neatly on the foldaway double bed, and went to attend to the feline, closing the room's sliding door behind him.

>—/

Prague, June 1992

Fast forward. Stop. Play. Vanesa emerged from the shower, the thick white terrycloth robe pulled tightly around her, her hair wound into another towel in one of those unfathomable, gravity-defying knots women seem to intuitively know how to create. Barefoot, the red toenail polish she favored contrasted sharply with the snowy robe.

The living room was warm from the day's heat. He sat on a plain-looking couch, staring at the slice of empty street visible from the flat's open window. He wore a short-sleeved shirt that accentuated his muscled arms. His hair askew, tears streamed down his face as he recalled the day's tragic events, finally mourning the loss of his friend after a day of repression. He looked up and saw her in the doorway, but didn't look away, unembarrassed by his tears.

Her demeanor softened as she walked across the room and stood in front of him. She reached down and wiped his tears away with a tentative hand.

He took the hand and pressed it to his cheek, feeling the warmth of the palm, the smoothness of the fingertips.

She pulled his head to her belly and stroked his hair.

He smelled soap and body lotion emanating from the warmth of the damp robe.

Her breathing quickened as she pushed his head back, untied the robe, and pulled him to her with gentle urgency.

They came together silently on the couch, he lost in the clean warmth of her breasts, she lost in thoughts unfathomable.

$$\rightarrowtail\!\!\!-\!\!\!\!/$$

Stop. Rewind. This was not necessarily how it happened. Vanesa claimed that nothing, in fact, had happened. She'd been annoyed at me for even alluding to impropriety on her part, and I believed her.

I felt terrible for doubting her, because I was supposed to trust her. What kind of supportive husband would suspect such things in the face of the horrors she'd witnessed? What kind of person would imagine ulterior attraction in a clearly dry, academic relationship with a fellow historian, especially given their shared trauma?

I believed her and apologized. I believed her because of who she was, because of what she sought. After all, who could suspect betrayal of someone who had clearly been so deeply, so grandiosely, so irreparably betrayed herself by those closest to her?

Yet it became clear that betrayal was itself, for the betrayed, an excellent instructor.

CHAPTER 19

RESIGNATION

Tel Aviv, 1978

After school let out, thirteen-year-old Vanesa and her schoolmates walked the narrow streets of south Tel Aviv, arm-in-arm in the cool spring afternoon, singing Izhar Cohen's quirky Eurovision hit A-Ba-Ni-Bi at the top of their lungs. They passed adults with transistor radios pressed to ears, eager for news of Operation Litani in Lebanon. She waved goodbye to the girls and entered her grandfather's shop. He acknowledged her arrival vaguely, and she made a beeline — as she did nearly every afternoon — for the refuge she'd constructed in an unused corner.

She had chosen the spot carefully. It was important that her grandfather Jakub, working only meters away yet mutely uncommunicative, could not see her. But she could see him clearly, if she craned her neck — a balding grey head bent over the workbench, scraping, cutting, sewing. She could also see out a corner of the dusty shop window to the street. She'd surrounded the fort with faded high-backed chairs, their frayed seats turned inward, and filled it with pillows from the living room couch. She had covered it with a ratty blanket retrieved from high in the linen closet, and populated it with her own friends — the animals she'd adopted and made her own.

Even though she knew it was babyish, she had named them all. David the hoopoe, his long bill hanging sadly down where it had been broken, was still regal and vigilant. Shula the hyrax had a permanent look of grief in her black eyes, having lost a cub to a marauding jackal, but her coat was so soft and lustrous. Kewpi the hedgehog was, of course, the villain of the group—as any hedgehog would be—and was forever picking on poor Hayim and Hedva, the shrew twins.

But it was Shlomit, the fox, who never stopped lovingly licking the neck of her cub, Shmulik, which Vanesa loved most. She would always take care of her cub. She would show the world how much she loved him. She would never retreat from his embrace in horrified silence, as if he were plague-ridden. She would never lock herself away and try to hurt herself. She would never *die*.

Since her mother's death the previous winter, Vanesa had spent more and more time in her fort. Michael didn't seem to notice her absence, even when she fell asleep, waking only at the sound of the Arab garbage collectors, who came banging trash cans and yelling to each other gutturally just as the sun was beginning to make the dim yellow streetlights redundant.

She'd wake up, tell Kewpi to leave the twins alone today, for goodness' sake, and run upstairs to get dressed for school. Racing down the building's stairs, she'd tear down the street, stopping breathlessly on the way at Moshe's kiosk to get her sandwich.

Moshe was a portly middle-aged man with a kindly face, a Time cigarette permanently dangling from one corner of his mouth, and small, pudgy fingers that deftly worked the cash register. He supplied most of her meals in those days—omelet sandwiches on a baguette in the morning, chicken schnitzel in a pita with humus on her way home from school, and bread and white cheese with cucumbers in the evenings. He also supplied her father's primary sustenance: cheap vodka.

Despite her erratic behavior, Vanesa Sr. had been the glue holding the Neuman household together. Without her, seams split, boards cracked, pipes sprung sudden leaks. Laundry was ignored until Vanesa learned to take her and Michael's dirty clothes once a week to Shoshana, the Yemenite woman at the laundry on Nahalat Binyamin street with the kerchief on her head and the dark powerful hands, who spoke such exacting Hebrew. Dishes piled up in the sink, beds were constantly rumpled, and dust bunnies danced gaily, without fear of sweeping, when the fresh ocean breezes of spring whirled into the flat's open windows.

Michael stopped going down to the shop to work with Jakub, leaving the older man to shoulder the burden, which he did in stoic silence. Each morning, every day of the week, including Saturdays, Jakub came down from his two-room flat at precisely 8:00 a.m., breaking for lunch at noon and stumping back up the stairs at precisely 5:00 p.m.

Thereafter, the door to his flat would remain locked, and Vanesa quickly learned that even her most pleading entreaties would not open it.

On Friday evenings, she would go to Uncle Tomas' small flat for an actual cooked dinner, usually a whole chicken with potato dumplings and fried onions on the side. She'd walk the two blocks back to the store after dark, her tummy full and warm, her head full of the stories Uncle Tomas would tell her of faraway places like Prague and Berlin. Then she'd let herself into the shop and curl up with a blanket in her fort, her dreams guarded by David, Shula, Kewpi, and the rest.

On this night, a light still shone in the shop when she came back from dinner. Jakub, working late on a rush job, looked up briefly when she came in. He smiled absentmindedly, then turned back to his workbench. Vanesa curled into her fort, shutting her eyes against the light, and mentally wished her friends a good night, a good sleep, and good dreams.

She was awoken much later by a loud slam, and the equally loud slurring of her father's voice. She'd heard him speak like this, of course, most often to himself and sometimes to her mother, but never to Jakub. Michael, as far as she could recall, never spoke to Jakub at all, belligerently or otherwise. She sat up and peeked silently out of the fort, seeing the alarmed expression in Jakub's eyes as he turned to face his son.

"You... you...." Michael spluttered drunkenly, unable to find the right word. "You... piece of garbage. How long do you think you can hide in here? Huh? How long before someone figures it out? Your art. Remember your art? Oh, you are a piece of work, you are. You feel safe here? Do you feel all warm and cozy, you here and your art there? Do you, you piece of garbage, you animal, you *shit*?" Michael raised an arm and swept the workbench clear.

Vanesa gasped, but Michael didn't hear her as he continued to rage.

Jakub cowered, head bent as if in prayer, hands trembling on the work bench.

"You wanna stay here? Maybe we could just put you on display. Then everyone can come see the great Jakub Neuman, *artiste par excellence*. What do you say about that, you evil shit? Yea? You know what? I think that's a really good fucking idea. Yes I do."

Michael's drunken voice rose to a hysterical pitch. His arms, at first flailing uselessly as if seeking an outlet, something to help them express the disgust they shared with his mouth, now became dexterous. He grabbed the closest of Jakub's wrists, immobilizing it against the workbench, and expertly drove a sharp awl through the flesh between forefinger and thumb. The awl sunk deep into the soft wood of the workbench.

Jakub's scream made Vanesa put her fingers into her ears in mute terror, although she never averted her eyes.

Michael swiftly repeated the action with the other hand.

Jakub made no move to resist.

Michael stepped back to admire his handiwork. Satisfied, he grunted, "You'll live," and staggered out of the shop.

Jakub was hunched over, red-faced and sweating, a vein standing out in his forehead as he gritted his teeth against the pain. He was alone, and unable to free his bleeding hands without ripping the flap of skin that each awl held. He searched the room frantically for assistance, and when he finally found Vanesa's own wide eyes peering from behind the chair backs, in shock at the violence they'd just witnessed, it was with utter surprise. He had forgotten she'd come in, had perhaps never actually registered her presence.

She met his eyes, one of the few times she'd ever actually done so, and saw not just a man in physical pain, pleading for relief. She saw the eyes of a man who knew he was damned. She saw resignation and utter self-loathing. She saw the eyes of someone who felt, who knew, that he completely deserved what he got.

> ⊁—⫟

Prague, June 1992

Vanesa watched the light flowing in the small bedroom's single window turn from streetlight-yellow to dawn-grey. Individual vehicle noises, so intensely audible in the lonesome dawn silence, rose jointly into a cacophony, morphed into a diesel-tainted buzz, and faded into the urban background.

The morning was bright and warm. The scars on her back pinched as she got up from the low foldaway bed, and her neck was stiff from the over-stuffed pillow. With a low morning groan, she fished a pair of shorts and a t-shirt out of the open suitcase next to the bed. After pulling on the shorts and then, more painfully, the t-shirt—*sans* bra—she opened the door to an empty yet cheerily sunny flat.

"Jonas?" she called, and received only monotonous traffic buzz, broken by an occasional loud horn or siren, in reply.

As she brushed her teeth, already fantasizing about finding a large mug of coffee waiting in the kitchen, the front door banged open. She stepped out into the hall, and one hand went automatically to her disheveled hair as Jonas came in, smiled sweetly, and said good morning.

His voice struggled to maintain the proper note of somberness in light of the events of the previous day, but was unable to completely mask his obvious pleasure at seeing her. His eyes wandered unconsciously down her body, and he quickly forced them back up to her face, blushing slightly at his own impropriety.

"I brought us some coffee and croissants. Hungry?"

Vanesa nodded, her eyes darting to his hands.

He clutched a greasy paper bag and a cardboard tray with two steaming cups of coffee. He smiled again, offered her a cup, and gestured for her to follow him into the kitchen.

They sat in the bright space, the kitchen windows flung wide to reveal a view of the cobblestone courtyard three stories below. They drank in silence as a warm summer morning breeze flowed through the kitchen.

Jonas's excitement at finding Vanesa awake, not to mention scantily clad, faded into the shared malaise of yesterday's loss. Finally, he spoke again, in a voice that betrayed sadness tinged with the sparkle of curiosity.

"I woke up thinking of how excited Marek was the night before you arrived. 'It's in the map!' he kept saying. He was laughing, giggling actually, like a schoolboy with a new toy. Finally he hung up, or maybe the phone fell. Agata used to prop it by his ear. In any case, he had to have been talking about the map on the ceiling. You got a good look at it before the police arrived. Did you recognize anything?"

Vanesa shook her head, silently conjuring the image she'd seen on Marek's ceiling and vaguely wishing she'd had the presence of mind to take a picture of it. The image in her mind's eye kept morphing into Agata's torn stocking, Marek's purple fingernails, the flies. *The flies!* She shook her head, as if to forcibly remove these extraneous snapshots from it.

When she finally spoke, her voice was still slightly scratchy from sleep.

"I saw what it *was*, but I have no idea what it *means*. What I am guessing is that whoever killed Marek and Agata was not thinking like a bedridden quadriplegic."

Jonas nodded in agreement.

Marek had been in the hospital bed with the expensive bedsore-relieving mattress for several months already, constantly on his back except for the daily physical therapy sessions. If the intruders had been looking for something Marek had *found*, the likelihood of that something being hidden in a drawer or cabinet was nil. They had probably left empty-handed, despite the fact that a clue—if it *was* a clue—was right above their heads the whole time. For what a bedridden person unable to even turn his head sees most is *the ceiling above his bed*.

"It was just last week," Jonas began, breaking the croissant-scented silence that had again descended over the kitchen. "Out of the blue, Marek called—Agata called for him, of course—and asked me to have a full-color poster-size blow-up of a map made for him. He had the map in his desk at the museum, he said. It was an original official map of Nazi-occupied Prague, once actually in use by the Central Office for Jewish Emigration. The Office ran crews that went around the city emptying the apartments of the Jews who had been deported. They employed local drivers and porters, of course, but this was, Marek insisted, the 'official' map, used by the Nazi overseers who would ride along. In theory, the crews were supposed to bring all property collected to the *Treuhandstelle*, the trustee committee of the museum, who would register, sort and appraise it. In practice, many items got 'lost' along the way. It was a good business for them, the Nazis. Although there were many middle class apartments with just furniture and appliances, there were also plenty of luxury flats, owned by people with art collections, antiques, things that couldn't be quickly converted into cash like jewelry, or easily transported. Most of that property was abandoned by its owners, and then resold. The proceeds partially funded the Office's activities, but mostly filled the pockets of the Nazis involved, along with a whole line of shady middlemen."

Jonas paused here, gauging Vanesa's reaction. Her face remained impassive, her eyes focused on the steam rising from the coffee, and he continued. "Marek insisted that the idea was a whim, and that nothing would likely come of it. I indulged him, of course. It took me several days to organize, and I... I... I am *such an idiot!*"

He sprang from the table suddenly, as if bitten, and knocked over his coffee cup. He raced from the room and down the narrow hallway.

Vanesa saw him round the corner and enter the small room in which she had slept, which also served as his office. She grabbed the nearest kitchen towel and mopped at the mess to the sound of scrabbling, of objects being moved, of papers being shuffled.

Jonas called apologetically, "Sorry! I am such an idiot. I made a copy of the map for myself. I completely forgot. One minute. Let me just... find... it.... Aha!"

He began speaking excitedly even before he reentered the kitchen. "Found it! I can't believe I didn't think if this yesterday night!" He spread a map the size of a small poster on the table, and continued.

"I remember thinking that the cartographer who created this thing was obviously color blind and dyslexic, not to mention completely lacking an understanding of scale. The coloring is odd, too, don't you think? Look at this dark orange background, the roads outlined in blood red, the parks and town squares colored a kind of sickly green. And it is so crudely drawn, with the handwritten street names. Some of the names have been 'Germanized,' like this street where three of the sites of the Jewish Museum are located. The name of the street is 'Old Cemetery Street,' because of the Jewish cemetery located there, but the Nazis changed it to 'Luython Street.' Apparently, even a reference to *dead* Jews was offensive."

He smiled wryly and fell silent. The silence blanketed the kitchen for several minutes, growing heavier as they both stared intently at the map spread out before them. Jonas got up to turn on the electric kettle, and continued speaking with his back turned.

"The area you're looking at is, of course, my neighborhood, Josefov. This is the very heart of what was once the Jewish ghetto of Prague. I'm sure you know the history. We are located...." He turned and reached over Vanesa's shoulder, intending to point out the location of his apartment on the map. The view down Vanesa's thin t-shirt from above stopped him in mid-sentence. "...uh... we're located... uh... right here. Yes."

He recovered, went back to his tea-making, and continued. "So, I tacked the map up on the ceiling above Marek's bed. Agata helped. Then he had me mark with thumbtacks the five buildings that made up, and still do make up, the core facilities of our museum: the Maisel Synagogue, the Pinkas Synagogue, the Klausen Synagogue, the Prague Burial Society Building—next to the cemetery—and the Spanish Synagogue."

He paused, and the kettle boiled and shut itself off. Leaving the two cups of tea on the small kitchen counter, he stepped out of the room wordlessly. He came back with a box of thumbtacks, which he set on the table. Without further comment, he searched the map carefully, and marked five locations with tacks, apparently unconcerned by the holes he was making in the rough kitchen table.

"As you probably know, these buildings were purposely preserved by the Reich, whereas such grand synagogues in other major cities were systematically destroyed." Jonas slipped unconsciously into lecture mode. "These buildings were slated to house the exhibitions of the Central Jewish Museum—what Hans Guenther considered his 'Museum of an Extinct Race.' They still do exactly that—minus, of course, the 'extinct' part. How ironic."

Jonas smiled again, but Vanesa paid little attention. She was staring intently at the points on the map, her eyes far away, trying to focus on what she'd seen on Marek's ceiling.

Jonas kept speaking, unaware. "That's all we know. Marek told me he just wanted to look at the map, wouldn't say what he was looking for. I guess he found it, in the end. Now we'll never know...."

Vanesa remained silent, still picturing Marek's ceiling. He'd apparently had Agata wind red string around the thumbtacks, turning the five points into an amorphous shape. She closed her eyes, focusing on the shape, manipulating it in her mind until, with banality greater than any literary anti-climax she'd ever experienced, and with blatancy worse than the most overt *deus ex machina* plot twist, the answer presented itself.

It was so simple that her first inclination was to dismiss it altogether.

How could the key to something that has confounded me for over a decade be so trivial? She opened her eyes to gaze at the map on the table, and upon realizing what she was looking at, felt neither relief nor catharsis, but rather profound embarrassment. *Am I* really *that stupid?*

"Yes, we will," she said, the energy drained from her voice. "We *will* know."

"What makes you say that?" Jonas countered.

Vanesa put her cold coffee cup on the kitchen table. "Because the answer is right here in front of us. All we have to do is figure out what it means, and why it was important enough that someone killed Marek for discovering it. Then, we have to make sure they don't do the same to us."

Jonas stared at her for a moment, appearing taken aback by her bluntness. He recovered and turned back to the map. "I'm sorry. I don't see it. What are you talking about?"

She smiled indulgently, the kind of smile typically reserved for a child in need of explanation about something self-evident to adults. Catching herself, she turned businesslike, and said simply, "Connect the dots."

Still Jonas stared, uncomprehending.

"Connect the dots," Vanesa repeated, more insistently. She grabbed a pencil from the nearby counter, and quickly sketched four lines on the map.

"What if, beyond its inherent runic meanings, the symbol was a key, created to fit this particular map? Each of the five buildings of the museum represents one endpoint of the symbol. And the sixth... taking into account that this map is not exactly to scale, and leaving a little room for creative interpretation, the sixth point should be right... about... here."

She reached over and added a fifth line to the map.

"So, we need to find out what is here, on the corner of Usergasse and Geistgasse. Any idea where that corner is, what was there during the war, or what is there today?"

Jonas shook his head, yet unable to make the short hop from understanding to action. "But there *is* no sixth site," he protested. "There's no historical record of a sixth museum site!"

Vanesa smiled her rueful smile again, this time making no attempt to check herself. "To that, my Ph.D advisor Professor Ben-Artzi would have said, 'history, my dear, is nothing but an endless process of factual revision.' Apparently, it is time we revise what we know of the Jewish Museum of Prague."

CHAPTER 20

ART

Prague, September 1943

Josef Polak walked hurriedly down Parizska Street, dodging puddles from the previous night's rain, his head bent forward as if either in deep thought or extreme haste. The citizens of Prague had come to wryly refer to this as the 'Occupation Walk.' In sharp contrast to delightfully circuitous pre-war strolls, which would eventually lead Praguers to their destinations, one now engaged in the Occupation Walk to get from one place to another as quickly and innocuously as possible. Life under the Nazis, as Praguers of all walks of life had quickly learned, necessitated the art of calling as little attention as possible to oneself.

A knock on the door, an official letter in the post, a rough accosting on a street corner — these were the stuff of nightmares. With the Occupation Walk, one felt momentarily above the rampant danger, as if invisible to evil, stepping lithely around it like a pothole or a pile of fresh dog shit. The Occupation Walk provided an illusion of control in a world spun far out of anyone's hands, especially those of 57-year-old portly Jews like himself.

Josef Polak passed the unimposing façade of the steep-roofed Altneuschul — literally the Old-New Synagogue — barely glancing up at Europe's oldest synagogue, its structure dating to the 1300's. According to legend, the body of the famous Prague Golem still lay in a secret attic *genizah* — 'hiding place.'

This was not a morning to pause and contemplate the richness of Prague's Jewish history, Josef thought, even though that was technically his job as curator of the city's Jewish Museum.

No, he corrected himself, *my job is to create an illusion for my overlords. I am to turn what is essentially cataloging Nazi booty into a coherent museological experience. It is my job to memorialize 1000 years of Jewish existence in Bohemia and Moravia – hundreds of thousands of lives – in museum exhibitions aimed at boors more tickled by the toot of the* shofar *than by the multifaceted, intellectually and spiritually rich society they're in the process of destroying.*

He could feel the eyes of the helmeted German soldiers on the corner of Siroka Street as he passed, and he unconsciously hunched further over in a vain attempt to make his bulky figure smaller. *Just a yellow-starred Jew out for a morning stroll, nothing to concern yourselves about,* he mentally projected.

No one stopped him.

He walked on, his thoughts now meandering to the opening of the Central Museum's, as it was now called, first exhibition in the Klausen Synagogue, barely six months previously. He had guided Hans Guenther, his rosy-cheeked baby face incongruous with the icy dead eyes above it, and Karl Rahm, his deputy, whose bored gaze occasionally broke long enough to allow a coldly intellectual curiosity to peek through. They had been genuinely interested in the exhibition, and Guenther had even tried to show off some of the Hebrew he'd learned. But they had been interested much as children could gaze with open-mouthed wonder at a giant anthill, and later gleefully burn members of that same species alive with a magnifying glass.

He passed sparse shop windows on the shady street. He reflected on the colorless Prague he'd discovered upon returning from his years as director of the East Slovak Museum in Kosice. Grey, lifeless, hunched and labeled – *this* was occupied Prague, he thought, as if the Germans had opened some hidden valve and drained the city's vivacity and color into the Vltava, where it dissolved like crematoria ash.

He rounded the corner of Jachymova Street, the maudlin thoughts still meandering aimlessly in his mind, and immediately dropped the Occupation Walk, coming to a shocked standstill.

Four swastika-flagged staff cars sat parked in front of his office at number 3 Jachymova. The short street was closed off at both ends by wooden barricades manned by jittery SS soldiers. It seemed the memory of Reinhard Heydrich's recent assassination still irritated their fingers like a rash, as they nervously caressed the triggers of their MP40s.

"Papers!" a soldier barked, eyeing him suspiciously. He took Josef's proffered identity card and consulted with his officer. The officer recognized his name and gestured with mock deference to let him through.

I am, after all, the personal pet of SS-Sturmbannfuhrer Hans Guenther.

Josef passed the barricade, moving quickly but without self-importance. He had no illusions about his value to the Nazi regime, nor his life expectancy. He was already dead, as were all his staff. What he'd yet to learn was merely the exact date that should, but likely never would, be inscribed on their gravestones.

His footsteps echoed loudly in the empty street, and a sick feeling settled into his stomach. An early morning visit from the "smiling executioner" could not in any way bode well, especially when Guenther arrived before him. He did not worry for himself; he was too valuable to Guenther, for the moment. It was his staff that concerned him. Guenther could easily have any or all of them, with one exception, deported or summarily executed with the wave of a hand. Twenty-four years his junior at age 33, Guenther's cherubic energy and snap early-morning inspections were no less renowned than his temper tantrums when displeased by their findings. And today, less than a month from the opening of the new exhibition dedicated to the incoming *Reichsprotektor*....

"Polak, you are inexcusably late," Guenther spat as Josef entered his office, hat in hand, having already removed it when he presented his papers to the guard at the building's entrance. Guenther sat behind Polak's desk, his feet up, his high black boots rhythmically bumping with demonstrative irreverence against a pile of leather-bound volumes with Hebrew titles. He stared at Josef, who now stood in front of his own desk with eyes downcast. Guenther leaned forward, picked up one of the Hebrew volumes, leafed through it, and tossed it aside.

"This type of slovenly behavior does not become a Jew of Polak's elevated status, does it, Rahm?" Guenther addressed the officer at his right, *SS-Obersturmfuhrer* Karl Rahm, his deputy and next in line to be commandant of Theresienstadt.

Next to Guenther's young, fresh visage, Rahm's heavy-browed face seemed even more ominously brooding. "No, *Herr Sturmbannfuhrer*, it does not." Rahm's curt reply accompanied a withering examination of Josef, like a gardener eyeing an intrusive weed.

"No, it does not, Polak," Guenther repeated. "Especially not three weeks before we open our new exhibition—exhibitions, that is—for the honorable Wilhelm Frick, our new *Reichsprotektor*. But apparently we are in luck, since judging by your leisurely arrival, everything must already be in order. Therefore, we shall now proceed to inspect these exhibitions, Polak. You will take us there now."

At this, Guenther sprung up from Josef's rickety wooden desk chair. His tall athletic frame filled the cramped office briefly as he strode rapidly out the doorway, long black leather coat flowing cape-like behind him, Rahm in tow.

Josef Polak trailed them out onto the street, trying to get Guenther's attention like a child pestering an irate parent. "But *Herr Sturmbannfuhrer*, these exhibitions are not yet complete! That is, they are of course in the very final stages of preparation, and will be ready well in advance of *Herr Reichsprotektor* Frick's visit. But perhaps *Herr Sturmbannfuhrer* would prefer to see them at a later time, after the finishing touches have been applied?"

At this, Guenther stopped and turned to face Polak, the master facing his over-excitable slave. "But Polak, of course it will be completed. Of that I have no doubt, since you know the consequences to you and your staff's families if it is not. But that doesn't mean I don't need to closely monitor your progress. Now, let's have a look at the Usergasse collection, first. Polak, call ahead and tell that Jew—what's his name?—ah yes, Neuman. Please tell Jakub Neuman that we will be visiting his collection, then join us at the site. You can walk. It's close."

Guenther turned from Josef and climbed into the armored staff car, speaking to Rahm as he did so. "You'll be quite impressed with this, an extraordinary collection and outstanding preservation efforts. This Jew is truly—"

The driver closed the heavy door behind them, cutting Guenther off mid-sentence.

The car pulled away, leaving Josef standing on the sidewalk, head downcast again, sweat stains dampening the underarms of his shirt. Yet when he looked up at the retreating Mercedes, he did so with eyes that blazed defiance, not shame.

>——+

Prague, June 1992

They took the short walk from Jonas' flat to the small street the Nazis called Usergasse, which was now, according to the tourist map they'd consulted, named Bilkova Street. The spontaneous outing sprang primarily from Vanesa's intense need to occupy her body in order to silence her mind.

She took into account that her map theory could be incorrect, but the discovery of the symbol's possible meaning may have brought her light years closer to the source of the mystery — closer, perhaps, than she was yet comfortable with. She had never considered relenting in her search, nor would she now. But neither was she convinced, deep down, that truth would be her salvation. This approach-avoidance conflict made her jumpy, and when she got jumpy she needed to work.

Vanesa normally would have conducted thorough background research – learning the historical names of the street, discovering what had been located there and what was there now, contacting current and past property owners, reviewing building blueprints from municipal archives — before dreaming of initiating a field survey. This situation, however, was unique... and uniquely pressing.

Jonas assuaged the hesitancy she vocalized, explaining over his shoulder on their way down the narrow stairs of his building. "After all, it *is* close, and we *are* talking about a public street in the middle of a major European city, in broad daylight." Reaching street level, he hurried through the heavy metal door.

Vanesa barely managed to keep up. She exited behind Jonas, and while she was still blinking in the blinding morning sunshine that flooded the narrow street, he stopped so abruptly that she collided with him.

He apologized and turned to steady her, concern on his face. "Wait a second. I mean, there probably is one thing we should resolve before we run off exploring, as it were. What exactly are we looking for? I mean, what's our exact working theory here?"

Vanesa recovered her balance and gestured that they should start walking. They fell into a comfortable stride next to each other.

She took a breath, and began. "Fair enough. I'd suggest we review the evidence, what little there is, and our suppositions. Stop me if I miss something."

Jonas nodded his assent, and they walked slowly toward the surmised sixth site of the Jewish Museum of Prague, and whatever shared fate it would presage.

Vanesa said, "One: I surmise, but don't yet have any proof, that my grandfather, father, and Uncle Tomas—none necessarily by choice—were involved in a Nazi endeavor that was somehow under the auspices of the Jewish Museum. The symbol in my father's diary, which we also saw in Terezin—presumably carved there by him prior to his return to Prague—and on the objects Marek showed us, can be considered direct evidence of this."

They walked along Siroka Street until they came to the Church of the Holy Ghost, just across from the ornate Spanish Synagogue, also part of the Jewish Museum. Jonas waved to the woman at the ticket window of the synagogue, who was barely visible through the line of tourists already queued to enter the facility, and received a smile of recognition in return.

Vanesa continued. "Two: given the extreme paucity of evidence found, I believe this organization operated in secret. This is supported by the fact that no records exist of my grandfather and father leaving Terezin in early 1943, and that the record of their transport to Auschwitz is incorrect, not to mention the number on Uncle Tomas' arm, which is exactly one number higher than the last number issued at Auschwitz. This type of record falsification is certainly conceivable, but could only be accomplished with support from the highest levels of the Nazi government."

They crossed to the small, sunny square across from the entrance to the Spanish Synagogue, and sat together on one of the wooden benches.

She immediately stood back up, pacing circuitously around the bench, as she ticked off the items she was discussing on her fingers. "Three: it seems the importance of this secrecy has not diminished, assuming that what happened to Marek and I was not coincidence. The fact that my father, grandfather and Uncle Tomas never revealed anything about their involvement supports this. This means that whatever the secret is, it retains its value until today, and...."

She sat back down heavily next to Jonas, and rested her head on his shoulder for some momentary comfort. "Four: based on our findings at Terezin, it is clear that the organization had to do with the preservation of life, or so my father believed at the time he carved the slogan into the bunk. This theme made a deep enough impression on him that he became semi-obsessed with the symbol.

"Five: from his diary, we know that my father met and interacted with a very diverse set of people, all Jews, from a large geographic area. I surmise that these people must have been connected with the secret endeavor, and thus the endeavor itself had to involve multiple individuals.

"Six, and lastly: we know that, despite official Nazi policy to the contrary, wealthy Jews were able to buy their way out of the Reich even late in the war years."

Vanesa stood, took another pensive lap around the bench, and finally turned to Jonas. She crossed her arms across her chest and looked down at him. When she spoke, her voice betrayed a modicum of self-appreciation, yet trembled as she realized the true scale of what she was saying.

"Conclusion: my original theory is correct. The organization in which my father, grandfather, and Uncle Tomas were involved was a conduit for Jews to buy their way out of the Reich, which needed to operate in secret because of the change in Nazi emigration policy after October 1941. The people that my father met and wrote about were on their way to freedom. This organization was like a Nazi-run underground railroad, on which Prague was the final stop before Istanbul. The primary goal of this organization, from the Nazis' point of view, was to systematically strip Jews of their property and get them out of the Reich. More likely than not, the personal pockets of the Nazi officials involved were filled far more rapidly than the Reich's coffers."

She sat back down and turned childishly to Jonas, seeking his support for her theory. To her disappointment, his dark eyes displayed only skepticism as his brow furrowed in thought.

Finally, he spoke. "Let's say I accept your theory. There are a number of potential holes in it, but let's say I accept it. If, as you say, the primary goal of this 'underground railroad' was the personal profit of the Nazis running it, then how does this 'sixth site' of the Jewish Museum come into play? Maybe this place we're looking for wasn't a 'site' after all. Maybe it was just a transit point, a generic way station in the railroad. Maybe there's nothing left of the site, just like there was next-to-nothing left of the memorabilia belonging to the unit that ran it."

Vanesa quickly countered, "I see your point, but I don't think they would have gone to the trouble of incorporating the site so cleverly into the unit's insignia if it was a simple way station. There had to have been, and must still be, something of significance located there—something of value, something worthy of boastful yet secret gloating, something that might warrant attacking curious historians, something that could... have to do... with...."

To Jonas's enquiring look, she held up the Vanesa Finger—the finger she held up when in mid-revelation, the finger that said, "Hold on, I'm thinking." When she was seventeen, the Vanesa Finger was inevitably followed by a sweet smile of understanding, but over time, the sweet smile had become a haughty smirk, a look of, "I figured out something that you should know. How is it that you don't?"

Her eyes glazed in memory, and she suddenly recalled her night of terror, hidden in her chair fort in the shop. What was it that Michael had referred to with such bile, such venomous accusation?

She leaned back on the bench and looked up at the squat church tower across the street. Finally, she finished her sentence with a single word: "... art."

"Art?" Jonas repeated, clearly puzzled. "Like literature or music?"

"No. Well, I don't know. Just art. Listen...." She told Jonas the story of her father's vicious attack on her grandfather.

"...so my father referred to my grandfather's 'art.' He asked him how long he thought he could hide it. What if this organization that was helping Jews escape was also collecting the *objets d'art* they confiscated? The other sites of the museum collected and displayed Judaica. What if the sixth museum site was a display case for invaluable paintings and sculpture? We could be talking about a collection worth hundreds of millions of dollars today, possibly more. Wouldn't this be worth keeping secret? Wouldn't this be worth killing for?"

Vanesa now stood and gestured dramatically, almost desperately, to emphasize her point.

Jonas rose too, perhaps to calm her, or at least to more effectively engage her, and they stood in the center of the square, their backs to the traffic entering the small roundabout from Vezenska Street.

Vanesa's voice rose another octave. "If you think about it, it fits perfectly with the 'Museum of an Extinct Race' theory. In the first five museum sites, we have what the Jews, with their quirky rituals and odd but clearly complex culture, had created. In the sixth site, we have the invaluable articles of mostly non-Jewish origin that they, in their ultimately pointless attempt to assimilate, attempted to possess, yet failed. It would be a testament to the Jewish race's substantive inferiority, and a shot in the arm to Nazi superiority."

She gave a small laugh, as if attempting to shrug off the stunning cliché that she now recognized as the possible goal of her quest. She stared up at the tall stained-glass windows of the Church of the Holy Ghost, in which Prague's Jews had once been forced to attend Catholic services. Here Jews had been coerced into publicly professing belief in another faith's version of God, yet most had secretly clung to their true beliefs, as had countless generations before and after in similar circumstances. She had never understood this tenacity. What principle, lofty or assumed, could possibly trump pure self-preservation?

Self-preservation, she truly believed, was morally justifiable, and it would have been this which had driven her grandfather's choices, whatever they had been. Lacking the faith that could engender real understanding, she turned from the sacred to the profane. And what could be more profane, she mused as she turned from the church back to Jonas, than to discover a motive as petty as money?

"To be honest, I can't believe I'm even considering this. Stolen Nazi art troves are the stuff of cheap suspense novels and...." The questions continued to effervesce. Could their collaboration in mere art theft have been the source of her father's shame, her grandfather's toxic silence, Uncle Tomas' mysterious misinformation? Would this not have been overshadowed by the pride of having preserved so many lives? Or was the shame of collaboration—she was becoming less averse to the word—sufficient in itself to silence them?

Either way, could Marek have died for something so... *common* as Nazi loot?

CHAPTER 21

THE YELLOW BRICK ROAD

Tel Aviv, June 1992

I first truly grasped that Vanesa Neuman was beyond my reach when she didn't respond to the increasingly urgent messages I left on Jonas's answering machine. I'd left a message the previous evening, and another the morning before that. Now, at nine in the morning in Prague, according to my calculations—the brilliant June sun had long ago risen in Tel Aviv—Jonas's calm and mild-mannered voice again suggested something in Czech, most likely that I leave a message.

The grumble of morning buses echoed between the Tel Aviv buildings like distant thunder. Sitting on our porch, I raised my voice to make sure I'd be clearly heard. "*Please* have her call me, just to let me know that...."

Until then, I'd still felt connected to—perhaps "responsible for" would be more accurate—this woman I'd loved for over a decade. It was already a tenuous connection, one whose thread was rapidly unravelling even as I hung from it over my lonely chasm, but I was not yet in free-fall.

Until then, I had believed I could maintain my grip on her by sheer force of will. Although her slippery pain would likely forever elude my understanding, in my over-confidence I clung until... until the thread finally snapped.

I replaced the receiver, shook my head, and stared down into my sludgy morning coffee. The lower portion of the teaspoon I'd left in the glass mug was invisible in the cloudy liquid, yet the top remained clearly defined. I rested my chin on my hands, staring from tabletop level into the cup, mesmerized by the optical illusion of the teaspoon handle floating in space. I suddenly understood that my Vanesa was the upper part of that teaspoon, untethered to the actual, the illusion of her love insubstantial ballast to weigh her down.

Vanesa's depths could never be plumbed—she was bottomless, without foundation, with no real attachment to me, or anyone. The truly sad part was that it was not her fault. Her parents could not help her forge emotional bedrock, their own foundations having been so brutally uprooted. The deluge that had swept them away continued to toss her, and she would never, ever, find a foothold from which to grasp my outstretched hand. She was capable of continuing to thirstily receive as much of my offered love as I could deliver, but would never be able to return it.

At that moment, with Jonas's voice still echoing in my ears, I accepted that not even the heaviest anchor could stave her unremitting drift. At that moment, Vanesa Neuman consciously became to me what she had perhaps always been—my lost love.

>——/

Prague, June 1992

"Well," Vanesa said quietly. "This place, whatever it is and whatever it represents, is not going to present itself. Let's get going."

Jonas was all too happy to comply, and led them deftly between the parked cars choking the sides of Vazenska Street. They left the square behind and turned into a pedestrian alley that led them, just one short block farther, to Bilkova Street. They leaned against the rail of the raised garden at the street's western end, as Jonas's gaze swept the short stretch of archetypical Prague street facing them. Somewhere between Kozi Street behind them, and Dusni Street some 100 meters in front of them, they might find more answers, more questions, or—equally likely—more danger.

Anger rose silently in him. "I'm a PhD, a researcher in a museum, not some Indiana Jones wannabe!" Then he saw again the surprised look in Marek's dead eyes, and he glanced at Vanesa.

Her own brow was furrowed introspectively, her eyes staring unfocused at the high-walled canyon of buildings in front of her.

Then he thought of another set of eyes, those of his Great Uncle, Tobias Jakobovits. His grandfather's brother had been a nebulous character in Jonas's childhood, revered by the few surviving Jakobovits family members, most of whom had returned to Prague after World War II, braving the grey and brutal decades of Soviet rule to remain in this land that had so clearly revoked their welcome. Although Tobias was larger than life, the family rarely discussed him. He remained a quiet source of family pride. Several books in Czech and Hebrew with his name on their spines sat on the family bookshelves, and a framed photograph of him hung on their wall, taken before the War. In it, a completely bald, full-cheeked man with a stern goatee half-smiled with a self-satisfied yet not conceited look, as if to say, "I think you understand, as I do. Now, prove it to me."

Tobias Jakobovits was fifty-one when the first Nazi soldiers crossed the Vltava into Old Prague, a prominent German-trained scholar and leader of the city's Jewish community. As librarian of the Prague Jewish community, he had been a natural candidate to take joint charge of the Jewish Museum with Josef Polak, he responsible for cataloging the hundreds of thousands of looted books that poured in from the far corners of Bohemia and Moravia, Polak in charge of art and Judaica. Tobias had conceived, organized, and even written the guide for the fledging museum's primary exhibit, first opened for a private showing to Hans Guenther and his deputy Karl Rahm in 1943.

Tobias Jakobovits was inseparable from the history of the Jewish Museum of Prague, had perhaps played a key role in this mysterious "sixth site," had perhaps known Vanesa's grandfather and father during the War.

Jonas had never revealed the connection to Vanesa, despite their growing intimacy. Perhaps she knew, he thought. Perhaps she simply assumed a familial connection, but was tactful enough not to mention it. He had never broached the subject for one simple reason: Tobias Jakobovits, unlike Vanesa's relatives, had actually been on Transport EU from Prague to Auschwitz, yet had never returned. His great uncle had, like Vanesa's grandfather, collaborated with the Nazis. *But Tobias paid the price*, he thought. *His death redeemed him from the stain*. Vanesa's grandfather and father had lived. Comparing them, he felt — even mentioning them in the same context — sullied Tobias's memory. Thus, he kept his silence.

Yet Jonas still felt the challenge of his Great Uncle's eyes, daring him to push the limits of his comfort zone. He saw a similar challenge in Marek's unseeing eyes, etched onto his mind, and he answered their silent challenge resolutely, willing himself to swallow his fear, determined to see the quest through.

As if sensing his reinvigorated resolve, Vanesa turned to him with a decisive nod, then turned back to survey the street. "Okay, here's what I think. According to our map—assuming my entire theory isn't just a case of wishful thinking—there's no question that this is the block we're looking for. But there are at least ten buildings here. The map would seem to indicate the far end of the street, at the corner with Dusni, but beyond that, we're on our own. With the sheer number of floors, not to mention basements, sub-basements, attics, outbuildings in the courtyards, we could literally search here for months, *if* we could even get access to all these places. Not very practical. Suggestions?"

Jonas, decidedly ready to do something, *anything*, to put his new resolve to the test, adopted a pragmatic track. "Yes, legwork. I'm afraid I don't see any way around pure legwork. I would suggest we go to the Prague municipality and retrieve the zoning maps of this street, and the building blueprints if possible—today, if you'd like. Then we go door to door, starting at the far end of the street. At each building, we ask for the building manager or caretaker. We can present my museum credentials—they will certainly agree to back me up on this—and explain that we're conducting a historical survey of the street, and ask if we may look around the building. If they agree, we do so. If they don't... well, we can cross that bridge when we come to it, as they say. I think we need to accept the fact, up front, that this could take not just months, but years."

>——/

Vanesa was silent. It had not occurred to her that the answers she sought could be so physically close, yet possibly so inaccessible. Swallowing the rising sense that she was taking her first tentative steps on her own Yellow Brick Road, she considered his suggestion of knocking on doors. She was impressed with the audacity of the idea, and subsequently incredulous at its naiveté.

She couldn't contain a chuckle. "Right. So, whatever we're looking for has haunted two generations of my family, possibly resulted in Marek and Agata's deaths, and was cause for me to be attacked twice. Now, you're suggesting that we simply canvas the street for the next several years? Why not just stop passersby and ask for directions to the secret Nazi art trove?"

"That could work, I suppose," Jonas deadpanned. "But I'd suggest we start my way."

Vanesa smiled at him saucily, then stood up and walked to the west end of the street. She confidently approached the intercom at the building's entrance, looked over her shoulder at Jonas, and rang the first buzzer she saw.

>——/

Like the fate of many great and grandiose long-term schemes before it, Jonas's plan for a years-long expedition on Bilkova Street was cut dramatically short. In fact, it became obsolete after only thirty minutes.

He systematically rang buzzers in the entrance of number 12 Bilkova, having been unable to convince even one tenant of number 10 to let him in.

Vanessa made her way to the next building on the opposite side of the street, having actually been let into number 11, searched the hallways and basement, and found nothing of obvious significance.

Jonas was just talking over the scratchy intercom to a woman of indeterminate age, but obvious recalcitrance, when Vanesa's urgent call rose from across the street. He quickly apologized to the woman, turned from the intercom, ran into the street and was almost run down by a passing taxi. Jumping back to the curb, he looked across the street toward Vanesa, who was standing by the dark grey double doors of the entrance to number 13, trying ineffectually to be discrete while pointing excitedly at the intercom and mouthing something he could not yet hear.

Jonas looked carefully both ways this time, and stepped into the street while glancing upward at the building's moldering but clearly once glorious edifice. It had perhaps once been the home of a wealthy factory owner, he thought, based on the four industrially-inspired crests visible through the years of accumulated soot, and the motto *Buh Zehnej Praci* — 'God Bless Labor' — boldly emblazoned across its highest point.

Vanesa pointed excitedly at the panel holding the intercom's black plastic buttons — an especially lovely work of iron filigree, its pattern intricate yet harshly geometric.

As he approached, Jonas glanced at it, then back at Vanesa in confusion. The intercom panel was a thing of calculated, passing beauty, not something one generally stops and minutely studies. She explained, and only when he turned back to the panel and actually scrutinized it, did he see what was concealed in the lower left corner of the complex pattern. He turned to Vanesa, smiling broadly in amazement. It was the symbol, cleverly camouflaged but unmistakable.

"Seek, and ye shall find," she said.

>——/

Dostoyevsky pondered whether heroes originated "in obscurity or plain sight." Perhaps heroes did not exist, bravery being contextual, not absolute. In any case, selfless action was only superficially selfless, driven by ego with dark and unfathomable, yet unquestionably self-serving, motives.

Thus, Vanesa and Jonas were not brave to persistently ring the intercoms of every unit in the building at 13 Bilkova Street until someone finally relented and let them in. They were not heroes to enter the rickety elevator, nor to press the button labelled "-1" for the basement, after gleefully discovering the symbol faintly scratched into the metal panel next to it.

They were not heroes because they had no choice.

Vanesa had no choice, in any case. The need to know had long trumped — or perhaps emanated from — her instinct for self-preservation. Either way, her actions constituted choice only in that she *chose* to roll the dice and accept the outcome, rather than waiting for someone else to do the same.

Perhaps the outcome should have been clear, for it was obvious that there would be danger. It was obvious that they would not be alone when the doors to the elevator opened onto the dimly-lit basement corridor, its pipes marching off into the gloom on wall and ceiling like infinite serpents, the air a miasma of old newspaper and rodent droppings. It was obvious that the two men with guns—Vanesa's old friends Vodka and Garlic—would be waiting for them. It was obvious that two more men, strategically located on each side of the elevator, would step behind them and press the rags soaked with Kolokol-1, the incapacitating agent developed by Soviets, to their faces.

Most obvious of all was that Vanesa's last conscious recollection before succumbing to the drug would be the heavy polished metal door embossed with the symbol she'd been chasing. It was the same door through which her father was never allowed to pass, the same door through which her grandfather had frequently passed. Now, it was the door through which she and Jonas were dragged by the shoulders of their jackets, two pairs of heels bumping rhythmically on the long downward-winding staircase. And it was the door that slammed tightly shut behind them with a finality as ominous as it was obvious.

CHAPTER 22

PLAN X

Outskirts of Prague, May 8, 1945

Hans Guenther grunted as the lorry passed, disregarding the muddy water it splashed in his direction; he could not possibly be wetter. He heaved himself out of the low weeds growing in the fetid ditch and slunk rapidly across Road 115. Panting, he took refuge in an identical ditch on the opposite side of the highway, brushing the mud from the yellow Star of David armband as he did so.

This is not how the plan was supposed to work! He cursed silently for the millionth time since leaving Prague in the unmarked staff car three days earlier. He was supposed to be in Italy already, or at least well on the way. The Red Cross papers were flawless, and they were all perfectly disguised as Jews—yet another use for the Jews, he had joked grimly to Ernst as they'd stripped off their SS uniforms. *Such versatile human material!* More than enough leftover Jewish clothing had been lying around the Central Office to clothe him, Ernst, Girzick, Guennel, Aschenbrenner, Weiszl, Fiedler, and Rolf. *Rolf!* Hans tried to forget the "I told you so" tone that tinged every sentence his brother had uttered that day.

Rolf had still blamed him for ignoring Eichmann's entreaties to make early escape plans, but Eichmann had shown up to the meeting dressed as a Luftwaffe corporal. *A corporal, for God's sake! Who could have taken him seriously, back in February?*

Now here they were in May. They needed to be careful to stick to back roads, hoping his knowledge of Hebrew would be sufficient to fake their way through the partisan checkpoints that were popping up across the countryside like poisonous mushrooms after a spring rain. Just a group of Jews escaping the evil Nazis in a stolen staff car, heading toward salvation and Allied lines....

Rolf had laughed at their predicament as they left Prague behind them, gunshots echoing ever louder from the city's center.

What Hans had not taken into consideration was that not all Czech partisans were philosemitic. In fact, the two men manning the roadblock east of Hlasna Treban—just a large hay wagon next to an impromptu pile of sandbags, most only half closed and bleeding dirt—had opened fire the moment they saw the yellow armbands. Their angry cries of "*Zabte zidy!*"—'kill the Jews'—was barely audible before the roar of their Mausers began. By the time their officer intervened, at least three of the eight Nazi-Jews had lain dead.

Hans had run, the bullets whizzing over his head as he dove through the underbrush and splashed into the Mies. He'd wished in passing that the river flowed in the opposite direction, back to Germany, and that he and Rolf could just float all the way home to Erfurt. He wiped the water from his eyes as he surfaced, and had enough time to glance back and see bodies hanging half out of the car, and to see his brother with hands raised, looking like the same scared little boy he'd been when the headmaster caught him stealing coffee from the teacher's lounge, to give Mama a break from the ersatz coffee she so despised. Hans had dove under the water again, and had let the current carry him slowly but inexorably back toward Prague.

Now, three hungry and cold days later, he crouched on the outskirts of the city. He'd followed the Mies—the Berkouna, he corrected himself, consciously trying to think in the Czech in which he'd become so fluent—until it joined the Vltava. He'd slogged most of the way along the riverbank itself, eating stolen turnips and sleeping under bridges. This was far from Plan B in desirability. He'd taken to thinking of it as Plan X.

Going west, he decided, once he was sure the partisans were no longer looking for him, would be too dangerous. Best to use his dirty countenance and lack of identification to his advantage—his papers had quickly dissolved in the waters of the Berkouna—and to blend in with the inevitable stream of refugees and work his way to... to where? He knew of the Bishop's organization in Rome, which could help him get to South America, and he'd heard there was help in Spain for SS officers on the run. But both of those options meant traveling west past Allied lines—too risky. On the other hand, all the resources that he, like every other senior Nazi with a gram of sense, had been squirrelling away since the tide of the war had begun to turn resided to the west in Geneva. He could perhaps access those remotely from whatever safe haven he later found.

Preserving life, he thought with no small amount of irony. *Preserving life.*

Looking around from the ditch, he now removed the Star of David, his thumb pausing to stroke the rough stitching. *So close*, he thought, and yet the legacy of Usergasse afforded some comfort. He folded the star into a pocket for later use, gambling that German forces still controlled Prague and that being a Jew was not in his best interests.

When he'd left the city, the battle around the Czech Radio building on Schwerinstrasse had just begun, after those damn Czechs had broadcast their pathetic call to arms, despite Karl Frank's clear warnings of bloody retribution. He'd seen the Junkers bombers circling the city, had seen the plumes of smoke, their lazy upward drift belying the inferno below. *SS-Obergruppenführer* Frank was not a patient or understanding man, and his back had been to the wall with the Russians closing in from the East and the Allies from the West.

Hans hoped the Waffen SS had shown the Praguers that Germany was still not to be trifled with, even on the eve of her certain defeat. Personally, he'd have been pleased to see Prague turned into another Warsaw.

He estimated it would be half a day's walk back to Usergasse, what the Praguers knew as Bilkova Street. He'd be there by late afternoon if all went well. He'd left a large contingent of his own men surrounding the site, with strict instructions to hold the position and ensure that the staff continued working, no matter what. He was banking on them still being there, and on their recognizing him before opening fire. Once safely inside, he would gather his resourceful Jews, his keys to escape. He would convey his plans, seal the basement, and leave under cover of darkness.

Preserving life, he thought again. *This time, my life.*

He stood, trying to ignore the rough wet pants that chafed his every step. He'd need to get used to simple Jew clothing, he supposed, at least for the foreseeable future. He straightened his cap, tucked his hands into his pockets, and began walking east along the dirt road that hugged the Vltava, toward the center of Prague.

>——*

Prague, June 1992

Awareness returned to Vanesa calmly, almost comfortingly. Her head rested lightly on the smooth cold surface, and she started at the realization that it was a polished marble floor. The room, too, was cool. It felt large, the echoes of little sounds bouncing toward her from afar: a pipe clanking, a light bulb buzzing, faint footsteps from above.

She opened one gummy eye, then the other, and sat up groggily. The familiar tug of the knife wounds grounded her, speeding her return to full consciousness and jogging her memory of the events leading up to that moment.

Jonas was already sitting up, straining to see past the boundary of the single spotlight under which they sat—their island in a sea of darkness.

Footsteps sounded, closer and sharper now. They circled the island of light like a shark before a feeding frenzy, menacing from a safe distance.

Without warning, a deep gravelly voice sounded. "Welcome, Dr. Jakobovits and Dr. Neuman, to Galerie."

She recognized the voice immediately—the voice from the scratchy international telephone line; the voice of the man who'd never shown up for their meeting under the marble statues of the Church of the Holy Savior; the voice of the man Uncle Tomas had called "a friend."

Two more spotlights clicked on in quick succession, revealing the voice's owner. The darkness behind him, however, remained impenetrable. A tall man with an erect bearing that belied his obvious advanced age, he projected an aura of unquestionable authority. Standing directly under one of the spots, his heavy brows overhung eyes that, when shaded, looked like the empty black sockets of a corpse. His white hair, strictly parted on the right side and combed over his obviously bald pate, capped an angular face whose narrow cheekbones slid downward toward the chin, creating a permanent derisive scowl. He wore a grey wool suit, and carried a wooden cane with a shiny gold handle that was tucked under one armpit, leaving his hands free—powerful-looking yet thin and bony with unusually long fingers. He held his palms together at midriff-height, rapidly and rhythmically tapping the fingers of one hand against those of the other, pinky to thumb, and back. *Tap up. Tap down. Tap up. Tap down.*

When he finally spoke again, his voice was softer, a voice clearly practiced in assuagement but lacking the sincerity that a discerning ear sought for comfort.

"We have been expecting you, of course, Dr. Neuman. Your persistence is, shall we say, admirable. We are not used to uninvited guests discovering our unique showcase. I must say, you have presented us with a dilemma."

The man began circling them again, this time in the splash of light and more thoughtfully, but with equal menace. He continued tapping his fingers. *Tap up. Tap down.*

Finally, he spoke again. "But I am being rude. Allow me to introduce myself. My name is Josef Weiszl, but you probably know me as *SS-Oberscharführer* Josef Weiszl, yes, Dr. Neuman?"

Vanesa nodded slowly, still recovering from the effects of the drug. She tried to speak, and found her throat too dry to produce anything more than a croak.

"Your throat is painfully dry, is it not? That's a known side effect of Kolokol-1. The Soviets never did manage to work out all the kinks in that drug, I'm afraid. Yours too, Dr. Jakobovits? Yes? Well, perhaps we can alleviate your pain, if not yet Dr. Neuman's. You've already met Andel, I believe. Andel, can you please give Dr. Jakobovits something for the pain in his throat?"

Weiszl smiled knowingly as he made this request, and the rhythm of his tapping increased as if in expectation. *Tap up. Tap down.*

Andel, whom Vanesa recognized as Vodka, stepped into the island of light in which she and Jonas were now standing, both having risen unsteadily to their feet when Weiszl first started speaking. Andel stood momentarily in front of Jonas, as if assessing, and then, in a fluid movement clearly born of intense practice, he reached one hand behind his back while simultaneously stepping forward. A large knife, one side evilly serrated, appeared in a flash, then disappeared again behind his back.

Jonas looked surprised. His hands flew up to his neck even as the blood flowed from his severed carotid. He made a sound somewhere between a gurgle and a hiss as he sunk to his knees, his hands desperately yet ineffectually clutching at his neck, trying to staunch the bleeding.

Vanesa unconsciously stepped back from the horror in front of her, her eyes darting to Weiszl's fingertips, which were tapping ever more urgently. *Tap up. Tap down.*

Within seconds, Jonas keeled over onto his side, lying motionless save for one leg that twitched like a marionette operated by some drunken puppeteer.

It was this scene, this vision of Jonas in the throes of violent death, which finally elicited the hoarse, desert-dry scream from her throat.

CHAPTER 23

LIFE ITSELF

Prague, May 8, 1945

Hans Guenther served as a senior military officer in the greatest military conflict—if any military conflict could be considered "great"—in the bloody history of humanity, yet he had never seen combat. He was a killer who'd never, until three days ago, been forced to face the mortal anguish of being hunted himself. He was a bureaucrat, a powerful pencil pusher, but also an avowed yet pragmatic ideologue. Ideology, he'd learned in the past seventeen years since he'd first joined the *Sturmabteilung*, the precursor of the SS, was a cloak that could protect him from the inclemency of the outside world, no matter what truths lurked within.

Which is not to say that Hans Guenther lacked truths of his own; he was, after all, a child of Erfurt, home of Welt-Dienst, one of the world's most prestigious anti-Semitic publishing houses. He had dedicated himself with youthful enthusiasm to his role as "the soldier of an idea," the defender of Aryans from the scourge of the *untermenschen*—the 'sub-humans.' He had believed—still believed, on some level—that Jews were the embodiment of the *untermenschen*. He had been, in his heyday, unhesitant in exploiting his power to curb their verminous spread.

Yet this power, he now recognized, would soon become a thing of the past. Luckily, he thought, it ultimately mattered little, because the least celebrated and most prevalent of motives had always lurked beneath his ideology: ambition. National Socialism had been the life raft that saved him from Erfurt's provincialism and promise of unemployment, conveying him to a new and glorious future.

He'd ridden that raft until its leaks could no longer be plugged, and now, as it sank fast, he had no intention of going down with the ship. Hans Guenther was superior, resourceful, strong, and committed. Whether he donned this ideological cloak or that, he thought, was unimportant. Perhaps it was simply time to throw off the old cloak. He smiled inwardly, for there were certainly plenty of other cloaks for the taking.

Did this make him a traitor? Was he betraying his country, his family, the people he'd commanded and who had believed his fiery words?

He pondered this as he peered around to ensure he was unwatched. The street remained barren. He turned back to watch as Prague's still-smoldering Old Town Hall gave an audible groan, and a northern section of roof collapsed with a satisfying crash. Then it was silent again, save the echo of an occasional gunshot, caught and tossed back and forth by the looming buildings above him like children playing ball.

Was there a scale that could measure the needle's steady climb from free thought, through dissension, and into the zone of betrayal? Where did betrayal start, and where did it end? Was his willingness to imagine a new path for himself after the demise of the Third Reich a betrayal? If indeed it was, did not the legacy he was leaving, the legacy that would remain secret perhaps for generations, somehow compensate for his actions?

He checked the street in all directions one final time, and left the cover of the streetcar. He moved toward Usergasse, careful to stay in the deepening shadows that blanketed one eerily quiet street after another. Prague was silent, yet watchful, a lion resting with one eye open. Bodies littered street corners, some still grasping weapons, others in contorted piles that spoke of a cursory effort at gathering them together for removal.

He climbed quietly over a barrier comprised of an overturned wagon and several charred couches, and checked his watch: nearly 8:00 p.m.

The *Sturmfuhrer*—second lieutenant—left in charge of number 13 Usergasse was dead, shot by a Czech sniper. Hans Guenther quickly discovered this when the jittery sergeant major now in charge nearly shot him, unconvinced of his true identity despite his knowledge of both the correct daily password and the sergeant major's name. A tense few minutes passed before he managed to approach the sandbagged position.

The building, thankfully, remained secure and undamaged. The sergeant major reported that the staff was still at work in the sub-basement.

Hans Guenther relieved the garrison, helping himself to the dead officer's sidearm, which the sergeant major relinquished with some reluctance. He wished them good luck, and descended the dark staircase to the polished metal door on which the unit insignia had been engraved. He paused at the top of the long staircase that curved down and out of sight, and drew a deep breath of the familiar scented air.

It had taken him three days of hell. He had lost his brother, the one thing he'd promised Mama would never happen. His country teetered on the verge of collapse, and he was on the verge of betraying beliefs that had guided him for nearly half his life. He would also likely be a wanted man very soon, but he was here now, he would make it right.

He had made it back to Galerie.

>——/

Prague, June 1992

Vanesa opened her eyes, her head again resting on the coolness of the marble floor. Had she fainted? Been drugged again? She couldn't tell. She raised her head and tried to shake away the dizziness as the blood rushed to her lower body, and looked around—still in the puddle of light, still surrounded by blackness.

Jonas was nowhere to be seen, nor was there any sign of him, blood or otherwise. He had been erased: as if he'd never crossed the street to her, as if he'd never smiled in that first meeting in the museum, as if they'd never entered the elevator, as if she'd been alone in this sea of darkness forever.

The thought jumped into her mind that perhaps she had.

"Ah, you are awake now, Dr. Neuman? Very good." The gravelly voice spoke from nearby.

The sound of his voice, combined with the two spotlights switching on again, caused her to start. She blinked at the sudden brightness.

Josef Weiszl sat on a folding chair just meters away, the gold-handled cane resting against one thigh, his arms comfortably resting on the chair's armrests, fingers engaged in their habitual tapping. *Tap up. Tap down.* He took a break from his tapping to motion regally with one hand to her right.

She turned and found a small bottle of mineral water, which she grabbed and drank greedily. After wiping her mouth with the back of one hand, she sat up straighter, finally able to speak in a hoarse voice. "Where is Jonas? Is he... dead?"

Tap up. Tap down. "You are an intelligent young woman, Dr. Neuman. What do you think? You, yourself, are only alive because you are the, shall we say, *pet* of my trusted colleague and friend. But make no mistake about it...." Weiszl stopped tapping and leaned toward her for emphasis. As he did so, his silver combover flopped forward, displacing his attempted gravity with a comedy at once humorous and terrifying. "Make no mistake: I will have my way, and your end will come shortly. As a courtesy to Hans, I will, however, be pleased to make it less... uh... dramatic, if you'd prefer."

He leaned back in his chair and resumed his ritual. *Tap up. Tap down.*

Vanesa forced herself to swallow her grief over Jonas, to take the terror of her predicament and Weiszl's threat and file it away for future consideration. She could not afford fear at the moment. She became conscious of the gooseflesh on her arms, and hugged them to her sides until it subsided. She glanced again at the impenetrable darkness surrounding her, and finally glared up at Weiszl.

Although her voice trembled, she mustered indignation and managed to add unmistakable scorn to her words when she finally spoke. "Josef Weiszl, staff member in the Central Office for Jewish Emigration in Prague. Reported to Hans Guenther. Believed to be currently living in Romania. For your direct responsibility in the murder of hundreds of thousands of men, women and children, you served, I believe, five years in a French prison?"

By way of answer, Weiszl nodded once deeply. A thin ironic smile crossed his lips as he leaned back, crossed one leg over the other effeminately, and resumed tapping his fingers. He raised one eyebrow sarcastically. "Justice will be served, will it not?"

Vanesa got to her feet, unsteadily at first, the tiles of the floor revolving crazily for a moment. She regained both balance and resolve, ignoring the familiar pull of the scars on her back, and stood straight, looking down at Weiszl.

Vodka stepped into the light, moving closer to protect Weiszl, then turned momentarily away from her, nodding reassuringly to someone in the darkness as if to say, "I've got this."

As he turned, she saw the gun peeking from above his belt at the small of his back. At length, she spoke again, this time with no trembling in her voice. "Since I was a girl, I daydreamed about coming face to face with someone like you. I conjured all kinds of Wonder Woman fantasies of what I would do, of how I would avenge what you and your ilk did to my parents. Now, I find my mythological nemesis to be a pathetic old man with a bad combover, who appears to take pride in his control over smelly beasts like that one—" She pointed to Vodka. "—who seem to enjoy pissing on young women and dragging them back to this... this ludicrous secret basement lair. Wonder Woman, it turns out, wouldn't have wasted her spit on your shoes. Nor would I. Now, will you let me leave, or at least answer my questions before you...." She paused, momentarily unsure of how to express the demise she was trying to avoid contemplating.

Tap up. Tap down. "Before I have you killed, you mean?" Weiszl said. "Yes, I will answer your questions, but first, I would like to hear what you already know of where you are, what you think I've been up to all these years, and who else has been involved. Will you indulge an old man?"

She frowned and shook her head like a parent dismissing a pestering child. "I won't play your games. I want to know what my grandfather and father were doing here during the war, and I want to know who the man I've called Uncle Tomas all these years really is. That's it. If you want to kill me without telling me, that's your prerogative. Somehow, I think you'd like to tell me your story, and that's why you want to hear my extrapolation of it. You're proud of whatever little blood shrine to the glorious past you've created here, and you'd like to impress me with it. So, why don't you do so? Show me, kill me, move on. You'll get little more satisfaction from me otherwise, you... you...."

Again, her words failed her. What sound could her throat possibly produce that would be powerful enough to express the overwhelming contempt, the resolute loathing she felt for this human monster? A bellow of rage? A preternatural scream? Abject retching?

To compensate, Vanesa ratcheted her voice up and adopted a goading tone, driven to score points even in this, the ultimate unwinnable game. Yet behind her rage, behind her fear, behind her grief at Jonas' death, her insatiable drive to understand still lurked. Her unquenchable need to satisfy her curiosity, no matter what the cost, overpowered and continued to trump mere visceral well-being.

"So, show me your art," she goaded. "Show me what you took from people who were so desperate to live that they'd give up any worldly possessions, and rightly so. Show me this source of pride of yours, so I can spit on it, because this may just be worth my spit."

Weiszl had remained impassive throughout Vanesa's diatribe. *Tap up. Tap down.* Now, he paused his tapping, again leaned forward in the folding chair and stared directly into her eyes. The combover stayed put this time. "My dear Dr. Neuman, as you appear to have answered all my questions during your misinformed tirade, I agree that it is only fair to answer yours. First, I would like to disavow you of what appears to be a gross misconception on your part about Galerie."

He leaned back again to consider his words, then slowly got to his feet, leaning heavily on his cane. "You see, Dr. Neuman, what is on display here is art taken during the war. Art comes in so many forms, does it not? Ordinary art can express a beautifully diverse range of emotions, reflecting so many facets of a human life. Art imitates life, they say, but in Galerie, things are different. The art here is utterly unique because it does not attempt to mimic life, but rather has successfully captured it. Galerie is not an imitation of life, Dr. Neuman, *Galerie is life itself.*"

With this, he snapped his fingers. Section by section, with a crash of electrical discharge at each illumination, the powerful spotlights in the vast hall around Vanesa sparked on.

She blinked away the sudden brightness, and the room revealed itself to her, deflating her swagger immediately. She again fell to the floor, this time on one knee, as if in perverse monarchical reverence. Silent tears blinded her eyes, and her mouth worked codfish-like, helpless to find words. Her hands rose to press hard against her temples, as if to block out the reality that confronted her. It was a reality she had always known on some level to be true, but had never dreamed of accepting.

Oh, Grandfather, she thought. *What have you done?*

CHAPTER 24

MUTUAL INTERESTS

New York City, 1938

Never before had Hans Guenther experienced actual awe. He had been impressed, surely, by the cold logic and organizational talents of his new boss in Vienna. He had been moved, certainly, by the Fuehrer's more impassioned speeches. He had been brought to tears on occasion by a powerful rendition of the Faust Overture.

But this... this was beyond anything he'd experienced in his twenty-eight years.

The heels of his black leather boots had echoed so loudly in the after-hours emptiness of the museum that he had to stop walking in order to address Henry Osborne, Jr., his esteemed guide, and son of the museum's recently-deceased and legendary president. The boots' *tock-tock-tock* stopped suddenly as they crossed the splendor of the Theodore Roosevelt Rotunda, which dominated the entrance to the American Museum of Natural History. From the gloom of the nighttime rotunda, Guenther stared past the twin brown marble columns into the brightly lit Akeley Hall of African Mammals. His mouth visibly dropped open as he walked forward.

He faced a herd of charging African Elephants. The ears of the bull elephant, which stood some three meters high, were thrown forward in rage. His angry trunk was an accusing finger pointing directly at Guenther's chest, his tusks two spears threatening imminent impalement, his black eyes open so wide that the wrinkles on their brows were like foothills to the mountain of his massive head.

Behind and to both sides of the elephant herd, brightly lit windows opened into alternate universes: a golden lioness licked her paws under an African sun; a wild boar mother watched over her young with evident maternal pride; a male gorilla asserted his lordship over a misty green mountainside. These, and eleven other universes, winked at Guenther from behind clear glass, each containing stunningly lifelike animals in meticulously recreated settings.

"They are so *real*." Guenther turned to Osborne, smiling like a child. The *tock-tock-tock* resonated with increasing urgency as he scurried from diorama to diorama, making a full round of the hall over the course of some ten minutes.

Osborne stood watching with mild amusement, until Guenther clomped back to him, standing under the imposing tusks of the lead East African Elephant.

"He was a genius, a true... how do say... *kuenstler*? Artiste, yes?" Faltering in his excitement, Guenther's heavy-tongued but rich English was barely understandable.

Osborne responded somewhat oratorically. "Yes, Carl Akeley was a genius, a true groundbreaker. This hall is truly his legacy. He developed techniques that could capture the subtleties of animal anatomy in detail far greater than traditional taxidermy had ever achieved. These animals were born twice, my father used to say: once at the hands of the Almighty, and once at the hands of Akeley." Osborne smiled wryly. "Of course, there are those who feel that wildlife is better observed in its natural environment."

"The natural environment? Who needs the natural environment?" Guenther waved a hand dismissively. "Do you not see, Herr Osborne? We can create our own natural environment. Akeley has demonstrated our true power, not just over nature's creations, but over nature itself. Look around you. Akeley didn't just recreate the natural environment, he captured it. He tamed it. He packaged and preserved something that will disappear—*wie sagt man?*—inevitably. He's showing us that we can possess the natural environment, dominate it."

At this, he enthusiastically threw out his arms to encompass the hall, then checked himself and reassumed the air of grave dignity he'd practiced since getting the news that he was to join the brief SS fact-finding delegation to New York. It had been an honor not only to have been chosen, but to have been chosen by *SS-Obersturmfuehrer* Adolf Eichmann himself, the head of Vienna's new Central Office for Jewish Emigration and a rising star in the Third Reich.

Osborne pushed his glasses onto his forehead and rubbed his eyes tiredly. "Yes, I can see how that could be interpolated from Akeley's work, the dominance of man over nature and whatnot. There was certainly an element of this thinking inherent in his generation's attitude toward nature. But you see, Mr. Guenther, this is simply not the case. Akeley, and even Theodore Roosevelt, with whom he hunted in Africa on several occasions, were actually conservationists. Yes, they were realists who understood that much of the natural world was inevitably, as you said, bound to be steamrolled by mankind. Yet they felt that killing and preserving species in places like this museum would ensure that they were not lost to posterity. Akeley Hall is not a symbol of man's dominance over the species of the world, but rather of man's respect for them. This is why Akeley himself, as you may know, worked tirelessly to create the first mountain gorilla sanctuary in the Belgian Congo. He did so out of love, not triumph."

Guenther straightened the black leather belt creeping up from his waist, pulled the black SS dress uniform coat down haughtily, and drew himself up to his full height. "Do you know, Herr Osborne, the primary difference between we Germans and you Americans? That is, those of you who are still of pure Nordic stock, not yet tainted by the plague of racial pollution that you seem unable, or unwilling, to stop? We both inherently grasp our superiority over the degenerate races—as you certainly know your late father did—and we both act in the interests of maintaining this superiority, much as your people did when you eradicated your native population in the previous century. The primary difference between us, as I see it, is that we National Socialists are unafraid to state publically what you prefer to hide behind populist and quasi-democratic rhetoric."

Osborne began to object, but Guenther politely raised a finger, indicating that he had not yet finished. "Herr Osborne, deep inside, you know who is master and who is subordinate. Look at the way you treat your Negros, your Jews? Looking at these dioramas, I am convinced that Akeley understood this, for who carried his tents and who emptied his chamber pots on his long African expeditions? How many hundreds of elephants did he kill before he found just the right specimens for this herd? Akeley's work is a monument to our race's domination over the lowest level of species, the animals. Herr Akeley paved the way, Herr Osborne. Now, we Germans can continue this work, but not in the darkness of back rooms and hidden workshops. We, Herr Osborne, have made the choice to overtly triumph, in ways you have not yet begun to imagine. That is why the world watches us so attentively, perhaps with bit of... how you say... *ehrfurcht!* Yes, awe... because it is only we who have the will to unashamedly monumentalize our domination over *all* the degenerate species, not just the animals."

>——/

Prague, May 8, 1945

"Neuman! Neuman! Get over here. Now, Neuman!"

Hans Guenther's voice, at first simply assertive, took on a manic quality as it rose in pitch. Now that he was on the verge of putting his plan in motion, it seemed suddenly imperative that it all happen now, immediately—no more time to wait. He took the dead officer's pistol from its holster. It felt reassuring in his hand.

"Neuman! Where the fuck are you, you stupid Jew?"

Jakub Neuman hurried across the hall from one of the recessed access doors that led into the display cases. Though a small man, unassuming in manner from years of practice serving people with the power of life and death over him, he nevertheless lacked the subservience that is the result of actual submission. With his thin and graying hair, and the dark circles ringing red eyes that radiated equal measures of exhaustion and grief, he was long past concealing fear. Too much had already been taken; there could be no more loss. His once-white apron was smeared with something dark red. He had been painting a background, and had not heard the *Sturmbannführer* calling.

He apologized and provided answers to series of rifled-off questions. Yes, he was almost finished with this last display. No, he didn't need much more time. How could he be of assistance?

Behind the grill with the Galerie symbol so intricately incorporated in its ironwork, Michael Neuman watched and listened wide-eyed, as he had so often done over the past two years.

Guenther waved the pistol dismissively at Jakub's apology. "Things have changed. Come with me into the workshop. Now."

As Jakub waited deferentially near the workshop entrance, Guenther crossed the hall and bent to retrieve a small folded note from under one of the display cases. He unfolded it and moved his lips as he silently read its contents, seeming to commit them to memory. He then re-crossed the hall and pushed past Jakub through the door marked "Staff Only."

Hans Guenther holstered his pistol and threw himself onto the stool by the workbench. He drew a metal stamp holder and small handful of dies from the back reaches of a bottom drawer. Each die was made up of needles approximately one centimeter in height, arranged on a small square of metal to form a number or letter. He hurriedly sorted through the dies while repeating the note's contents under his breath, inserted the characters A-25379 into the handle, and locked them into place. He had already rolled up the sleeve on his left arm to the elbow, and poised the device on the outside of his forearm, when Jakub hurried in.

"Get me some ink," he commanded, and Jakub hurriedly complied. Gritting his teeth, Hans plunged the stamp into his arm, removed it, and then wiped away the blood with his handkerchief. He took the proffered bottle from Jakub and poured it over the wound, massaging the liquid into the open cuts.

"Well," he said, grunting in pain to Jakub. "There's no turning back now, is there? Don't you people have some kind of ceremony, welcoming me as one of your own? Or do I have to actually undergo circumcision to receive that honor?"

He gave a wry smirk, wiped the excess ink away with his handkerchief, and folded it to create a makeshift bandage, which he deftly tied using his right hand and his teeth. Then he turned back to Jakub.

"Now, listen to me, and sit down. Yes, yes, right there. Go ahead. It seems to me that we have quite a bit in common at this point, you and I. Primarily, we want to live, and we want to avoid any, shall we say, repercussions of our work here. Would you agree with this? Yes? Very well, I suggest that in light of the change in circumstances, it would be in our mutual interests to cooperate closely, at least for the time being. Do you concur? Yes? Then here's what I propose...."

CHAPTER 25

BETRAYAL

Prague, June 1992

In her conscious, deeply self-aware and oft over-examined mind, Vanesa had expected to find a museum-like gallery. She had expected to find paintings hung on walls with intricately-framed grace, statues on unobtrusive stands scattered dramatically throughout the hall's open space, glass-topped display cases containing jewels or valuable Judaica. She had expected to be disgusted at the ostentation. She had expected to be indignant, yet not truly surprised, at the gall of displaying these invaluable works of art, these things of inherent beauty which had been paid for in such ugly currency.

What she discovered when the lights crashed on was nothing she had expected, and everything she had known.

She stood in the center of a vast oval hall of green marble, which was ringed by glass windows. She knew instantly—as would any child of a prominent taxidermist, who grew up with taxidermy journals and coffee-table books scattered around her living room—that it was an exact and seemingly full-scale reproduction of the famous Akeley Hall in the New York Museum of Natural History.

Immediately behind her, in the center of the hall, a large wood-paneled platform was ringed by benches. It was the display from which, in New York, Carl Akeley's famous herd of angry-eyed African Elephants charged at visitors. Here, a group of ten or more tallit-clad orthodox Jews stood facing her, eyes upcast. They watched with obvious reverence as their rabbi, his back to her, held a Torah dramatically aloft—the traditional *hagba'a* after the reading of the scroll. The life-size figures stood in a highly detailed cutaway model of the interior of Prague's inimitable Altneuschul.

From her place on the floor, she could clearly make out the worshippers. Their faces, each unique, were incredibly realistic, showing blemishes, scraggy beards, and acne scars. Their hands—some with clean nails, others with the permanent dirt of manual labor, some calloused and hairy, others smooth—held prayer books, fingered the fringe of prayer shawls, or rested lightly in pockets of coarse cloth trousers. Their presence was at once powerful and realistically mundane, giving the viewer the voyeuristic sense of intruding upon a real-life scene.

She swept her eyes around the room, counting the expected fourteen glass-windowed displays. Behind each, people went motionlessly about their vastly different business. To her left, a robed oriental carpet merchant with long sidelocks haggled with a customer over an intricately woven rug spread at their feet in a cramped shop, throughout which carpets hung. To her right, a housewife in a head scarf kneaded bread on a rough wood table in a dark one-room house. One lock of hair flopped down over her sweaty forehead. Her husband pored over a book by candlelight at the other end of the table, and three children played on the narrow bed in the background. In another window, a purple-robed bride, resplendent in what Vanesa recognized as a traditional Moroccan wedding headdress, sat in a red velvet chair, receiving her brightly dressed guests as her mother and father proudly looked on. Children with mischievous smiles, some clutching cookies, peeked out from behind the chairs. Beyond the wedding party, a group of men in grey wool suits debated around a polished conference table in a well-apportioned library.

And there were more... so many more.

She stood, taking in the vastness of the room. With a sudden gasp, her eyes focused on the American GI with the gold Star of David at his neck, sitting on the hood of his jeep. The name "Moe" rose to her lips unconsciously. Then she saw the sunburned young man riding a donkey in an olive grove and mouthed the name "Zvi." More names came to her, on and on: Rivka, the housewife kneading bread; Moshe, the carpet merchant; Jakob, the Austrian Zionist leader.

She knew these people from her father's stories. These were the people her father had met. In the horror of this place, even as his father had been working on his twisted "art," young Michael had taken it upon himself to preserve, in his own way, their lives.

She'd known, of course. It had been the one explanation of her grandfather's, her father's, and Uncle Tomas' mysterious past that she'd been unwilling to consciously consider all along, the one explanation that actually made sense. She'd understood immediately after the lights clicked on, because it was so obvious. She understood that behind these glass display cases, within these painstakingly realistic dioramas, were not wax or clay figures, not models of people, but rather perfectly preserved, meticulously mounted, and intricately displayed *people*. *Actual people.*

She recalled the symbol's runic meaning, "life from death," and the writing on the bunk in Terezin, *Zachrana zivota*. She should have known. Oh yes, the words had meant "preserving life," but not as she, nor indeed any sane person, would have ever dreamt of interpreting them.

$$\rightarrowtail\!\!-\!\!/$$

Tel Aviv, 1980

Fifteen-year-old Vanesa sat dejectedly on the building roof, her back to the solar water heater panels, her feet dangling precipitously over the littered courtyard two stories below. The presentation had gone poorly, to say the least. It was her fault, was it not? How could she have expected the other 9th-graders at *Ironi Vav* high school to look past the visceral and see the art—to pause, try to understand, try to respect what her father and grandfather did for a living?

Theirs was a respectable art, a science in fact, and not a bad living. Her father was one of the top taxidermists in Israel, sought after by the country's universities, private collectors, and avid hunters alike.

Her father labored in the shop scraping hides, sculpting frames, or poring over heavy anatomy textbooks every day, sometimes until the early dawn hours. He could work for a week perfecting the malevolent snarl of a Rock Hyrax or the suspicious scowl of a Jackal. He was so sensitive to detail that a single feather out of place on the tail of a wide-eyed Osprey mount could drive him to distraction. What was not to respect?

"There are many things, *Kotě*, that people are not ready to hear or see," Uncle Tomas had warned her when she told him of the class assignment to present her father's profession. "There are things that we should not expect them to understand — about what we do, about what we've seen, about who we are."

She'd had no choice. The assignment was what it was, and it had gone well in the beginning. She'd been confident as she stood in front of the class. Her new jeans — bought, if not especially for the occasion, then at least with it in mind — flattered her budding figure, and her usually unruly hair had behaved marvelously that morning, newly tamed by a home perm. She'd carefully arranged the display on the table next to her, and covered it with a sheet she'd filched from the linen closet. She spoke clearly and passionately about the history of the art, and the other students paid attention, at first.

>—⫻

"Although taxidermy dates back to ancient times, its modern history began with Carl Akeley, who is considered the father of modern taxidermy. Akeley was born in 1864 and died in 1926. The years following his early death, from disease while on an expedition to Africa, are regarded as the true heyday of 20th-century museum taxidermy. Akeley perfected new techniques to ensure anatomical accuracy in mounts. By doing so, he helped raise taxidermy from a perversely-regarded preservation technique for hunters and collectors to an art of international prominence. His idea to display mounts in highly accurate habitat dioramas, instead of just glass case displays, became the standard of museum presentation worldwide. Toward the end of his life, his prestige was so great, and his work was so highly regarded, that he was given free rein to design and stock the massive Hall of African Mammals in New York's American Museum of Natural History, which still bears his name."

Here Vanesa paused and looked around the classroom. All eyes were still upon her as she smoothed her blouse demurely, made sure to keep her chin up, and continued.

"The Prague Museum of Natural History commissioned hundreds of mounts in the early 1930s. Many of these mounts were prepared by a particularly renowned Prague taxidermist—my grandfather, Jakub Neuman. His shop was in a courtyard just off Wencelas Square, only a block away from the museum building.

"From the late 1920s until his deportation to Theresienstadt in 1942, my grandfather's shop, Neuman Taxidermy, served as a Mecca for Prague's hunting and naturalist community. It may sound funny today, but in those days, naturalists firmly believed that killing and mounting wildlife was a legitimate act of conservation. This was the ideal that Akeley and his students brought to taxidermy—a true love of life, a deep respect for the natural world, and a powerful drive to capture its beauty."

A few students had begun to look out the window, seeking something to occupy their increasingly bored minds.

Vanesa continued, now more philosophically. "You see, this was a time of domination—of man over nature, and later, of man over man—as the Nazis took over Europe. The fact that preservation came only after destruction, and was actually impossible without it, was not something that would have occurred to my grandfather and his contemporaries. At that time, man was master over nature—it was a given."

More than half the class was now fidgeting, or passing notes, and even the teacher looked distracted.

Vanesa shuffled her note cards nervously, and decided to skip her review of ancient taxidermy and Egyptian mummification. She dropped the curiosities of Victorian taxidermy—anthropomorphic mounted kittens playing croquet; Herrmann Ploucquet's unabashedly grotesque taxidermic adaptation of Goethe's fable Reinecke the Fox; and of course, "El Negro," the African man who had been preserved and displayed in the 1830s by two French taxidermists.

She skipped, in fact, the entire remainder of her presentation. Instead, in what seemed a good way to regain the attention of the class, she simply stepped away from the table and tugged the sheet off with a circus master flourish. The effect was, to say the least, dramatic.

A collective gasp rose as the students took in the display, which showed the mounting process from carcass to finished mount. When the first whiffs of decay from the still-curing hedgehog pelt, which comprised the display's first stage, reached the first row of students, the gasp turned into a collective groan of revulsion. A chorus of "Ewwww!" — begun by the girl in the second row and picked up by the other girls — grew as they took in the inside-out, cleanly-scraped pelt with its blankly inquisitive empty eye sockets. The boys in the third row began mock retching, and the whole class followed suit. One boy ran dramatically over to open all the classroom windows, holding his nose. Another affected falling off his chair, clutching his throat. Someone called out, "It smells like a dead Wookie!"

That's when the laughter swelled, the blood rushed to Vanesa's face, and the tears welled up in her eyes.

She had never considered her father's profession different in any way. Taxidermy was just something he did, no different than a plumber, or a cloth merchant. The fact that her stuffed animals, since she was a little girl, had actually been *stuffed animals*, had never seemed odd to her.

At some point, every child first glimpses her father's flawed humanity, first wipes away the stardust to reveal scratches in the paternal veneer. As the surprise dissipates, this glimpse ultimately grows into either empathy or rancor.

For Vanesa, squinting into the sun's last rays as they caressed the crumbling concrete of the Tel Aviv rooftops, with the echoes of her classmates' laughter still ringing in her ears, this discovery gave rise to something altogether different. As thoughts of her father swirled through her brain, she felt neither love nor hate, neither respect nor derision.

Rather, she was consumed, inexplicably yet unquestionably, by overwhelming shame.

>—/

Prague, June 1992

It was not shame that Vanesa felt as the shock subsided, however. It was rage. The blasphemy of Galerie was a betrayal of everything the triumvirate of men in her life — Jakub, Michael, and Tomas — had ever done on her behalf. Every touch, every word, every kindness — all were tainted, negated, scorched beyond recognition.

She shuddered as the truth sank in deeper. She had loved these men. She had trusted these men. She had admired, respected, and emulated these men.

Josef Weiszl's voice broke her reverie. He stood there smiling, cane tucked under his arm, fingers tapping again. *Tap up. Tap down.* "So what do you think of our *'tableaux morts,'* Dr. Neuman? I like to think of them thus, since they are the antithesis of *'tableaux vivants,'* yes?" Weiszl stopped tapping suddenly, as if fatigued, and lowered his cane. He leaned heavily on it as he moved to her side to take in the hall, his gaze of reverence a counterpoint to hers of disbelief.

"Your grandfather was a talented man, was he not?" The old man's eyes twinkled with evil merriment through his fatigue, and he even chuckled to himself. He was enjoying her stupefaction, and pleased at the efficacy of his dramatics. "Yes, it is amazing what you can elicit from an artisan, with the right persuasive tools. In this case, the lives of your father and grandmother proved a most powerful incentive. Oh yes, he was quite reluctant to work with us, in the beginning. A pity that your grandmother — Alena, was it? — paid the price for his reluctance. A nasty disease, Typhus, and so prevalent in Theresienstadt."

Her anger suddenly softened. Of course, her grandfather had been forced to choose. What would she have had him do, watch his wife and son starve, be tortured, be murdered? Was this not the true nature of collaboration? Not choice, but coercion? He'd simply had no choice. Perhaps. Yet as she looked around at the intricacy of her grandfather's art, the painstaking accuracy, the loving detail, she saw not mere artisanship but artistic pride. He had loved these creations, not for who they had been, but for what he had made of them.

Thus Jakub's deal with the devil, even if signed under extreme duress, was not in pure self-preservation, and thus indelibly tainted everything it subsequently touched. Her father, her mother, herself? After all, Jakub had lived — lived to see a grandchild grow, lived to see countless sunsets over the Mediterranean, lived to build a business, to build a life in a strange new land where Jews were sovereign. He'd done it all on the ruins of these poor people, the subjects of these sick tableaux. How could he? Would death, even that of his family, not have been preferable? Was this not the essence of betrayal, she cried internally. On the other hand, would she herself have had the courage to act any differently?

Weiszl's grating voice again interrupted her tortured musings. "At least you gained an 'uncle,' did you not? It is not every Israeli girl that can claim such an illustrious historical figure in her inner circle. But wait...." Weiszl paused, noting her uncomprehending look.

He was now close enough that she could smell his faint yet clearly expensive cologne.

"Surely a historian of your caliber has by now figured out who this 'Tomas Marle,' who played such a significant role in your young life, truly was, no? Certainly he was not—" He chuckled again, pointing to the third display case to Vanesa's right. "– that young Czech Jew, the original Tomas Marle, who actually was a Czech partisan when we obtained him. No, not him, since he's still here. Although his identity, not to mention his similarity in height and build, were of infinite assistance to my commanding officer, *SS-Sturmbannfuhrer* Hans Guenther, your 'Uncle Tomas,' on the last day of the war."

He chuckled again, pleased with his own dramatics.

She cut short Weiszl's levity, however, with a sudden and vicious kick at his cane.

He crumpled heavily to the floor.

Vodka, who had been lurking nearby, was on her in an instant, gun in hand. Assessing the situation with eyes that showed street smarts, if not outright intelligence, he quickly stuffed the gun back in his belt and grabbed her, pinioning her arms as she lunged toward the old man again.

Garlic emerged from the shadows to help Weiszl, who was unhurt, to his feet, brushing the old man's suit off ineffectually as he did so.

"Bastard! You fucking bastard! You took them all from me! I loved them! You killed them all!" Vanesa's incredulity had turned to rage with the old man's goading, and she lost any semblance of restraint. Yelling incoherently and struggling mightily in Vodka's powerful grip, she managed to butt him with the back of her head.

Having finished helping Weiszl, Garlic stepped forward at Vodka's prompting and neatly punched her in the stomach.

She doubled over, partially deflated, but continued to struggle.

Garlic produced a pair of handcuffs, deftly twisted her arms behind her back, secured her wrists, and pushed her away from him.

She fell to the floor, and there she remained.

Weiszl straightened up and smoothed his combover, vainly attempting to regain his previous dignity. There was no finger tapping now. "You little kike whore," he spat in a low voice that bristled with the hatred of a street fighter. "I should simply kill you now, as I wanted to when you first came to Prague. Hans only wanted me to scare you off, and he was furious when my colleagues got a bit overzealous in Terezin. In any case, before Hans become 'incommunicado,' shall we say, I made a promise on my honor and I am nothing if not an honorable man. Now, if you please will sit down here...." He indicated the wooden bench, directly under the upraised Torah in the central diorama.

Vodka picked her up and roughly pushed her towards it.

"I will tell you the story, as Hans wished," Weiszl said. "Then we will be done with you."

CHAPTER 26

GALERIE

Prague, June 1992

SS-Oberscharfuhrer Josef Weiszl sat down next to Vanesa, who slumped uncomfortably on the hard wooden bench. Her arms ached from Vodka's rough yank, the handcuffs were beginning to chafe her wrists, and her hands felt swollen and strangely, numbly detached. Trying to hide her pain, she sat up with difficulty, blew an itinerant strand of hair from her face, and stared at Weiszl with an undisguised loathing, as if the illusions he had so casually shattered had become daggers that she repeatedly stabbed into him one by one.

Weiszl stared back at her, unabashed. He regarded her for several long minutes, pensively resuming his ritual. *Tap up. Tap Down.* Finally, as if just noticing her obvious discomfort, he motioned to Vodka to approach. "Andel, I believe that Dr. Neuman's temper tantrum has passed. Has it not, Dr. Neuman? Very well. If Dr. Neuman promises to behave, you may remove the handcuffs, Andel. Thank you. After all, it's not like she'll be going anywhere, correct? There is only one door to Galerie, and it is locked and guarded at all times."

Vodka approached, groped her unabashedly as he removed the handcuffs, and then retreated.

Weiszl again stood. "I think it would be more illustrative if we took a stroll. Will you join me, Dr. Neuman?"

He waited expectantly for her to comply, and she did so, rubbing her wrists as she rose. He led her to the first display on their left, in which an attractive young woman in her twenties sat playing a cello in a flat that resembled Jonas's. A look of intense concentration mixed with subdued triumph on her smooth and eerily realistic face, her brow furrowed as if she was successfully working through a particularly challenging cadenza. Her skirt was pushed back to expose shapely legs whose clearly defined calf muscles were taut from the effort of holding the cello. A view of Prague Castle, shrouded in grey rainclouds and real enough to make a viewer momentarily forget the sub-basement venue, was visible from the window behind her.

"Rachel was our first," Weiszl reminisced. "Of course, we had to keep her for almost a year, until your grandfather was finally persuaded that he had no choice but to use his skills to assist us. Hans shopped for her for several months in late 1942. He finally found her in Mauthausen—the camp, of course, not the village. Such a lovely specimen, don't you think? So young, so liberated, so free-thinking—truly the quintessence of Prague Jewry. We got to know each other very well during that year. Very well indeed." His voice trailed off, its lascivious innuendo unmistakable.

Controlling her urge to throttle Weiszl, Vanesa looked carefully around the room and took in the minute details, although not yet sure what she was seeking. She noted the bronze plaques next to every display in the hall. This one contained the young woman's full name, Rachel Glaser, her date and place of birth, education, profession, and a short backgrounder on Jews in the diorama's setting, in this case pre-war Prague.

Weiszl shook his head as if dispelling the memory. He looked at his watch fretfully, clucked his tongue in dismay, and continued. "Let us get on with this. Time is short and I have a long trip back to Bucharest tonight. Where were we? Oh yes. So, Hans first approached your grandfather in early 1942. Neuman was still living in Prague at that time. There was really no question as to which taxidermist would be most suitable. He was truly renowned in the taxidermy and naturalist community, his reputation sterling, his work beyond compare. It had to be him, but he was quite recalcitrant. It took several months on half rations in Theresienstadt to bring him around. Starving, not to mention watching your wife and child starve, can be a powerful motivator. But I think it was the transport of your grandmother's family to the east—they ended up in Maly Trostenets, I believe—that really clinched the deal. This was my idea, of course. Hans had by that time entrusted such logistics to me, as he did throughout the project until the end of the war. In any case, when Neuman finally relented, we left his Jewess in Theresienstadt as insurance, but let him bring his boy back here to Prague. We brought them here, as they say, 'off the books,' so as not to leave a paper trail that might raise questions. Later, Hans even made sure that their names were included in the last transport from Theresienstadt to Auschwitz. Pity he didn't manage to get his own included, but he of course did not then know he would need to. In any event, we brought them here in early 1943. A very cold winter, I recall."

They had moved on to the next display, the Iraqi carpet merchant—Moshe Mizrahi, the plaque declared. Weiszl continued his monologue, but Vanesa focused on the recessed door next to this display, and similar doors next to all the others. Did these lead just into the display cases, or was there a service corridor behind them, perhaps with an exit to the street?

Weiszl continued, and she listened, divided between morbid fascination and an urgent drive for self-preservation.

"This specimen was difficult to obtain. I myself oversaw the covert operation in Baghdad, which was not part of the Reich, as you know. We wanted a recent sample of Babylonian Jewry, and, you see, Hans insisted on absolute authenticity for all the displays. All the specimens you see here are real people, displayed in situ, as they actually lived. I visited Mizrahi's store myself, and worked closely with your grandfather on the details of this tableau. The level of detail, I think you'll agree, is outstanding.

"However, in this display, unlike others, you'll note that the subject is facing the side, and his face is partially obscured. This is because he was unfortunately disfigured in the collection and shipping process, which was not as delicately handled as it could have been. Your grandfather quickly learned that, unlike animals, whose pelts are quite resilient even several days after death, human skin is far more difficult to preserve. It turns out that human corpses make poor mounts, and signs of violence are difficult to eliminate in the mounting process. After Mizrahi, we decided it was imperative that future subjects be brought gently, willingly, and alive, back to Prague."

As they moved to the next display window, Vanesa surreptitiously tried the handle of the access door. Locked. Would the rest be similarly inaccessible? She needed a quick exit option, some way past Vodka and Garlic, who were closely shadowing her and Weiszl, carefully watching her for signs of renewed violence. She clenched and unclenched her hands, still feeling the stiffness brought on by the tight cuffs.

Weiszl led her to the next window, and stopped. It was Moe, the American GI, posed against the backdrop of an Allied encampment, smoking a cigarette while leaning on an actual olive drab, white-starred Willys jeep. A Star of David pendant hung on the chain with his dog tags over the neck of his dirty white undershirt. Vanesa leaned forward and could just make out the "H" stamped into the corner of the tags, the US Army's designation for Jewish soldiers at that time.

"Mojzis Jehlicka. He called himself Moe, I believe, and came from some small town in the American Midwest. We collected him from Berga, where they were keeping the Jewish POWs at that time. He came quite willingly when we offered him a warm place and food. After several months here, his physical condition had improved sufficiently to enable us to harvest and mount him. Perhaps you'll be pleased to hear that your grandfather consistently and adamantly refused to take part in the harvesting, although he did provide us with the detailed conditions that needed to be upheld, in order to optimize the mounting process."

Weiszl now motioned to the remaining eleven windows. "The rest, most of which you'll note include multiple specimens, were collected under the auspices of RSHA Referat IV-B4\7g. From late 1943, we became a recognized section in Eichmann's sub-department IV-B4. Although we were a confidential section, as the 'g' for '*geheim*' in our section nomenclature indicates, Eichmann was so taken with Hans' vision that he ensured our provisioning and funding right up to the end."

Weiszl's blatant bureaucratic pride reminded Vanesa in passing of their former boss's testimony in his trial in Jerusalem. Eichmann, she had long suspected and now knew for sure, could not have been merely benignly evil, as thinkers like Hannah Arendt portrayed him. To actively further an agenda like Galerie demanded a special kind of evil—rabidity that, although perhaps concealable, incorporated no trace of "banality."

Weiszl continued enthusiastically. "With funding and administrative infrastructure, we were able to entice whole groups of Jews from the far reaches of the Reich to come to Prague of their own volition, healthy and intact. We even created fake travel papers for them from their origin to Istanbul—always through Prague, of course. We were, to some measure, self-funded. Once in Prague, our subjects would go through the Central Office's standard procedure, signing away most of their remaining assets like any other emigrants, willingly surrendering their valuable property on the promise of safe passage out of the Reich. They would be held upstairs in this building, 'awaiting transport.' We had a special team that would discreetly harvest them one by one. Separating the children from the parents for harvesting was a bit messy, as we needed to avoid generating stress, which could damage the preservation process. We learned to overcome this, as you can see from the quality we achieved in tableaux like this one, our Moroccan wedding party."

Weiszl had led her to the next window, labeled "Azoulay Family Wedding," and pointed out the subtle details with obvious pride: the inlay in the furniture, the authenticity of the costumes, the subtly joyful expressions on the bride and groom's faces, and the mischievousness looks on those of the children.

"Yes, yes, they are completely real, too," Weiszl assured her.

Vanesa, sickened but still hyper-alert for any hope of salvation, suddenly drew in a breath.

Weiszl, interpreting her gasp as a sign of awe at his previous revelation about the children in the display, nodded as if to acknowledge the compliment, and turned to move on. He was clearly enjoying this.

But Vanesa's eyes were not on the children. They were locked on the air vent near her feet. Around one meter square, it contained the same intricate ironwork as the grill at the entrance to the building, with the Galerie symbol subtly incorporated into its pattern. *"I came down to see him through the air duct, the one with the symbol in the grillwork,"* her father had written in his story about Moe. He'd mentioned the grill in other stories, too. She quickly scanned the hall. This was the only opening of its type she could see.

Unaware, Weiszl led her on to the next display, a winter *shtetl* street scene. The plaque read "The Jewish Shtetl of Krenau, Poland, 1943." Weiszl began a droning explanation about the display that had clearly been delivered numerous times, how its subjects were actual residents of this former part of the town, how each was depicted in his or her natural occupation—the butcher behind his counter, the beggar on the stoop, the old lady pulling her shopping cart—all actual people, all preserved for eternity just as they had been.

Vanesa nodded sagely, trying to add the right tinge of revulsion to her expression in an attempt to disguise the fact that her mind had grabbed the torch of hope and was sprinting off into the distance, trying hard not to look back.

Perhaps in an attempt to protect his son from the "work" in Galerie, Jakub must have made the sub-basement off-limits to Michael. The air duct had to lead to the upper floors, if Michael had used it to surreptitiously access Galerie. Not "had to lead," she cautioned herself, because her father's actual physical situation almost fifty years ago was anyone's guess. But "would likely lead" was good enough for her, given the circumstances. She doubted she'd find a better option, and Weiszl's tour was already nearly half over.

The duct would have been big enough for her father at age twelve, so she could probably fit through it. But what if its egress, wherever that was, had been sealed off over the course of the years? This would make sense, since the preservation of the covert museum for so many years must have necessitated absolute secrecy, and all physical traces between Galerie and the outside world would have had to be strictly eliminated. Could she gamble her life on the chance that it hadn't? They would kill her if she didn't get away, and she would only have one chance to do so. One chance, she thought, her eyes darting back to the *shtetl* display.

We all get one chance to choose the right path, do we not? Did my grandfather thus choose? Do our choices define us, or we them? The questions poked through her fear like thorns in a cotton shirt, pricking her with increasing pain even as she attempted to shift away from them.

Weiszl gently took her elbow and urged her to the next window, farther away from the duct. "Jakob Ehrlich Addressing a Session of the 14th World Zionist Conference, Vienna, August 1925," the plaque read.

This was the display she'd seen when the lights first came on. In it, grey-suited and mustachioed Zionist leaders listened raptly to the anti-Nazi Erlich against the backdrop of the Flag of Israel. Erlich, she recalled, had been a prominent Jewish leader known to have been murdered by the Gestapo for his outspoken anti-Nazi views in the period before the Anschluss, the annexation of Austria by Germany in 1938.

As if anticipating her question, Weiszl nodded enthusiastically. "Yes, it was really him. Himmler had kept him all those years, and provided the family with an alternate body. When he heard from Eichmann of Hans' plan, he made us a gift of him. Ironic, is it not?"

She stared stony-faced at Weiszl, choosing not to dignify his sick self-satisfaction with a response, and using the silence to glance longingly back to the iron grill, two displays behind her. Weiszl again took her elbow, urging her forward, and when she hesitated, Vodka gave her a small shove from behind. The grill was getting farther and farther away. She needed to arrest the tour's progress long enough to somehow distract the three men, get to the air duct, remove the cover—assuming that was even possible—and get inside, all before they grabbed her.

"What about my father?" she blurted, grasping at the first idea that popped into her head. "Where was he, this whole time my grandfather was working on these... these... displays?"

Weiszl looked at her with surprise, as if he'd forgotten she could actually speak, then answered brusquely. "He wasn't allowed down here. There is only one way in here, and the door was locked, with guards at the top of the staircase day and night. He knew nothing of what went on here. I don't really know where he was or what he did. Jakub took care of him, although Hans did develop a certain fondness for the boy. I still think Michael was part of the reason Hans stayed in Israel, instead of continuing on to Syria as he'd planned. Then you came along, and it was clear to me that Hans actually liked his life in Tel Aviv. You were the 'new Jews,' he once told me, nothing at all like the old ones, and quite empirically fascinating to him."

Weiszl turned to move forward, switching back to tour guide mode. "Now, let us continue to the next display. I think you'll agree that here we truly reached new levels of realism...."

He droned on as if on auto-pilot, as if she was part of a group of... of... who? Who would come to this type of place for a tour? She forced herself to focus, and suddenly felt as if a light bulb had just lit up over her head. *Weiszl doesn't know about the stories! Uncle Tomas never told him. This is my key!*

"Yes, he did," she said simply.

Weiszl turned around with annoyance at her repeated interruption of his carefully polished monologue.

She continued. "He did know, my father. In fact, he kept a diary, in which he recorded everything he knew. It's safe in Tel Aviv with my lawyer. He has instructions to turn it over to the Simon Wiesenthal Center if I don't return safely. I did the same with my research notes. I left a copy with a colleague of Marek's in the Jewish Museum."

She paused for effect, letting the implication of her words sink in, and continued pensively. "I wonder if they'll give you a show trial when they catch you, like Demanjuk. I mean, he was just a low-level guard, but you are a big fish, an Eichmann groupie who's never been tried for this particular crime. Then again, they might just kill you when they find you, to save trouble." She was dangerously twisting the knife, but she had nothing to lose.

Weiszl looked momentarily flustered, wobbling against his cane as if there had been a sudden, highly localized earthquake under his feet, but he quickly regained his poise, waving her away as if she was a pesky fly. "You're bluffing, and it's pathetic. You have no leverage, Dr. Neuman. Don't try to pretend that you do."

Vanesa's historian brain kicked into hyper-analytical mode. Out of options, she had to play this out, so she shot back. "Very well. Then how did I find this place, Herr Weiszl? I mean, the physical location was fairly easy, but how did I know of Galerie in the first place? I may have lacked an exact understanding of your deplorable crimes here, but what was my first clue to its existence? Tomas—that is, Hans—didn't tell you how I knew, did he? Just that I was coming. How did I know, if not from my father? Do you think Tomas, Hans Guenther himself, told me?"

Weiszl dropped his calm façade and motioned Garlic over. He whispered urgently into the latter's ear.

Vanesa caught the phrase: "...do it *now*. I don't care what time it is there!"

Garlic scurried off to do his master's bidding.

Just a bit more, Vanesa thought, and she'd have her chance. She took a cautious step toward Weiszl, not enough to threaten him, but enough to accentuate the impact of her words.

"Who do you usually give tours to, anyhow? Is this place some kind of underground neo-Nazi shrine? Do you have reunions here? Bachelor parties? Inductions with secret handshakes? Do you sit around and sing the *Horst Wessel Lied*, drink beer, and get all teary-eyed for your lost Reich? Or do you meet here and plot how you'll reestablish it, you and your storm troopers there?" She gestured to Vodka, and continued with sarcasm. "I suppose you could've had a chance, if only peeing on the enemy was lethal."

Now, finally, her expertise in the goading and nagging arts came to practical use.

Weiszl whirled on her, his face livid. He leaned forward, one hand heavily on his cane, the other pointing directly at her face, and snarled, "You listen to me, you little bitch...."

Before he could continue, Vanesa lunged forward and again kicked the cane out from under him.

Again, he crumpled to the floor, and again Vodka rushed to assist him. Only this time, Vodka encountered her outstretched foot as he passed, and went sprawling, nearly landing on top of Weiszl.

Still not enough time to make it to the duct, she thought, nor any chance of taking on the prone Vodka directly. He was too strong, and was already getting to his feet. She had to outwit him to gain control of the situation. But how?

Jumping at the next idea that popped into her head, Vanesa darted around Vodka to Weiszl, and began viciously kicking his inert form, as if enraged.

Weiszl curled into a fetal ball, trying to protect himself.

Vodka, now on his feet and clearly distraught at having failed to protect his charge, grabbed Vanesa, flung her away, and bent to help Weiszl.

She let herself be thrown aside, careful to retain her balance. As soon as Vodka's back was turned, she pounced on him from behind and deftly removed the gun he'd left causally tucked in his belt. Before either was aware of what was happening, she had cocked the pistol loudly and trained it with a steady hand on Weiszl and Garlic, who both stared in dumb shock at her audacity. Keeping the gun on them, she began backing toward the duct cover, some twenty meters away.

"Move or make noise, and I may not get you both, but I was a very good shot in the army." Vanesa's cold eyes, steady hand, and matter-of-fact tone left little doubt of her willingness to follow through on this threat.

Weiszl looked up at her from the floor, and said simply, "Do what you will, Dr. Neuman. There is no way out except through that door, which is still guarded." He jerked his head in the direction opposite her current path.

"Perhaps," she said simply, crossing the stretch of floor to the grill in just seconds. It blessedly came free with just a tug, clattering to the hard floor with a noise that echoed loudly in the empty hall.

Weiszl quickly straightened up, and seemed to immediately understand her intention and its apparent chance of success. Mustering his lost dignity, he brought a hand with affected nonchalance up to his forehead, and smoothed his comb over back in place. He fixed her eyes, and said, almost with amusement, "You won't get me, and the legacy of this place will live on, in any case."

Vanesa sunk to her knees, ready to back into the duct without lowering the gun. She met Weiszl's gaze, unblinking. She took in his pathetic insouciance, no longer convincing in any way, and the snarling hatred plastered on Vodka's face. She took a final look at her grandfather's warped legacy—this Galerie which would soon, she hoped, be a sick secret no longer.

"A journey of a thousand miles must begin with one step, *Herr Oberscharfuhrer*," she said simply, and backed into the darkness of the duct.

CHAPTER 27

NO QUESTIONS

The graphic designer calmly working on the new logo for Prague Telekomunikace had never considered herself the screaming type, but when a foot came through the plasterboard wall to the right of her desk, she let out a shriek that would have put Fay Wray to shame. Cowering in the corner of her cubicle, she watched as the rest of Vanesa's gun-toting, white-dusted body broke through the hole, vowing to herself to never, ever mix cocaine and alcohol again.

When they finally arrived, Abbot and Costello, the two Prague police detectives, were incredulous both at Vanesa's ghostly appearance and her story. They were also experienced enough to thoroughly check it out.

Thus Vanesa Neuman found herself at the center of three murder investigations and a very public scandal surrounding the existence of Galerie, a Nazi shrine created by none other than Adolf Eichmann and run by a prominent SS war criminal in the very heart of Prague, right under the noses of the Czech police and intelligence services. Galerie was known, it turned out, to nearly everyone *except* law enforcement. Throughout Europe, a visit to Galerie had for decades been a mandatory part of initiation rites into numerous right-wing nationalist and neo-Nazi groups.

Vanesa was stuck in Prague for several long months as the wheels of the Czech justice system creaked forward at geological speed. She lived in Jonas's apartment with the gracious permission of his family, who had semi-adopted her in their grief over the loss of their son, and worked from Marek's old office under the auspices of the Jewish Museum.

>——/

I spoke to her infrequently, and saw her only when she finally returned to Tel Aviv.

Did she allow herself to grieve for Jonas, I wondered. In his apartment, surrounded by his things? What about Marek? What about her father, whom she was finally able to understand and forgive? What about her grandfather and Tomas?

I never asked her about Jonas, not really wanting to know. For Marek I know she had felt deep friendship. As for her grandfather and Tomas, she soon made her feelings about them abundantly clear, both in word and in deed.

Neither Czech nor Romanian intelligence, nor investigators from the Simon Wiesenthal Center, ever caught up with Weiszl, who apparently had a well-prepared contingency plan in case of discovery. They never found Vodka and Garlic, either, despite Vanesa's best efforts working with a sketch artist to create an accurate portrait of each. Apparently, two neo-Nazis with poor personal hygiene and a single first name between them was not enough information for the Czech police to go on. Ultimately, they shut down the investigation.

Galerie was taken apart, its subjects returned to their respective families or communities for burial in accordance with Jewish law.

Vanesa never told anyone about Uncle Tomas' true identity, nor his role in Galerie.

>——/

One winter evening in early 1993, Vanesa Neuman walked back through the door of our Tel Aviv flat, a very different Vanesa than the girl whose fragrant, smooth, white neck I had first tasted by the Wisconsin lake shore eleven years previously.

I asked her several months later, the night before we were due to make our first appearance at the Tel Aviv Rabbinate to start divorce proceedings, if she was happier now that she knew. Did she think her life was better, would be better, knowing what she knew about her father and grandfather? How could it possibly be easier for her to consider her future, having been so deeply betrayed, and now forced to carry the burden of her grandfather's unforgivable crimes? Wasn't she sorry — I simply couldn't stop myself from asking this — that she'd ever even started down the road that led her to Galerie?

She looked at me sideways with the Vanesa Eye, a sardonic, almost sassy half-smile on her face. The Marlboro Light dangling from the corner of her mouth danced rhythmically as she spoke, and she squinted against its smoke. "Honey, you've got it backwards. For once, I'm carrying nothing — not betrayal, not hatred, nothing. My father was a child, who was faultless but forced to carry my grandfather's guilt. How can I blame him? My grandfather was despicable, from any perspective, and he paid — yes, we all paid, but he paid more dearly — for his crimes with a miserable life, a life lived in half-truths and constant dark silence. He clearly, desperately needed love, but could never reach far enough to receive it – from me or anyone. He was despised by his son, whose existence he poisoned despite having chosen to work on Galerie for my father's benefit in the first place. He carried the burden of my grandmother's death. I realize now that in his frailty, my grandfather betrayed only himself and his humanity, not me. He did inhuman things, yet I was a witness to his inhuman life. Was his inner prison any worse than a Czech or Israeli prison would have been? Was he truly better off alive than dead?"

That's when I understood, because even in the shadow of the horrors she'd seen and to which her family had been party — for the first time in Vanesa Neuman's twenty-seven-year existence, *there were no questions.*

EPILOGUE

Pardesiya, February 1993

This time, she strode the two kilometers from the bus stop with neither worry nor pain, but with single-minded purpose. The winter wind slapped the dark, dripping Eucalyptus trees in angry gusts, ripping loose and carrying away leaves both live and dead in a gusty tantrum. Vanesa's long hair, left loose in her urgent haste, was similarly whipped by the wind. She brushed it angrily from her eyes for the umpteenth time, set her teeth, and walked on.

There was only one alternative, she'd reasoned over the long months in Prague. Tomas would never be brought to justice, not in his current state. There would be no actual trial for this half-dead defendant, and even if there was, there could be no true punishment. Any public exposure of the horrendous crimes of this senior SS officer who had lived as a taxpaying, normative Israeli for fifty years, would serve no purpose other than to unnecessarily blacken her father's name and pointlessly inflame public opinion. It would all be another superfluous exercise in national self-justification, she thought angrily.

Israel had undergone its Holocaust catharsis and had moved on. Today, while the few remaining elderly Holocaust survivors went hungry in squalid flats, living on insufficient state pensions, tens of members of parliament and tens of thousands of Israeli high school students paraded tearfully at Auschwitz every year, wrapped in Israeli flags and watching

Israeli Air Force fly-overs. A fraction of the expense of these symboli-cally important yet undeniably photogenic visits could easily ensure the comfort and safety of the few remaining survivors.

This, thought Vanesa as she rounded the corner and walked through the gate into the Lev HaSharon Holocaust Survivors Hostel, *does not hap-pen. Why?*

When facing the horror of the Holocaust, it was still easier to strip it of corporeality. It was simpler to regard its inanimate symbols rather than its fading, yet still living, human face. One could look at the remains of Auschwitz, and see the piles of shoes and eyeglasses — tangible, hor-rifying, yet less emotionally threatening than Moshe, the ninety-year-old Auschwitz survivor, with his liver-spotted hands, creaking walker, ratty slippers, and empty refrigerator.

Dehumanizing the horror made it more palatable, simpler to explain. Yet it also empowered the horror with symbolic anonymity. A symbol lacked the frailties and subtleties of a person, and was as such more mal-leable. It was far more difficult to use Moshe to justify actions or ideas. Auschwitz, as a symbol, was far more effective.

That is exactly what we do, thought Vanesa, pushing open the screech-ing aluminum door, and wincing at the acrid stench that burst from the building, as if eager to escape its own potency. *We use Auschwitz to both cynical and positive ends, and in ignominious self-interest we choose to abandon Moshe because his actual usefulness is, after all, limited.*

There was, as usual, no attendant in reception. The chipped Formica covering the reception counter had begun to peel in grey flesh-like strips from the floor up. Notably absent was the formerly ubiquitous voice of Henya, calling her lost son home for dinner. A thick silence now hung over the facility, with only distant voices and a vague clatter of dishes audible from the direction of the common room. Lunchtime.

Her shoes squeaked on the just-washed floor, the smell of disinfectant struggling vainly to overcome that of excrement. Neither of Tomas' two roommates were in the room — *Hans' roommates,* she reminded herself, gritting her teeth. One bed was neatly made, apparently unoccupied. On the second, a wad of sheets with a clearly yellow tint moped on one corner of the grey-striped mattress.

Tomas lay in his usual place, sagging bedsprings visible over the dusty floor, catheter bag bulging with dark urine, rumpled pajamas clearly unlaundered. Hearing the squeak of her shoes, his eyes turned in her direction. A look of joyous recognition flashed through them, but was quickly replaced by confusion and then fear when he met her cold glare.

Vanesa checked the hallway in both directions, found it still deserted, and moved toward his bed. As she passed the unoccupied bed next to his, she took its pillow, clutching its edges so tightly that her knuckles turned white.

There was truly only one logical course of action, she had decided— one way of obtaining a semblance of justice for her father, for her mother, for all the subjects of Galerie and their families, for the entire Jewish population of Bohemia and Moravia, for that matter, over which this sick man had wielded the power of death. She would exploit that which he had taken from her family—literally the only remaining possession this poor excuse for a human being had to give.

She raised the pillow to her chest and moved toward the bed. All her anger at Weiszl and his henchmen, her grief over Jonas and Marek, her fury at her grandfather's horrific choices, her pity for her father who never had the chance to choose, and her sorrow for her mother who had been unable to move forward from the horrors of her past—all this propelled her arms upward and forward toward the prone figure in the bed.

Hans' eyes now registered mortal terror as he understood her intentions. His bowels let go, and the room filled with the potent smell of shit.

"I know who you are, and I know what you did," she said simply, through clenched teeth.

As she positioned the pillow just above his face, already smelling his sour breath, the tears began to course down her cheeks. The muscles in her arms stood out as she pressed the pillow between her hands... and deftly positioned it behind his head.

Then, not with any semblance of forgiveness, but rather with a simple recognition of the frailties of human flesh that affect us all, Vanesa Neuman set to straightening the bedclothes.

—THE END—

BOOK CLUB GUIDE

1. *Galerie* tackles the emotional issues facing the children of Holocaust survivors. Would you call the relationship between Vanesa and her parents "loving"? Could Vanesa's parents – and by extension other Holocaust survivors – be expected to have the skills to create a loving environment for their children, in light of the horrors they lived through? Could they be expected to have the capacity to love at all? Could their children hope to develop such capacity? Their children's children?

2. Were you surprised at the true nature of Galerie? At what point did you realize that Vanesa's grandfather was not "preserving life" in the way that she had originally hoped? Do you think that a museum exhibit like Galerie is farfetched, given that the Museum of an Extinct Race was a historical reality? Why or why not?

3. The secrets revealed in *Galerie* about Uncle Tomas' wartime actions are shocking. At the same time, he played a sorely-lacking positive, kind, and truly human role in Vanesa's childhood. Does this good offset the evil we discover about him? Was Vanesa's kindness toward him in the book's Epilogue – after she knew who he was and what he did - justified, in your opinion?

4. Vanesa's grandfather Jakub collaborated with the Nazis in the most horrific way imaginable, yet did so with the aim of saving his family. Were his actions morally defensible in any way? Why or why not?

5. Vanesa's father, Michael, was old enough to understand what Jakub and Tomas were doing in Prague, and clearly knew that Tomas was actually Hans Guenther. Despite this, he kept his silence over the years, never revealing the secret to the authorities after the war. Was he wrong to do this, even given the dire consequences it would have had for his own future had he done so?

6. *Galerie* is uniquely narrated from Vanesa's husband's point of view. He is never named, and his perspective is simultaneously semi-omniscient yet blatantly subjective. Why do you think that author chose to tell the story from this perspective? Did you feel that this added or detracted from the novel's engagement or emotional impact?

7. *Galerie* probes the nature of filial relationships tainted by what we'd likely today refer to as Post-Traumatic Stress Disorder (PTSD). Are there lessons we can learn from the Holocaust that could help us treat or relate to the children of modern-day PTSD victims?

8. In human history, and certainly in the modern world, there is no shortage of tragedy and suffering – some of it on a terrifyingly massive scale. Is the Holocaust over-discussed? Should it be considered singular in scope and horror? Should it be a litmus test by which we measure other human tragedies, and if so, does this diminish its impact?

ACKNOWLEDGEMENTS

Everything in *Galerie*, with the very notable exception of Galerie itself and the Neuman family, is true or based on actual historical events and characters.

The Jewish Museum of Prague was indeed taken over by Adolf Eichmann's "Central Office for Jewish Emigration" in 1941. The office in Prague was headed by Hans Guenther with the assistance of his deputy Josef Weiszl and others. Among Guenther's responsibilities were the museum, which he ran with a large Jewish staff managed by Josef Polak and Tobias Jakobovitz. The entire staff, with the exception of Hana Volavkova (see below) was murdered in Auschwitz in late 1944.

Hans Guenther was ostensibly shot dead on May 5, 1945 by Czech partisans at a roadblock, as he was attempting to escape to Italy or Spain. There are claims that he actually got away, but no proof of this has been presented, to the best of my knowledge. For his prominent role in the destruction of Czech Jewry, Josef Weiszl did indeed serve five years in prison, and his whereabouts thereafter are unknown.

Holocaust researchers—including those at the museum itself—still debate whether the museum was ever overtly dubbed or even privately considered to be the "Museum of an Extinct Race." But it is my unscholarly belief, based in large part on Hana Volavkova's definitive work "A Story of the Jewish Museum in Prague," that there could be no other explanation. Volavkova, the sole survivor of the wartime museum staff (see the list below), presents her evidence from a museological point of view, arguing that the aim of the collections created during the Nazi years could be none other than to systematically present Jewish life *ex post facto*.

Akeley Hall is still a highlight of the New York Museum of Natural History, and its opening in 1936 did indeed raise the esteem of taxidermy immensely. Techniques based on Carl Akeley's work are still in use by taxidermists today. From Egyptian mummies to currently-offered preservation services of questionable legality (and good taste), human taxidermy has been practiced for millennia, although no large-scale endeavor such as Galerie has ever been attempted, to the best of my knowledge.

This book would not have come into being without the assistance of one very special young man, who retained an interest in moving the project forward even when I got tired of it. Thank you, Segev Greenberg, for your patience as we trekked around Prague and Terezin, living on pizza and self-dubbed "pigeonburgers," for your ideas whenever I was stuck, for asking me at every opportunity, "So, how's the book going, Dad?", and for reading every single draft written. I can't wait to start our next project.

Special thanks to Magda Veselska of the Jewish Museum of Prague, who provided me with the full list of wartime museum staff and answered my pesky questions via email. Thanks also to Sima Shachar and Oded Breva of Beit Terezin (the Theresienstadt Martyrs Remembrance Association), the research staff at Yad V'Shem, Dr. Jan Bjorn Potthast, and Marek Taborsky, whose outstanding WWII Tour of Prague and follow-up answers via email added so much to my research. Thanks to Petr Brod for his Czech language insights and valuable information about Prague, and to my circle of beta-reader friends and family who provided crucial yet loving input and critique on the first drafts of Galerie. And of course, thanks to my editors, Michelle Berry and Lane Diamond, whose combined plot insights and grammatical acumen really brought the final version of Galerie to life.

Finally, an especially warm and loving thanks to my wonderful, beautiful, and incredibly supportive wife, Michal, without whom none of my books (not to mention my very rewarding and full life) would ever have come about.

Steven Greenberg
Kadima, Israel
August 2015

APPENDIX

Staff of the Jewish Museum of Prague, 1941-1944

This book is dedicated to the brave men and women who staffed the Jewish Museum of Prague during the Nazi occupation, and who were sent to their deaths as thanks for their conscientious and thorough work preserving the legacy of Bohemian and Moravian Jewry. *Yehi zechram baruch* — may their memory be blessed.

Specialist Staff

Jakobovits Tobias, Polak Josef, Engel Alfred, Fischhof Franz, Flesch Josef, Formankova Etja, Konirsch Berthold, Lieben Salomon Hugo, Pollak Josef, Popper Bedrich (Friedrich), Reiner Karel, Richter Hugo, Woskin-Nahartabi Mosesx, Lausmann Grete, Lederer Bedrich (Fritz), Lendecke Marketa

Administrative Staff

Crkovska Bedriska, Demelova Alice, Eisler Johann, Fischhof Edith, Friedlander Ruzena (Rosa), Gobiet Edith, Gottlieb Lev, Heydukova-Slaninova Ruzena (Rosa), Hraska Marta, Jakobovits Berta, Kampert Gertrude, Kantor Marketa, Kohn Marta, Kolisch Bohumir (Gottfried), Lieben Sophie, Masin Marie, Neumann Bohumil (Gottlieb), Novak Marta, Pospisil Zdenka, Schramm Vilma, Smutna Ema (Emmy), Sojka Walter, Tauchmann Hana, Teichmann Blanka, Voticka Zdenka, Woskin Tamara, Zizius Lily

BIBLIOGRAPHY

In addition to countless and lengthy articles, online and off, in English and in Hebrew, and many hours in the Yad V'Shem archives in Jerusalem, I read extensively to ensure that the setting and characters in *Galerie* were as realistic and historically accurate as possible, most notably:

Works of Non-Fiction
1. Albright, Madeleine - Prague Winter: A Personal Story of Remembrance and War, 1937-1948, Harper, 2012

2. Arendt, Hannah - Eichmann in Jerusalem: A Report on the Banality of Evil, , Viking, 1963

3. Epstein, Helen - Children of the Holocaust, Putnam, 1979

4. Kirk, Jay - Kingdom Under Glass: A Tale of Obsession, Adventure, and One Man's Quest to Preserve the World's Great Animals, Henry Holt and Co., 2010

5. Larson, Erik - In the Garden of Beasts: Love, Terror, and an American Family in Hitler's Berlin, 2011

6. Milgrom, Melissa - Still Life: Adventures in Taxidermy, Houghton Mifflin Harcourt, 2010

7. Redlich, Gonda - The Terezin Diary of Gonda Redlich, Saul S. Friedman (Editor), University Press of Kentucky, 1999

8. Volavkova, Hana - A Story of the Jewish Museum in Prague, Artia, 1968

9. Weiss, Helga - Helga's Diary: A Young Girl's Account of Life in a Concentration Camp, W. W. Norton & Company, 2013

Works of Fiction

1. de Rosnay, Tatiana - Sarah's Key, St. Martin's Press, 2007

2. Gutfreund, Amir - Our Holocaust, Toby Press, 2006

3. Harris, Robert - Fatherland: A Novel, Random House, 1992

4. Waldman, Ayelet - Love and Treasure, Knopf, 2014

5. Weil, Jiri - Mendelssohn is on the Roof, Harper Collins, 1992

ABOUT THE AUTHOR

Briefly....

I am a professional writer, as well as a full-time cook, cleaner, chauffeur, and work-at-home Dad for three amazing young children, and the lucky husband of a loving and very supportive wife. Born in Texas and raised in Fort Wayne, Indiana, I emigrated to Israel only months before the first Gulf War, following graduation from Indiana University in 1990. In 1996, I was drafted into the Israel Defense Forces, where I served for 12 years as a Reserves Combat Medic. Since 2002, I've worked as an independent marketing writer, copywriter and consultant.

More than You Asked for....

I am a writer by nature. It's always been how I express myself best. I've been writing stories, letters, journals, songs, and poems since I could pick up a pencil, but it took me 20-odd years to figure out that I could get paid for it. Call me slow.

After completing my BA at Indiana University – during the course of which I also studied at The Hebrew University of Jerusalem and Haifa University – I emigrated to Israel only months before the first Gulf War, in August 1990. In 1998, I was married to the wonderful woman who changed my life for the better in so many ways, and in 2001, only a month after the 9/11 attacks, my son was born, followed by my twin daughters in 2004.

Since 2002, I've run SDG Communications, a successful marketing consultancy serving clients in Israel and abroad.

Please stop by and connect with me at any of the following sites:

Website: **www.stevengreenberg.info**

Facebook: **www.facebook.com/stevengreenbergauthor**

Twitter: **www.twitter.com/GreenbergSteven**

Goodreads: **www.goodreads.com/author/show/534479.Steven_Greenberg**

LinkedIn: **www.linkedin.com/in/sdgcom**

WHAT'S NEXT?

ENFOLD ME

This timely and relevant novel, examining a world in which the Middle East has changed radically, is coming in a new second edition in the spring of 2016. For more about this book, please visit the Evolved Publishing website at **www.evolvedpub.com**

Fear. It remains a constant focus of life in the Middle East: what we have, what we could lose, what others might or did take away from us.

The question is, do you control your fear, or does it control you?

Daniel Blum—scientist, father, soldier—has many reasons to fear. He lost more than he knows when the modern State of Israel fell, following a massive earthquake and Iranian-led attack. Torn from suburban family life and a budding career, Daniel is alone and scarred, enduring subjugation and terror in Hamas-controlled Northern Liberated Palestine.

Together with George Farrah, a figure from his past, Daniel journeys deep under the Carmel mountain, through Egyptian-controlled, quake-ravaged Tel Aviv, and ultimately to the ruins of a secret government research facility. Haunted, Daniel strains the bonds of duty and family as he confronts a world he no longer understands, discovers unintended consequences of his actions, and plumbs the true depth of his loss.

In the Middle East, tragedy on a biblical scale has been, for millennia, the starting point of many dark journeys. The first dystopian Israeli fiction in three decades to be set in a realistic post-Israel Middle East, *Enfold Me* is a compellingly cold journey, a cruel snapshot of a society in disintegration, and an examination of how one person can be both perpetrator and victim of tragedy.

MORE FROM

EVOLVED PUBLISHING

For lovers of literary sagas with a fantastical feel (suitable for readers 13 and older):

THE DAUGHTER OF THE SEA AND THE SKY
By David Litwack

This literary journey exploring the clash between reason and faith, and the power of hope and love, is now available. For more information about this book, please visit the Evolved Publishing website at **www.evolvedpub.com**

After centuries of religiously motivated war, the world has been split in two. Now the Blessed Lands are ruled by pure faith, while in the Republic, reason is the guiding light – two different realms, kept apart and at peace by a treaty and an ocean.

Children of the Republic, Helena and Jason were inseparable in their youth, until fate sent them down different paths. Grief and duty sidetracked Helena's plans, and Jason came to detest the hollowness of his ambitions.

These two damaged souls are reunited when a tiny boat from the Blessed Lands crashes onto the rocks near Helena's home after an impossible journey across the forbidden ocean. On board is a single passenger, a nine-year-old girl named Kailani, who calls herself "The Daughter of the Sea and the Sky." A new and perilous purpose binds Jason and Helena together again, as they vow to protect the lost innocent from the wrath of the authorities, no matter the risk to their future and freedom.

But is the mysterious child simply a troubled little girl longing to return home? Or is she a powerful prophet sent to unravel the fabric of a godless Republic, as the outlaw leader of an illegal religious sect would have them believe? Whatever the answer, it will change them all forever… and perhaps their world as well.

Praise for *The Daughter of the Sea and the Sky*:
"The *Daughter of the Sea and the Sky* by David Litwack is a stunningly constructed story of a young girl who is deeply troubled but goes out of her way to help others. Tender yet tense, it is a story that explores the issue of faith and reason, and the wisdom and discernment to choose between right and wrong. David Litwack's exquisitely crafted story is thoughtful, passionate and simply delightful." – *Khamneithang Vaiphei*

"This is a tale of the heart and soul, of the beautiful yearning for meaning, and of how it can be found in the union of faith and reason, as well as in creativity. Everything, Litwack seems to say, points to Spirit. In this novel, nature itself embodies the spiritual world. The farm's overseer, Sebastian, knows this well, for he has been at the farm for many years, and is completely attuned to the rhythm of the seasons. I'm delighted to have truly found nothing negative to say about this book. *The Daughter of the Sea and the Sky* is a beautiful, moving novel, one that I predict will become an instant classic, especially in the literature of spirituality. It is a novel to be treasured and re-read many times, not only for its beauty, but for its thought-provoking treatment of universal themes." – *A Night's Dream of Books*

"First off, let me start by saying this book is something special. I don't say that often, but there is something un-pinpoint-able and undefined that is wholly beautiful, endearing and magical about this book and the story. I'm going to lay this at the author's feet. If this author brings out another book, you can bet I'll snap it up as soon as it's in print, because I can tell from this one alone that me and David's books are going to be lifelong friends." – *Elle Lainey*

For lovers of traditional literary or contemporary southern fiction (suitable for readers 16 and older):

HANNAH'S VOICE
By Robb Grindstaff

This up-market literary fiction, exploring the extraordinary events of
one girl's life and struggles to be understood, is now available. For more
information on this book, please visit the Evolved Publishing website at
www.evolvedpub.com

CARRY ME AWAY
By Robb Grindstaff

This literary coming-of-age novel from the author of the critically-ac-
claimed *Hannah's Voice,* and featuring the unique and memorable Carrie
Destin, is now available. For more information, please visit the Evolved
Publishing website at **www.evolvedpub.com**

Description of *Hannah's Voice*:

When six-year-old Hannah's brutal honesty is mistaken for lying, she
stops speaking. Her family, her community, and eventually, the entire
nation struggle to find meaning in her silence.

School officials suspect abuse. Church members are divided—either
she has a message from God or is possessed by a demon. Social workers
interrupt an exorcism to wrest Hannah away from her momma, who has
a tenuous grip on sanity.

Hidden in protective foster care for twelve years, she loses all contact
with her mother and remains mute by choice.

When Hannah leaves foster care at age eighteen to search for Momma,
a national debate rages over her silence.

A religious movement awaits her prophecy and celebrates her return.
An anarchist group, Voices for the Voiceless, cites Hannah as its inspira-
tion. The nation comes unhinged, and the conflict spills into the streets
when presidential candidates chime in with their opinions on Hannah—
patriotic visionary or dangerous radical. A remnant still believes she is
evil and seeks to dispatch her from this world.

Hannah stands at the intersection of anarchists and fundamentalists, between power politics and an FBI investigation. All she wants is to find her momma, a little peace and quiet, and maybe some pancakes.

One word would put an end to the chaos... if only Hannah can find her voice.

Praise for *Hannah's Voice*:

"Grindstaff's prose is unadorned, deft, carefully constructed — but I think what sets this novel apart is its humor. Grindstaff has a knack for portraying the drama of Hannah's dilemma in a way that makes you giggle." – *P.B. "Pete" Morin*

"Grindstaff's writing is pure, and free of the hyperbole and love for one's own words that often get in the way of a good story. His deft handling of the character and personality of Hannah at two distinct stages in her life showcases his mastery of language and characterization. He carefully chose each word to show the ten year difference in Hannah's life while staying true to who she really is. That is no small feat." – *Lanette Kauten*

"This book is so well written and Hannah is so compelling, her voice lingers in my mind long after I have finished reading. If *Hannah's Voice* doesn't end up on the bestseller's list, on every notable list... I will be shocked." – *Michelle L. Johnson*

"There are books that are interesting, and then there are books that you just can't put down. This is one of those books. Something in Mr. Grindstaff's writing style is reminiscent of Flannery O'Connor. He captures the quirks of Southern characters while maintaining their humanity. It would have been easy to write so many of these as stereotypical comical buffoons, but he avoided the easy way out." – *The Self-Taught Cook*

"*Hannah's Voice* is a beautiful story, and I'm going to tell you about it, but before I do: seriously, you guys, read it. I'm not kidding. You'll be changed forever, inside... it's not a book with such strong thematic material that it will make anyone cringe, but it will be burned into your brain for eternity in such a delightful way. Touching, moving, funny, awesome. I can't say it enough: this book is revolutionary, and the best thing I've read in years. Awesome. AWESOME." – *Naomi Sarah*

Description of *Carry Me Away*:

Carrie Destin, a biracial military brat, learns the injuries she sustained in a car accident will prove fatal before she reaches adulthood. She accelerates her life and sets aggressive goals: college, connecting with her Japanese roots, and the all-consuming desire to find her soul mate. A kid from nowhere, she travels the world with her Marine father and Japanese mother.

Facing an abbreviated life with a brash attitude and a biting, sometimes morbid sense of humor, Carrie races to graduate high school at age fifteen. College is her marker of adulthood, when she can smoke in public and order dessert before dinner. She tosses out her adolescent wedding scrapbook for a funeral plan. A teenage crush on Paul, a family friend and a widower seventeen years her senior, develops into a fantasy that takes on a life of its own.

As she outlives the original prognosis into her early twenties, her life goals evolve—always short-term. The longing for love stays constant, yet she walls herself off from others. Relationships end in betrayal, abandonment and violence. When love reveals itself, she pulls away, fearing that an early meeting with Death is on the horizon.

Carrie's frantic desire to experience life before it ends spirals out of control, leading to a physical and emotional collapse. Her grandmother's wisdom points her toward acceptance, but first she must break through her walls before she can give the gift of 'til-death-do-us-part.

Praise for *Carry Me Away*:

"After the wonderful *Hannah's Voice*, my expectations were pretty high. I was not disappointed. Robb Grindstaff's second book, much like his first, is a grand achievement of literary talent and it should easily cement him on many people's 'can't wait to see what he releases next' lists." – *Allison M. Dickson*

"Grindstaff has produced another masterpiece on par with *Hannah's Voice*! Carrie's life is all about racing forward, while she herself stands internally still, convinced she'll die before she has a chance to live. She tries to experience every aspect of life, but refuses to let the experiences in on a deeper level, and it's heart-wrenching, vivid, and realistic. I feared with Carrie, I cried for her, and I begged her to quit TRYING so hard to live, and just LIVE. Like *Hannah's Voice*, Grindstaff's characters are beyond real. Carrie has a special place in my heart. You'll never meet another character like Carrie, who packs the most life possible into every page of every chapter." – *Nola Sarina*

"I used this book to escape from the business of my everyday life, to allow me to reconsider all the things going on around me, and help me focus and see things in a new light. Most books don't do that. This one did." – *Naomi Leadbetter*

An award-winning historical glimpse inside American Indian culture (suitable for readers 13 and older):

CIRCLES
By Ruby Standing Deer

This award-winning, critically-acclaimed Native American Indian Historical Fiction novel is now available. For more information, please visit the Evolved Publishing website at **www.evolvedpub.com**

SPIRALS
By Ruby Standing Deer

This much anticipated sequel to the award-winning *Circles* is now available. For more information, please visit the Evolved Publishing website at **www.evolvedpub.com**

STONES
By Ruby Standing Deer

The third book in the Shining Light saga has arrived and is now available. For more information, please visit the Evolved Publishing website at **www.evolvedpub.com**

Circles:

With much of the world still undiscovered, a small band of people live a peaceful life, until the dream vision of a young boy, Feather Floating In Water, changes everything. Only nine winters old, Feather's dreams turn his seemingly ordinary childhood into the journey of a lifetime. He must help his people face a terrifying destiny from which they cannot turn away. He must find a way to make his people listen.

Bright Sun Flower, the boy's grandmother, guides his beginnings, teaching him about the Circle of Life, and how without it, no life can exist. But he needs a bigger push, and gets it from a grey wolf and a Great Elder. The boy's journey leads him to discover that the Circle of Life involves all people, all living things, and not just the world he knows.

In the end, an ancient People guide the boy in his visions, toward an unexpected place hidden from outsiders.

This story is steeped in American Indian life, in their beliefs and humor, and in their love of family. It shows how we might benefit from the old ways today.

Praise for *Circles*:

"This novel of historic fiction is a must for any fan of Native American history, or seeker of knowledge, or lover of life. It is expertly crafted with vivid imagery and characters that will become beloved. If you don't know what it means to sing someone home, prepare to swallow hard. It is heart warming and moving. Truly a thing of beauty." – *T.W. Griffith*

"Gorgeous language, an inspiring story, and unforgettable characters--Circles has it all. I fell for this book in the very first chapter when we're introduced to Feather Floating In Water, and I didn't fall out from under its spell even after I had read the final word. I found myself "thumbing" back through the pages to read particular passages just like I return to my favorite poems." – *Yvonne Rupert*

"From the first chapter, truly the first paragraph, I was transported into the lives of the characters, feeling their joys, pains, their lives. The gentle way in which the author writes, you feel deeply fulfilled. Your soul expands as you read, you wish for it to continue forever." – *Rosaleen MacQueen*

"In today's age, where everything is delivered at a high speed pace, we have a book that slows us right down and allows us to take a breath as we follow the simple life of an American Indian people at the time of the conquistadores. If you want to read something that is not formulaic, but original and captivating, then this is your book." – *Silby Grant*

CPSIA information can be obtained at www.ICGtesting.com
Printed in the USA
LVOW01s0102160915

454370LV00011B/47/P